MURDER COMES

Celia Heyworth is a success~~~ ~~ ~~~~~~~,
popular at work and with her neighbours, who
has decided to remain in the quiet town of
Cannonbridge after her husband's posting to the
north of England. Not on the face of it a likely
murder victim, but when her body is found
battered in her own kitchen, and another
woman's is found at the bottom of the stairs, DCI
Kelsey is left with the task of finding a motive for
the double murder.

The obvious culprit is the estranged husband,
with money or another woman the motive, but
Kelsey finds the field more crowded with suspects
than he'd expected. What about the strange
young man who used to spy on Celia Heyworth
from a neighbouring garden? Or one of her fellow
workers who is concealing a murky secret in his
basement? As the case grows in complexity and
the suspects multiply, Kelsey wonders if he will
ever get to the bottom of it. But there is to be
another tragedy before the surprising truth
emerges.

In *Murder Comes Calling*, popular author Emma
Page has produced another thoughtfully written,
cleverly plotted crime novel which will keep
readers guessing to the very end.

MURDER COMES CALLING

Emma Page

HarperCollins*Publishers*

Collins Crime
An imprint of HarperCollins*Publishers*
77–85 Fulham Palace Road, London W6 8JB

First published in Great Britain
in 1995 by Collins Crime

1 3 5 7 9 10 8 6 4 2

© Emma Page 1995

The Author asserts the moral right to be
identified as the author of this work

A catalogue record for this book is
available from the British Library

ISBN 0 00 232564 0

Set in Meridien and Bodoni

Photoset by Rowland Phototypesetting Ltd
Bury St Edmunds, Suffolk
Printed and bound in Great Britain by
HarperCollinsManufacturing Glasgow

FOR THE ONE AND ONLY,
WITH MUCH LOVE,
AS ALWAYS.

CHAPTER 1

On a sunny Friday morning in mid-July, the windows of Melco Polymers, on the Lydhall industrial estate, stood open to the breeze. Lydhall was a thriving northern town of considerable size; the industrial estate covered several acres on the edge of town. Melco had started life there some forty years ago, rising from modest beginnings to its present position in the forefront of the industry. The handsome building now housing its head-quarters occupied a prime site on the estate.

In her office on the first floor, Sarah Brooke was talking on the phone to one of Melco's stockists, jotting down salient points. She was a good-looking young woman of twenty-eight, athletically built, faultlessly groomed, elegantly dressed. She exuded an air of single-minded force and direction. She had been transferred to Lydhall from an outlying branch two years ago.

When she had finished her call she looked over her notes, pacing about the room, thinking over the conversation. Her steps took her across to the window where she stood frowning, cogitating.

A car drove on to the forecourt and the driver got out. Sarah's train of thought came to an abrupt end as she saw who it was: John Heyworth, one of the managerial staff on the sales side, returning, no doubt, from some visit to a customer or supplier. He didn't glance up at her window but strode briskly off towards his office. She sent an intense, searching gaze after him, until he disappeared through a doorway.

She didn't immediately return to her notes but remained by the window for some little time, motionless, lost in thought.

Later in the morning, John Heyworth went along to see Miss Forster, the personnel manager, to discuss details of a forth-coming measure of reorganization in his department. Heyworth was a tall, well-built man of forty, with a serious cast of countenance.

He had a useful talk with Miss Forster, an astute spinster in late middle age, who had built her life around the firm. Her sharp eyes missed little of consequence that went on under its roof. At the end of their discussion she walked out into the corridor with Heyworth. 'And your own situation?' she asked with a casual air. 'Will your wife be moving up here soon?' Promotion had brought Heyworth to headquarters six months ago, from the Cannonbridge branch, a hundred miles to the south. He was still occupying the rented furnished flat he had taken on arrival. It had been understood then that his Cannonbridge house would be put up for sale, his wife would be joining him as soon as possible and they would set about finding a house in Lydhall. But month had succeeded month and there was still no sign of Mrs Heyworth.

'There have been one or two difficulties,' Heyworth replied easily. 'Nothing that can't be sorted out. I'm sure Celia will be here before much longer.' He gave her an amiable smile and turned to go.

The instant they parted company the smile vanished from his face; his jaw set in a grim line as he went off along the corridor.

I wonder how Sarah Brooke's going to take it when Mrs Heyworth arrives on the scene, Miss Forster thought with anticipatory relish as she returned to her desk. Sarah had first encountered John Heyworth eighteen months ago, when he had come to headquarters on a routine visit. Miss Forster had noted then the impression he had made on Sarah. As she had also noted the play Sarah had made for him during the last six months. She didn't see Sarah as a wholehearted career woman, but as someone with a clear vision of the kind of life she wanted to lead – and no objection to that life being sustained entirely by the efforts of a husband. She could envisage Sarah turning her back without regret on her career, settling down happily to a secure and comfortable domestic future as a wife and mother, content to leave all subsequent career strivings to the man she married.

I wonder what Mrs Heyworth is like, Miss Forster pondered as she resumed her seat. Would she be any match for Sarah Brooke? Sarah would undoubtedly fight every inch of the way for what she wanted. I don't know if she's managed to nobble

Heyworth yet, Miss Forster thought, but I'd wager good money she'll get him in the end, one way or another.

Shortly before noon, Sarah Brooke put her head round the door of Heyworth's office.

'Lunch?' she inquired on a note of lively invitation.

He glanced up, smiled and nodded.

'A quarter to one?' she pursued. 'Meet you in the car park?'

Again, he smiled and nodded.

She withdrew her head and was gone.

Southview, the Heyworths' house in Cannonbridge, was an Edwardian villa of medium size, near the upper end of Grasmere Avenue, in a pleasant residential suburb. All the houses in the avenue were detached, of varying dates and sizes.

The Heyworths had no children and for the first few weeks after John had left for Lydhall Celia had lived alone in the house. She had a full-time job which kept her busy and at first John came back every weekend. Then his visits became less frequent and she began to feel lonely on her own.

A girl at her hairdresser's, a junior named Beth Knight, a girl Celia had taken a liking to, told her one Saturday morning, during a shampoo, that she would have to leave her digs shortly. Her landlady had died suddenly and the house was being put up for sale. Beth was seventeen, a country girl, from a village twenty miles away. She had worked at the salon since leaving school.

On a good-natured impulse Celia told Beth that if she was stuck she could have a bed at Southview for a week or two, until she found somewhere to suit her. Beth was delighted at the offer and moved into Southview a few days later. That was almost four months ago now and Beth was still at Southview. John Heyworth had been far from pleased when he discovered his wife had, as it were, taken a lodger, at a time when the house should be going on the market. But the arrangement had otherwise worked well and Celia had never regretted her impulse. Not only had Beth proved to be a congenial companion, invariably cheerful, helpful about the house, but she had also turned out to possess an unexpected talent: she enjoyed cooking and was good at it. She had very soon taken over the kitchen, a development which precisely suited Celia, who had little liking for cooking herself.

On Monday morning, as on every other working day, Beth sprang out of bed the instant her alarm sounded. It was never any hardship for her to greet each new day. She loved her work and was doing well at it; she never minded the long hours on her feet. She had always wanted to be a hairdresser and had her sights firmly fixed on a salon of her own, in the not too distant future. Her looks would have been ordinary enough, except that Nature had blessed her with one superb gift, the best of all assets for an aspiring hairdresser: a superb head of hair, luxuriant and wavy, in a beautiful shade of auburn.

Celia Heyworth's mood on waking was only a little less sprightly than Beth's; she was certainly not at all reluctant to face the start of another week. She had a good job at British Braids, a thriving concern on the industrial estate. She had worked there for four years, from shortly after her marriage. She had already achieved promotion and was currently hopeful of another step upwards. She hadn't the slightest intention of quitting her job to join her husband, and had never had any such intention.

She was thirty years old, Cannonbridge born and bred. She had lived at home until the deaths of her parents who had died within a few months of each other, five years ago. She had been content in those days with a run-of-the-mill office job.

She had one sister, Abbie, six years older. Abbie had left home in her late teens and was living with a boyfriend when the parents died. Celia had felt very much alone after their deaths, with no centre to her life, no drive or purpose.

Not long afterwards she met John Heyworth, ten years her senior. He was solid and steady, ambitious and hard-working. He seemed to offer a solution to her problems of loneliness and lack of direction. They were married a few months later.

During the years she had lived at home, Celia had always been compliant and dutiful. Her father had been a strong-minded man and she had unquestioningly followed the example of her mother in always deferring to him. Her view of marriage was highly conventional. On her wedding day her vision of the future had automatically included children.

But it wasn't long before that view began to alter, in the reality of her new life. The firm she was working for was taken over shortly after she married and she lost her job. She found herself another almost at once, with British Braids. The new job was a good deal more stimulating, as well as paying better. For the first time she began to take a real interest in her work. She ceased to think in terms of a job and began to think of a career. Thoughts of starting a family receded from her mind – though not from John's.

She discovered as time went on that she had little in common with her husband and less and less wish to subordinate her own interests and desires to those of any other person. Maybe she shouldn't have married at all; she certainly wasn't drawn to any other man.

But her nature was kind and she would never wish to inflict hurt if it could be avoided. Nor had she any taste for argument or confrontation. John had never done anything to harm her; she had no reason to be antagonistic towards him. She was delighted when the vacancy arose at Melco headquarters and John thought of applying for it. She at once encouraged him to go after it, allowing him to take it for granted that she would move house and join him if he got the job. What she actually hoped for was to be able to ease herself out of the marriage after John left for Lydhall. He would grow accustomed to the separation, he might meet someone else up there. She wished him well, she would like him to be happy. She saw no reason why the marriage shouldn't drift peaceably to an amicable ending.

Now, on this Monday morning, her step was light as she left her bedroom. She had a particular reason for wanting to get to work today. Further expansion was planned at British Braids and new appointments were to be made. Celia had her eye on one of them. She was positive she could do well in the post and had said as much on Friday to her boss, George Drummond. He was not a man to go in for snap decisions but neither would he let any matter drag on unresolved. He had had the weekend to mull over what she had said and she was pretty sure when he came in this morning he would have made his mind up either to move her another step up the ladder or advertise the post along with the other vacancies.

She glanced at her reflection in the long mirror on the landing, pausing to adjust the set of her jacket about her shoulders. She was an attractive woman, with dark hair and bright blue eyes. She was, as always, carefully groomed and neatly dressed, but beyond that she had little interest in her appearance; even as a girl she had never been overmuch concerned with her looks.

She went downstairs to the kitchen, where Beth had prepared breakfast. Over the excellent coffee, Beth broached the subject never far from her mind of late: would Southview be going on the market soon? Should she start looking for somewhere else to live?

'You don't need to worry about that,' Celia assured her with a smile. 'You won't find yourself turfed out at a moment's notice.'

Beth couldn't refrain from putting a further question: 'Do you think you'll be moving to Lydhall in the autumn?'

There was the briefest of pauses before Celia answered calmly: 'I very much doubt that I'll be moving up there at all.' Her tone and manner made it plain she wasn't going to enlarge and Beth, never one to press, was content to let the matter lie.

On the dot of 8.15, as every weekday morning, Celia edged her car out through the gates of Southview, with Beth beside her. As she drove past Rosemont, the sizeable late-Victorian house next door, the last house at the top of Grasmere Avenue, she caught sight of her neighbour in his garden. Ronald Marriott was dressed ready for work in a dark grey suit and white shirt. He was chasing after his stepson, Ben, a bright, lively boy, rising five. Ben flung a look of mischievous defiance over his shoulder as he raced for the shrubbery; they were both laughing. They slowed at the sound of the car and glanced out. Marriott waved to Celia and Beth in a friendly fashion and seized his opportunity to pounce on his quarry. Ben gave a cheerful wave of his own in the direction of the car as Ronald bore him off indoors to where his mother was waiting to get him ready for the kindergarten he attended.

Celia made her usual detour to drop Beth off at the salon and then continued to the industrial estate. She immediately set about her work with resolute concentration, determined to banish distracting thoughts of what the boss might have decided over the weekend.

It was an endless hour before Drummond sent for her. She went rapidly along to his office where she found him standing in the doorway, talking to Wilfrid Probyn, the firm's chief accountant. Both men smiled at her as she approached. She felt at once that was a good sign but she daren't give free rein to her hopes as she stood to one side, waiting for Probyn to go.

At last he took himself off and she followed Drummond into his office. He was smiling again; it must be good news. She drew a long, quavering breath.

'I've thought over what you had to say,' Drummond began when they were seated. 'I believe you would do well in the new job. But there's one point I feel bound to raise. I've no wish to pry into your personal affairs, but I must ask you: how long would you intend staying with the company if you were promoted? Do you not intend at some stage to join your husband in Lydhall?'

She was prepared for the question. She eyed him squarely. 'No, I won't be joining my husband,' she responded in a voice of iron resolve. 'I have every intention of remaining in Cannonbridge.'

CHAPTER 2

The next avenue higher up from Grasmere, running parallel to it, was Coniston. The second house from the upper end of Coniston Avenue, directly in line with Southview in the avenue below, was Leacroft, a substantial, turn-of-the-century dwelling. It had been built by a prosperous local retailer by the name of Cormack who had established on secure foundations a business specializing in the provision of family clothing. The house and business were now owned by his sixty-four-year-old grandson, Thomas Cormack. In recent decades the business had widened its scope to include an increasing proportion of good-quality fashionwear, as well as household linens and soft furnishings.

At five o'clock on Monday afternoon, Thomas Cormack was still at work in his office at the business premises near the centre of Cannonbridge. It would be five-thirty before the shutters went up, and a further twenty minutes before Thomas drove home for supper, always served punctually at six-thirty. His wife Ellen, seven years his junior, had been employed in the business until her marriage. The couple had had one child, a girl, whom they had named Faith. When Faith was barely sixteen she had given birth to an illegitimate child, a son, named Simon.

In the kitchen at Leacroft, Ellen Cormack, a tall, bony woman with greying hair severely dressed, was preparing supper. Shortly after five she heard the door of Simon's bedroom open and close, his footsteps on the stairs – as she had often heard lately at this time of day, since Simon had come home from university at the end of term.

He would have left the house without a word to her but she called out as he crossed the hall: 'Are you off out, Simon?'

He called back in reply one solitary syllable: 'Yes.'

She didn't ask where he was going. If she had asked he

wouldn't have told her. 'You won't be late back for supper?' she called.

Another syllable in response: 'No.'

The front door opened and closed and he was gone.

Simon was nineteen years old and had just finished the first year of a course in business studies. He had worked hard and was doing well.

During the latter part of his time at school he had spent part of every holiday working in various departments of the family business. Between school and university he had devoted a full year to the firm. Thomas had been more than satisfied with his progress. Simon had not only worked diligently but had conducted himself with propriety and discretion, expecting no favours, never trading on his position. The staff had respected him and had liked him well enough, though he was never on close terms with any of them – quite correctly, in Thomas's opinion, as Simon would one day head the firm, a fact of which both Simon and the workforce were well aware.

During university vacations, Thomas was content that Simon should spend only three or four mornings a week in the business, acknowledging that the lad must have time for his studies, as well as for concerns of his own, now that he was growing up. Thomas knew that Simon was genuinely interested in the business and enjoyed the time he gave to it. He knew also that Simon felt a need for broader experience and intended, after finishing at university, to strike out into the wider world of commerce for a time before settling down one day to run – and probably expand – the family business. Thomas saw the wisdom of the plan and thoroughly approved of it.

Now, when the front door closed behind Simon, Ellen drew a long sigh and returned to her task with an abstracted air, looking back into the past. Simon had been reared from birth, not as the Cormacks' grandson, but as their son. Until the age of thirteen he had unquestioningly believed Thomas and Ellen to be his parents and Faith his older sister.

Faith had been a pretty girl, dark-haired and blue-eyed. Thomas and Ellen were a strictly religious, churchgoing couple and had been horrified to discover her condition when she was two months pregnant. There could be no question of marriage as Faith wouldn't be sixteen for several months and in any case stubbornly refused to name the father of her child. Her parents

15

were immovably opposed to abortion, which they considered the most heinous of sins.

But neither did they have any liking for scandal, and after much prayer and cogitation they came up with a plan. Faith's opinion in the matter wasn't sought; her part now was merely to do as she was told.

Ellen took her away to stay with Ellen's mother in Scotland, telling everyone she was going in order to look after her mother, who she said was in poor health. In due course Ellen returned to Cannonbridge with a baby, whom she gave out to be her son, born in Scotland. As Ellen was no more than thirty-eight at the time, there was nothing intrinsically improbable in her story and it never provoked disbelief. She also gave out that Faith had taken a strong liking to both Scotland and her grandmother. She had found herself a job up there and had decided to stay on with the old lady, whose health, according to Ellen, was now much improved. Faith would be able to keep an eye on her.

Time went by. Once or twice a year Faith came back to Cannonbridge for a short stay, to see her parents and the son who believed her to be his sister. Simon was a quiet, well-behaved child, intelligent and quick to learn. He was always strictly disciplined, in no way troublesome. Thomas and Ellen spared no expense in their determination to do their best for him.

When Simon was seven years old, Faith went on a coach trip to France. A violent storm blew up as the coach travelled south. There was a motorway pile-up, with horrific casualties. Faith was among those killed instantly.

Six years later, Simon moved on in the normal course of things to his next school, the best independent day school in the vicinity. He settled in without difficulty and was soon making friends, acquitting himself well in studies and sports. During his second term he was at home one day, recovering from a cold. Ellen was out shopping and Simon decided to occupy an idle hour with one of the little snoops round the house he sometimes indulged in when opportunity offered.

In Thomas's study he once again tackled the bureau which had always stoutly resisted him. This time he was delighted to discover that by some oversight a ring of keys had been left in a lock. He was soon glancing swiftly through the long drawers,

16

fingering through various papers, careful to leave no trace of his prying, keeping an ear open against Ellen's early return. He found little of interest.

He lowered the drop-front and turned his attention to the pigeonholes and the set of small drawers on either side. In one of these drawers he came upon a bundle of certificates: the birth certificates of Thomas and Ellen; their marriage certificate; Faith's birth and death certificates.

And one more certificate, last of all: his own birth certificate.

As he studied it with proprietary interest his expression altered suddenly. He frowned in puzzlement, looked up and stared at the wall, astounded and bewildered. He read the certificate through again. And again.

All thought of listening for Ellen's return, restoring the bureau to the state in which he had found it, vanished from his brain. When Ellen came in shortly afterwards she found him still in the study, standing by the open bureau, the certificate in his hand. He didn't look at her, didn't speak. She took the certificate from him and sat him down beside her. She embarked on an explanation which he received in silence.

In the difficult days that followed, Ellen and Thomas did their best to clarify, to justify. On each occasion Simon heard them out with his face averted, staring down at the floor. He asked no questions, made no comment. After a week or two of this unrewarding exercise the subject was dropped and never again referred to between the three of them. Simon made no mention of it to a living soul. To the outside world he was still the Cormacks' son but from that time on he never once referred to them as his parents. In speaking directly to either of them he never used any name at all.

Two things had cut particularly deep into his soul that morning. The fact that he could clearly remember his mother and had liked her but had never been allowed to learn their true relationship while she was alive. The second, deeper, cut had pierced him beyond any possibility of forgiving or forgetting when he saw what had been entered on his birth certificate in the space reserved for the father's name. A single bald word had been set down: UNKNOWN.

When he looked at himself in the mirror he saw that his clean-cut features, his grey eyes and fair hair, hadn't come to him from Faith, nor from Thomas or Ellen. They could only have been a legacy from that long-vanished unknown who had risen up from the bureau drawer.

After that monstrous upheaval things settled down at Leacroft, though they could never again be as they were before. Simon worked harder than ever at school and was never in any kind of trouble, but he grew quieter than ever. His friendships withered away and he lost his place in the school sports teams. He treated his grandparents with unvarying, distant courtesy.

Today, as he closed the gates of Leacroft behind him and crossed the road, he saw coming towards him a girl he knew: Lorraine Beattie. At the sight of him her face broke into a smile and she quickened her pace. She was eighteen years old, pretty enough, with pale blue eyes and a clear skin. Left to its own devices, her hair would have been an unremarkable brown but the regular application of a colour shampoo had endowed it with gleaming chestnut lights. Her clothes were of good quality, chosen with care and taste; she wore them well. She walked with a springy, athletic step. She took excellent care of herself, practised aerobics, played a proficient game of tennis and was a strong swimmer.

She was on her way home from the high-class fashion boutique where she worked. Monday was never busy at the boutique and on slack days the manageress usually allowed one or other of the employees to leave early. Today it had been Lorraine's turn. She always walked home when the weather permitted, believing it helped to keep her in trim.

She lived with her widowed mother in a cottage a few minutes' walk from Coniston Avenue. She knew Simon through the local church they had both attended since childhood. She had been out with him a couple of times since his return from university at the end of term, the initiative on both occasions coming from her.

'I'm glad I bumped into you,' she said brightly by way of greeting. 'I was going to call in to see if you fancied coming to the theatre this evening. One of the girls at work gave me two complimentary tickets. She was given them herself but she can't use them and they're only for this evening.' She mentioned the play, which was on a tour of the provinces, in hopes of going into the West End later on. 'It's a good cast,' she assured him.

Yes, he would like to go to the theatre. He would pick her

up at seven-fifteen. He had his own car, a present from Thomas and Ellen on his eighteenth birthday.

Lorraine went off home, smiling to herself. Simon didn't glance after her but turned into a narrow footpath leading down between the gardens. He followed the path to a point a few yards short of its emergence into Grasmere Avenue. On his right was an empty property that had belonged to an old man who had died recently. The house had been up for sale since the end of May but the property had been neglected for some time and had attracted little attention in a sluggish market.

Without pausing, Simon let himself in through a side gate. The garden was a good deal overgrown. A tall horse chestnut tree in abundant leafy growth spread its branches by the far rear corner of the house. He swung himself nimbly up on to the lowest branch and scaled the tree with ease and speed, reaching the spot close to the top that he had appropriated on previous forays. It afforded him, through the leaves, a view of various parts of the garden and premises of the next-door property, Southview. He was well camouflaged in his casual gear of green T-shirt, brown slacks and dark trainers.

He looked at his watch as he settled himself comfortably into his eyrie, twenty-five feet above the ground. He had three-quarters of an hour before he need think of scrambling down again to set off back to Leacroft. He would never dream of presenting himself late or unwashed at the supper table. And this evening he must also allow time beforehand to smarten himself up for his visit to the theatre with Lorraine Beattie.

Mrs Beattie worked from eight till three as a care assistant in a superior private nursing home. She had been back from work some time and was busy in the kitchen when she heard her daughter's key in the lock.

Lorraine and her mother had always been close, with an excellent degree of mutual understanding. Lorraine came looking for her mother now, her cheeks flushed, her eyes bright, to say she was going to the theatre with Simon Cormack. Mrs Beattie was delighted at the news and Lorraine darted off upstairs to take a shower, decide the all-important question of what she was going to wear, and set about the meticulous preparation of her face and hair.

Downstairs in the kitchen, Mrs Beattie resumed her task with a thoughtful air. No casual outsider, seeing the two of them together, would take her for Lorraine's mother. She was a stocky, square-shouldered woman, plainly dressed; her face had never been her fortune. She had been brought up on a Cannonbridge council estate. Her husband, a shop assistant, had died young, when Lorraine was a baby. There had been no pension from his employment and she had had to struggle along as best she could. She had no close relatives and the only relative of her husband's that she knew of was a cousin who lived locally with his wife and schoolgirl daughter.

Through the difficult years Mrs Beattie had always found it a deep and abiding pleasure to watch Lorraine growing up, so pretty and ladylike; always dutiful and cooperative, never wild or rebellious.

What Mrs Beattie yearned for now, above all else in life, was to see Lorraine settled, comfortably and securely. And, if that could be thrown in as a bonus, happily, as well.

CHAPTER 3

Promptly at 5.15 Ronald Marriott left his office in the centre of Cannonbridge to drive home. He worked as an investment consultant for a highly reputable financial services firm with a number of branches in the area. He was twenty-nine years old, above average height; always well groomed and well turned out, with his share of good looks.

His stepson, Ben Griffin, was playing in the Rosemont garden, watching out eagerly for his return. The moment Ronald garaged his car, Ben was there, waiting to be swung off his feet, high in the air, laughing and shouting. As they walked across to the house, his hand in Ronald's, Ben chatted merrily about his day at kindergarten. The front door opened and Phyllis Marriott appeared on the step. A small, slight woman, with pleasant, everyday looks; she was eleven years older than her husband. She came down the steps, smiling, to greet Ronald. She gazed lovingly up at him and gave him a tender kiss.

Ben had brought some of his artistic efforts home from kindergarten for his mother to pin up on the wall of his playroom and he was anxious now to show them off to his stepfather. Phyllis stood in the hall, watching the two of them climb the stairs, Ben prattling cheerfully. She never ceased to be gladdened at the way they got on so well; in so many marriages a stepchild seemed to prove a source of discord rather than harmony.

She clasped her hands together in a rush of mingled joy and anxiety. She was just beginning to entertain hopes that she might be pregnant. Nothing would give her greater joy; it was all she needed to complete her happiness. She had feared it might be too late to look for motherhood again. How delighted Ronald would be to have a child of his own. As yet she had said nothing to him. She would hug her secret to herself for another few weeks, until she felt more confident of a successful outcome. It would be cruel to raise hope too early in Ronald, only to have that hope dashed by some mishap. It hadn't been easy for her to conceive and carry a child in her first marriage and now, on the threshold of middle age, things were bound to be even more tricky.

She turned from the hall and went along to the kitchen. She had married Ronald two years ago, after eighteen months of widowhood. She and Ben were already living in Rosemont, which had been her home throughout her first marriage. Her first husband had lived there all his life, as had his father before him.

Ernest Griffin, Phyllis's first husband, twenty-five years her senior, had owned a wholesale business in Cannonbridge, dealing in carpets and other floor coverings; the business had been started by his grandfather. Ernest was a man almost wholly absorbed in his business; Phyllis had worked for him since leaving school. His first wife, a meek, domestic creature, died when he was fifty; they had never had children. Ernest very soon became aware of the need to fill her place. He looked about for a speedy and trouble-free solution to his problem and his eye fell on Phyllis. Competent and loyal; good-natured and unassuming; industrious and supportive; no fancy ideas; unlikely to make demands on him. He need surely look no further.

Phyllis had never had a boyfriend, had never expected any man to seek her in marriage. She was amazed at the proposal, delighted and flattered, overcome with gratitude and happiness. She lost no time in accepting and had never for an instant regretted it. Nor had Ernest ever regretted his decision; Phyllis had proved the most devoted of wives.

Ernest had had one totally unlooked-for bonus after almost nine years of his second marriage: the birth of a son. It came at a time when he was sorely in need of good cheer. The economy was sliding towards recession. The housing market was running down; folk were staying put. And when they stayed put they didn't go out and buy new carpets or any other floor covering. The more business dwindled, the more Ernest worried and the harder he worked.

Benjamin was eighteen months old when his father fell across his office desk one afternoon with a massive, fatal heart attack. Phyllis sold the business for what she could get. There wasn't much of it left by the time everything had been settled. But she had the house. And, she was relieved to discover, a substantial lump sum, together with a regular income, from the life insurance Ernest had taken out many years before and had always kept up.

In the course of seeking financial advice on the investment of her capital, Phyllis met Ronald Marriott. As well as sound advice he gave her a good deal of personal attention, something she had never had from Ernest Griffin – or any other man. She was very soon head over heels in love, an overwhelming experience, totally new to her. When the idea of marriage began to rise in the air between them she could scarcely credit her good fortune.

She took Ronald to meet her only surviving relative, her widowed mother, who lived not far from Cannonbridge. Her mother took an immediate liking to Ronald and was very favourably impressed by his quiet courtesy, his attentiveness and thoughtfulness, his attitude to Ben. She rejoiced to see the bloom that now graced her daughter and she gave the marriage her wholehearted blessing.

There seemed no reason to wait. Ronald had no family of his own to consult; both his parents were dead. The wedding took place six months after Ernest Griffin's death and Ronald moved into Rosemont.

Now, as Phyllis set about her tasks in the kitchen, half her mind was still abstracted. Nothing must go wrong with this pregnancy – if pregnancy there should prove to be. Ronald loved Ben dearly and Ben, who no longer had any memory of his father, now looked on Ronald as his father and never thought of calling him anything other than Daddy. But Phyllis knew, all the same, how much a child of his own would mean to Ronald. If she could grant him this wish it would be some recompense for all the happiness he had given her.

And a child of his own would surely bind Ronald fast to her for ever.

No one worked late at British Braids. George Drummond liked everyone off the premises sharp at 5.30. He had no intention of killing himself by overwork and no wish to encourage any of his staff to do so.

Promptly on time, Celia Heyworth drove out of the car park. Her mood was still elated. She wanted to pour out her good news to someone, but Beth wouldn't be in till bedtime – she was going to her friend's house after work. I'll ring Abbie after supper, Celia decided, see if she can spare the time for a good long chat. There was no one she could talk to more freely than her sister. Abbie had a good head on her shoulders, a down-to-earth view of life. She would be delighted to hear of Celia's new promotion; she had been pleased from the start when Celia had first begun to think seriously about her work.

Abbie Yates was in business herself. She owned and ran a successful pet-grooming salon in Wychford, a small town ten miles from Cannonbridge. She had parted company last autumn with the boyfriend she had lived with for some years. She was currently on her own and happy to be so.

Celia's expression was relaxed and happy as she reached Grasmere Avenue and turned in through the gates of Southview. She was totally unaware of the pair of eyes looking down at her from the horse chestnut tree in the next-door garden.

Wilfrid Probyn, chief accountant at British Braids, had pulled out of the car park immediately after Celia and headed for home. He followed Celia's car for the greater part of the way, until she turned off into Grasmere Avenue, then he continued for another minute or two, bringing him to Sebastopol Gardens. Halfway along the gardens lay his house, Nightingale Villa, a handsome Victorian dwelling, named not after the songbird but after the Lady of the Lamp; the house had been built shortly after the Crimean War. Wilfrid had lived there all his life.

As he drove in he saw his wife's car standing by the front door, ready for her next foray into her endlessly busy world of guilds, institutes, leagues of friends, every kind of organization offering counsel, aid or fellowship. Wilfrid garaged his car and let himself into the house. He was forty-eight years old, of middle height, strongly built. His thick, wavy hair was of a brown so dark as to appear almost black; he sported a trim moustache. The expression of his brown eyes was mild and amiable.

As he closed the front door behind him he heard his wife's voice floating out from the open door of a room along the hall. The room had been his father's study; Eva had lost no time in appropriating it after their marriage.

Wilfrid went along the hall and paused by the open door. Eva was on the phone, talking to one of her many co-workers. She was solidly built, two years younger than Wilfrid. By no means ill-favoured, dressed and groomed in a fashion that suggested no shortage of means and a measure of good taste. She gave

Wilfrid a little smile, slipping a hand over the mouthpiece. 'We'll be eating in half an hour,' she told him. 'Then I'm off out.' He nodded and smiled in acknowledgement, then he turned towards the staircase to go up to his bedroom.

Eva's bedroom, the best bedroom in the house, lay across the landing from Wilfrid's; she had claimed it from the start. They had been married five years. Neither had been married before or had any serious romantic attachment. What little connubial traffic had ever existed between the two bedrooms had by now ceased. Not only were there no children of the marriage, there had never been the slightest suggestion on either side that there would, could or should be any.

They had come across each other at a local carers' support group, at a time when both had frail, elderly parents to look after. Wilfrid's mother had been bedridden for some years before the end. While Wilfrid was out at work every day, his father, though himself in poor health and plagued by arthritis, had attended to the invalid, with some help from a retired nursing auxiliary living nearby.

After Wilfrid's mother died, his father failed rapidly. He went into a nursing home, where he lasted only a few weeks.

Eva had nursed her widowed mother for the last ten years of her life. Her mother died twelve months before Wilfrid's mother, but Eva went on attending the carers' meetings. She had by then belonged to the group longer than anyone else and was highly knowledgeable in all matters relating to members' concerns. She had also for some years served as secretary and continued to do so.

Eva had an older sister, married, with children, living in a nearby town. By virtue of her domestic commitments, the sister had absolved herself from any responsibility for the care of her mother, blithely allowing the entire burden to fall on Eva's shoulders. It was therefore with a profound sense of shock that Eva learned, after her mother's death, the contents of her will. The matter had never been discussed between them, her mother being a formidable old lady, not inclined to welcome questions on such topics. Eva had taken it for granted that she would inherit the bulk, if not all, of what her mother had to leave. It never crossed her mind that she might not be able to go on living in the house, in the style she had always enjoyed. She discovered with dismay and disbelief that the house – a dwelling of no great size or value – had been left jointly to herself and her sister. The furniture and all other household goods, together with all personal possessions – again, none of great value – were to be divided between them. All her mother's investments and savings went to the grandchildren.

Eva's sister wasn't disposed to wait for her legacy. The house was at once put up for sale and the household and personal effects shared out. From her half of the house proceeds Eva bought herself a tiny flat, investing the remainder to bring in a little income, nowhere near enough to live on. She didn't relish the prospect of living alone in cramped quarters on straitened means for the rest of her days and cast about for an acceptable alternative.

Before staying at home to nurse her mother, Eva had worked as a shorthand typist for a local firm. She could take a retraining course and look for employment, in competition with women far younger, very much at home with all the new technology. Eva wasn't much taken with the idea. Nor with the notion – should she be lucky enough to find a good position – of having to go out to work, day in and day out, till she reached retiring age.

Time went by but she couldn't bring herself to apply for work. One by one she sold the pictures she had inherited, the ornaments, items of jewellery, surplus pieces of furniture. She was reaching the end of her stock of saleable articles and was beginning to contemplate the fact that she would soon have to make inroads on her slender capital, when Wilfrid Probyn's mother died, followed soon afterwards by his father. Eva had never been a close friend of Wilfrid's; neither of them had any close friends. But she turned her gaze on him now and saw what looked very like deliverance from her difficulties: a good-natured, amenable man, invariably courteous and obliging, the owner of a highly desirable house, holding down a well-paid job. She set smartly about translating design into action, before anyone else might snap him up, employing what charm she could muster to veil her unswerving purpose.

Wilfrid never stood a chance. He had barely got round to realizing his domestic freedom when another, more powerfully constructed cage began to close around him. Within a short space of time he found himself, somewhat to his astonishment, standing beside Eva in a register office, exchanging vows.

Now, on this Monday evening, Wilfrid duly presented himself at the supper table. He ate with a good appetite; Eva was an excellent cook. She chatted animatedly over the meal, telling him which particular organization was claiming her for the evening. The talk soon turned to the forthcoming production, scheduled for late autumn, of a Gilbert and Sullivan operetta, to be put on by the local amateur operatic society, which they had both joined soon after their marriage.

Wilfrid had an agreeable bass voice, not quite powerful enough to carry a leading role – which in any case he would never have wanted, not relishing the limelight it would entail – but more than adequate for a place in the chorus. Eva never appeared on stage; she had no singing voice. But she was a competent pianist, one of half a dozen in the society, greatly valued as accompanists for rehearsal.

Casting for the operetta had now been completed and work would begin shortly on the production, though not in earnest before September.

As soon as the meal was over, Eva took herself off, leaving Wilfrid to his usual chore of clearing the table and washing up, a task he fell to cheerfully. As he busied himself he contemplated the evening ahead. There was nothing demanding his attention in the garden, which had been laid out long ago by his father, to produce maximum effect with minimum labour. He might read the paper or watch TV. He could make a start on some of the operetta songs – his piano playing wasn't in the same league as his wife's, but it served well enough to accompany him for private singing practice.

But he well knew he would set about none of these things. What he would actually do as soon as he had finished in the kitchen was what he invariably did when he was alone in the house and opportunity offered: he would go down to his hobby rooms in the basement. They had been his exclusive territory since his schooldays; that had been made very clear to Eva from the start. He had taken her down there once and once only, to have a look round, at the start of their marriage. He had informed her that he would keep the rooms clean and in good order; there would be no need for her to concern herself with them in any way. Eva had raised not the slightest objection. She made it plain she had no desire to go poking round in basements or to assume responsibility for a cleaning chore some-one else was willing to undertake. She had never set foot down there again.

A gleam came into Wilfrid's eye at the prospect of the evening before him. He began to sing as he attacked the rest of the washing-up.

The meal Mrs Beattie had prepared was light but sustaining, well balanced and nutritious. Lorraine took care never to lay down a single ounce of surplus flesh and her mother cooperated fully in all her dietary endeavours.

Mrs Beattie was humming a tune when she took her place at the table. 'That song's been running in my head for the last half-hour,' she told Lorraine as she began to serve. 'They were playing it on the radio. It was very popular at one time. "Ramona", it was called. There were a lot of girls christened Ramona after that song.' She gave a reminiscent smile. 'There was a girl called Ramona lived at the end of our road, when I was at school. She was a few years older than me. She came from a decent, hard-working family; her father was a ticket-collector at the railway station.'

She passed Lorraine her plate. 'There were no flies on Ramona. She married well, she did very nicely for herself. She was only eighteen at the time; the boy was a couple of years older. He worked for his father, in the family business. He got Ramona into trouble.'

She served herself and began to eat. 'A lot of parents in that position in those days would just have paid the girl off or footed the bill for her to have an abortion on the quiet, but not this lad's parents. They were very strict churchgoers, very high-principled folk, the kind that think abortion no better than murder. They rushed the pair of them to the altar. Ramona couldn't have a white wedding, of course, or a big reception, but I dare say she thought that a small price to pay for what she got out of it.'

She poured the coffee. 'From all I ever heard, the marriage worked out very well. I certainly don't think the boy had any reason to complain.'

She passed Lorraine her coffee. 'What time did you say Simon was calling?'

'A quarter past seven,' Lorraine told her.

'You might like to ask him round for supper one evening,' her mother suggested on a casual note. 'I could make something special, leave everything ready for you, then I could go round to Madge's.' Madge was a woman she worked with. 'I wouldn't be in your way.'

28

CHAPTER 4

At twenty minutes past seven, Beth Knight left the hairdressing salon and set off for the ten minutes' walk to the house of her friend, Teresa Anderson. The time at which she left the salon varied a good deal. It was never before six, except on Wednesday, early closing day. Sometimes it was as late as seven-thirty.

She was hungry after the day's work, looking forward to the substantial supper Teresa would have ready for her. Teresa was six months younger than Beth and was still attending a local comprehensive school, hoping to go on to take a domestic science course. She wasn't interested in boyfriends. During term-time she worked Saturdays and some evenings at a health-food shop, working there full-time in the school holidays; term would be finishing in a few days. The two girls had met through the local church they both attended.

Beth's route took her through the centre of town. As she neared the theatre she caught sight of Simon Cormack approaching the building from the car park. At his side was a girl Beth recognized: Lorraine Beattie. She knew Lorraine slightly from church and as an occasional customer at the salon.

Simon she knew rather better. She had been out with him a few times during the Easter vacation. He had suddenly stopped seeing her, without any word of explanation, nor had he been in touch with her since coming home at the end of the summer term. Not that this had caused her any real distress; her heart had been in no way involved. But she had been somewhat puzzled. She had liked Simon and had thought they had a pleasant, easy relationship. She had found him quiet, with good manners; well read, interesting to talk to, with views of his own on a wide range of topics.

As the pair drew near, Simon's eyes met Beth's and she gave him a friendly smile. He didn't smile back. The pair turned to enter the theatre. Lorraine glanced about and her gaze fell on

Beth. Again Beth smiled and again received no answering smile. Lorraine gave her a long, cold stare before going into the theatre.

A further five minutes' brisk walking brought Beth to the quiet residential district where Teresa lived in a trim semi built between the wars. Michael Anderson, Teresa's father, was tinkering with his car, by the garage. He looked up at Beth's approach and gave her a warm smile and a friendly greeting. He was a tall, lean man of forty-four, with a genial manner. Teresa was his only child. His wife had died two years ago, of viral pneumonia, after a very brief illness. He worked as a methods engineer at British Braids; he had been with the firm several years.

Beth stood chatting to him for a moment. 'Teresa's upstairs,' he told her. 'She's making new curtains for her bedroom. She picked up some material in the sales.'

Beth went into the house and up the stairs to the landing, where Teresa was seated at her sewing-machine, whirring busily away. She was a cheerful-looking girl with a pleasant, open face. She had been greatly distressed by the death of her mother and had set herself afterwards to run the house and take care of her father, who had been hard hit by his loss.

When Beth had duly admired the gaily coloured material, Teresa left her task and they went down to the dining-room where Teresa had laid supper for them both; her father had eaten earlier. It was a fine, warm evening and the casement windows stood open to the breeze. Beth glanced out at the garden to where a man wielded a hoe between the rose bushes. He looked up and saw her; he smiled and raised a hand in greeting. She waved back and he bent again to his work. 'I see Alec's here,' Beth said lightly as she took her seat at the table. Alec Morgan was so regular a visitor these days as to be almost a fixture in the Anderson household. He had been a friend of Michael Anderson's since childhood. Alec had been a quiet, industrious child, with considerable artistic ability. He had gone on to art school, trained as a silversmith and set up in business on his own. For some years he had succeeded in making only a slender living, but the rising tide of prosperity in the eighties had swept him up and borne him to a point where he was able at last to contemplate marriage. He chose a high-spirited, pretty girl, considerably younger than himself, with few inhibitions about spending his money or making liberal use of credit cards.

When recession followed boom, Alec believed at first it would be temporary. He struggled on, hoping to survive until the tide turned again. But the recession persisted and deepened. His wife had little taste for retrenchment and before long packed her things and left him, for other arms and richer pickings. Alec was beaten at last to his knees and suffered a nervous breakdown. He was unable to work and the bank foreclosed. He lost both his business and his home.

That was back in the New Year. He spent some time in the psychiatric unit of the local hospital, where Michael Anderson visited him regularly. When Alec was well enough to leave hospital he moved into a boarding house found for him by the unit, where the landlady kept a benevolent eye on lodgers sent to her in this way. He lived on social security benefits, not yet sufficiently recovered to be able to look for work. He couldn't relax enough to read, listen to the radio or watch TV for long but found a measure of peace and tranquillity in performing simple tasks at his own pace for his landlady or Michael Anderson, knowing his efforts would be received in a friendly, uncritical fashion.

Neither Michael nor Teresa found his frequent visits in any way intrusive or irritating. Alec made no demands, but worked quietly and without fuss; it was easy to forget he was on the premises at all. Teresa liked him and felt sorry for him but she had given up offering him a meal or other refreshment as he would accept nothing of any kind in return for what he did, being determined not to impose in the smallest particular. The only liberty he would permit himself was to draw a glass of water from the kitchen tap when he was thirsty.

After supper the two girls went upstairs to resume the curtain-making. At her usual time, a quarter to ten, Beth's thoughts turned to going home. 'I'd better be off,' she told Teresa. She heard the back door open and close, the sound of voices as Teresa's father and Alec Morgan came into the house.

She helped Teresa tidy up and then went down with her to the kitchen, where the two men stood talking. Alec looked over at Beth. He was of medium height and wiry build, not bad-looking in an unremarkable way, with a quiet, closed face and nondescript colouring. 'I'll walk you home,' he offered, as he did every time Beth visited. It didn't take him much out of his way and Beth had no objection to a male escort, although she wouldn't have felt nervous walking home alone.

Alec never said much on the way to Grasmere Avenue. Beth usually did most of the talking, chatting easily about trifles. Light showed from the ground floor when they reached Southview. Alec waited until she had let herself into the house and then melted away into the shadows.

On Friday evening Beth had a phone call at Southview from a young man she had known since childhood. His name was Neil Leighton; his family lived along the lane from hers. Beth had always liked him but he was four years older than her, a gap that had seemed vast not so long ago. He worked for a chain of discount stores and had just been transferred to Cannonbridge.

Beth was delighted to hear from him. Yes, she would very much like to go out with him. Yes, tomorrow evening would suit her fine. He arranged to call for her at seven-thirty, to take her out for a meal.

She was ready and waiting next evening when he rang the doorbell. She asked him in for a moment to introduce him to Celia, then they went off down the path to his car, parked by the gate. They chatted easily, neither of them aware of the pair of eyes gazing down at them from the horse chestnut tree in the next-door garden.

Outside a pub on the outskirts of a town fifty miles from Cannonbridge, a small team of men engaged in buying antiques, travelling the country, knocking on likely doors, sat at a rustic table, drinking beer and studying a map spread out before them, debating where to go next.

There were five of them in the team. The leader, Joe Selwyn, was a big, heavily-built man, turned fifty. He had a shrewd face and an amiable manner, a look of unshakeable composure. The rest of the team consisted of two brothers, cousins of Joe, both in their thirties; a brother-in-law of one of the pair, around the same age; and a newcomer to the team, a young man of twenty-four, by the name of Darrell Wilding. Darrell had sharp brown eyes and an air of jaunty confidence. He wasn't related to any of the others; he had been on the road with them only since April. Joe Selwyn had been a good friend of Darrell's father – dead some years now – and had taken Darrell on, out of that

32

old friendship, when Darrell lost his job with a removal firm. Darrell had taken easily to the trade and the way of life.

The week just finished hadn't been too successful for the team. The brothers wanted to push south now, but the brother-in-law favoured the Welsh borders. Darrell was all for Cannonbridge. 'No shortage of money there,' he declared. 'I reckon we could get a good three weeks over there, taking in the villages as well. Plenty of good pickings in those villages.' He knew the area from his removal days. He had carried many a choice piece of furniture, many a fine painting and valuable ornament, for householders leaving or setting up home in Cannonbridge or the surrounding countryside.

Joe Selwyn spoke only after the others had had their say. And when Joe opened his mouth that was invariably the end of the matter. He stabbed a finger down at the map, at a part of the country he always had a fancy for at this time of year. A solidly prosperous region; beautiful stone-built villages, thriving market towns. A racecourse centrally situated; some well-known training stables in the area – Joe was a lifelong follower of the sport of kings.

'That's where we're off to next,' he announced with finality. He drew a finger round his chosen territory. 'We'll take a month over it. We'll move on to Cannonbridge after that.'

CHAPTER 5

The summer slipped by. Shortly after ten-thirty on the evening of Friday, 20th August, as John Heyworth put his key in the door of his rented flat in Lydhall, he heard the phone begin to shrill in the hall. He hurried in and picked up the receiver.

'Thank goodness I've caught you at last,' said a distressed female voice at the other end. 'I've been trying to ring you for the past two hours.' He recognized the voice; it belonged to his uncle's housekeeper, a competent, kindly woman in her sixties. His uncle, Ivor Heyworth, the older brother of John's dead father, was only a couple of years away from ninety. He was a retired bank manager, living in a small house in Gosford, a town some thirty miles from Cannonbridge. He had been a widower for many years; there had never been any children of the marriage. John had called to see him regularly for a good many years. The last time was three weeks ago, when he had found his uncle well and cheerful.

'I'm very sorry to have to tell you your uncle died just after seven this evening,' the housekeeper said with a break in her voice. The doctor had been in to see him only two days before, on his regular weekly visit. 'The doctor was very pleased with him,' the housekeeper added. 'He said your uncle was going along nicely for a man of his age. I gave your uncle his tea as usual, this afternoon. He seemed perfectly well. He sat in his armchair afterwards, watching TV.' Her voice broke again. 'I looked in later, just to see he was all right, the way I always do, and I saw at once that he'd gone.' She began to cry a little as she spoke. 'It must have been very peaceful. He hadn't moved.' She drew a long, quavering breath. 'It was the best way to go. He would have hated a long illness.'

'I'll leave here first thing in the morning,' John assured her. 'You're not to worry about anything. I'll see to it all.'

When he replaced the receiver he went along to his bedroom

34

and took down a travel bag. He would stay over Saturday night, return Sunday evening. There would be a good deal to see to. He should be able to get a word with his uncle's solicitor sometime tomorrow morning. John knew almost nothing about his uncle's affairs; the old man had always been extremely cagey. He had his pension from the bank and had lived comfortably, though by no means extravagantly, in his snug little house.

John knew of no close relatives to be contacted, but there was a niece of his uncle's wife's who had always kept in touch with him. John had occasionally encountered the niece at his uncle's house. She was an amiable woman, not far off sixty now, with grown-up children and half a dozen grandchildren. He knew his uncle had made a will, as the old man had spoken of it some time ago. He had given John to understand that he had appointed his solicitor sole executor. Of the contents of the will John knew nothing. The bank pension would, of course, die with his uncle, but he had probably had some savings – though he may have had to draw on them, or even exhaust them, as the years went by. The house should fetch enough to fund whatever provision Uncle Ivor had made for his house-keeper. He was sure to have provided as well as he could for her; she had cared devotedly for him for over thirty years. Anything left over would probably go to the wife's niece, or possibly to the niece's children, or grandchildren.

As he closed the travel bag it suddenly struck him that with his uncle gone he no longer had a single living relative that he knew of. He was an only child, born late in his parents' marriage; both of them now dead. It gave him a strange feeling to think he was the last of the line, a line that must, like every other line, stretch back into the misty beginnings of mankind. He stood motionless in the middle of the room.

Children, he thought; children are the answer; otherwise it all ends in nothingness. He felt the relentless press of the years upon him.

But there was still, surely, time enough. It was far from too late.

Shortly before noon next morning, John left the solicitor's office in Gosford and walked back to his car. His expression was deeply thoughtful, with a lingering trace of surprise.

Most of what the solicitor had had to say had been very much

35

as he had expected. The housekeeper had been left a generous lump sum, together with a handsome annuity. The matter of her future accommodation would present no difficulty. She was a native of Gosford, with a number of relatives living locally. She intended going to live with her younger, widowed sister in a pleasant residential suburb of the town. His uncle had left legacies for his wife's niece, her children and grandchildren. There were donations to charities and to his local church.

The residue of the estate had been left to John. He had been somewhat surprised at this, but not greatly so. He had thought his uncle might leave him something: his books, maybe, his pictures, or his furniture.

But what had surprised him, what had jerked his eyes wide open when the solicitor had gone on to explain in more detail, was the size of what that residue promised to be.

Ivor Heyworth had, it seemed, been a canny investor from the start. He had acquired over the years a shrewdly selected and well-diversified portfolio. Even in old age the habit of investment had remained, as an absorbing hobby. Far from having to draw on his savings, his capital had steadily increased, right up until his death. The final sum John could expect to receive would be very substantial indeed.

He got into his car and set off back to his uncle's house. The time had come to settle matters one way or another with Celia; things had been allowed to drag on for far too long. He would be down again on Friday for the funeral. He could combine that with one or two business calls in the area, for Melco. He could stay at Southview over the weekend – the bank holiday weekend, that would be. Three full days should surely, in all conscience, be enough for Celia to make up her mind, once and for all.

He set his jaw in a hard line. Until Celia had reached her decision he would say nothing to her about Uncle Ivor's death. And most particularly he would utter not a syllable about his uncle's will, the size of the estate, his own totally unexpected good fortune.

On Saturday evening Beth and Neil Leighton sat over dinner at a quiet country hotel, a few miles from Cannonbridge. They had been out together several times in the last four weeks.

After the waiter had served the coffee, Neil leaned forward

and took Beth's hand. 'I'll miss you,' he said fondly. 'I wish it was you coming with me tomorrow.' He was leaving on Sunday afternoon with a male colleague from the store where he had worked before his transfer. They were off on a three-week touring holiday in one of the less tourist-ridden parts of Spain; it had all been arranged months ago.

Beth had taken a week of her annual leave in June and had spent it at home, with her family. She would be taking her remaining two weeks during the first half of October, going home for the first week and then down to Devon to spend the second week with relatives.

She smiled tenderly at Neil. 'I'll expect you to send me a postcard,' she said lightly.

He gave her fingers a loving squeeze. 'I'll send one every day. But don't expect the first one too soon. They take a lot longer to arrive from abroad than you'd think, even sending them airmail.'

By noon on Sunday the skies had clouded over and the temperature had dropped several degrees; there was a threat of rain in the wind. The team of antique dealers set off for Cannonbridge in the late afternoon, Joe Selwyn at the wheel of his car, the two brothers in a car they shared, and the brother-in-law driving the team's van, with Darrell Wilding sitting beside him. They were making for comfortable digs Joe knew of old. They had done good business lately and were looking forward to even better times over the next few weeks.

A sprinkle of rain spattered the windscreens as they reached the outskirts of town. It didn't dampen their spirits. Fine weather tempted folk out of their homes; rain and wind tended to keep them indoors, ready to answer a knock at the door.

While Beth was round at the Andersons' again on Monday evening, Celia Heyworth rang her sister for a chat. Abbie was going off on holiday and Celia wanted to catch her before she left. Abbie's business was doing increasingly well and she now employed three assistants, sensible, hard-working young women. She could enjoy her holiday with an easy mind, knowing the business was in good hands. She was treating herself to a cruise along the Norwegian fjords. She was leaving on Wednesday morning and would be away nine days.

'I had John on the phone half an hour ago,' Celia told Abbie. 'He says he'll be down this way on business, on Friday. He's going to call in here. He wants to have a serious talk with me. He sounded very determined.'

'You can't go on stalling for ever,' Abbie put in, but Celia ignored the interruption and went on: 'I told him it would have to be in my lunch-hour – it's the only time I can manage.' She gave a little laugh. 'That way I can keep it nice and short. There won't be time for him to lay on too much pressure.'

'Didn't he suggest staying over the bank holiday weekend?' Abbie asked.

'He would have done,' Celia said, 'but I got in first and managed to head him off. I didn't relish letting myself in for a non-stop barrage over three days, so I told him I was going away for the weekend. I said Beth had invited me to her home, to meet her family; we'd be leaving as soon as Beth got in from work on Friday evening. I said I'd be busy from the time I got in from work myself, right up until it was time to leave, so our talk would have to be at lunch-time or not at all. He wasn't best pleased but he said if that was all I could manage then it would have to be lunch-time.'

'And are you going home with Beth for the weekend?' Abbie wanted to know.

Celia laughed again. 'No, I'm not. Beth's not going home herself, she's staying here. She has to work on Saturday. And she wouldn't find anyone at home if she did want to go there – they're all off to the sea for the weekend, they've been lent a caravan by friends.'

'It's about time you got things settled with John,' Abbie said, on an older-sister note of rebuke. 'You should tell him the truth about what you've decided, fair and square. He has a right to know.'

Lorraine Beattie was always up betimes. On Tuesday morning she stood in a patch of sunlight by her bedroom window, contemplating with deep satisfaction the result of the pregnancy test she had just carried out: undeniably positive. She drew a long breath and stared ahead, charmed by visions of the future.

Sounds from below floated up, breaking into her thoughts. She must go down at once and tell her mother.

She went swiftly from the room, out on to the landing. She

was about to dart down the stairs but checked herself, with a little smile. Must start taking care, might as well begin now. A very valuable pregnancy, this; a great deal riding on it. She placed a steadying hand on the banister rail and sailed sedately down to the kitchen, still smiling.

Celia Heyworth's car was no longer in its first youth and on Wednesday morning it signalled the fact by obstinately refusing to start. Celia rang the garage and was told someone would be over later in the morning to take a look at it. She glanced at her watch as she replaced the receiver. 8.25. Her neighbour, Ronald Marriott, always left for work at 8.30 on the dot. She and Beth hurried across to Rosemont and found Ronald's car drawn up by the front door. He came out of the house almost at once.

Celia launched into a rapid explanation of her plight. Could they beg a lift from him? It wouldn't take him out of his way.

'No trouble at all,' he responded amiably. 'Glad to be of help.'

Celia gave him a warm smile of thanks. As they set off she inquired after his wife. She had had a brief, passing chat with Phyllis a week or two back. Phyllis had disclosed with delight that she was expecting a child in the spring.

'I'm afraid she's had to go into hospital,' Ronald said in a tone of anxiety. 'We're hoping it's going to be all right, she won't lose the baby.' Phyllis had felt unwell yesterday afternoon and had phoned her doctor. He had come round at once and told her she must go into hospital right away, there was a serious risk of miscarriage. Ben had been out in the garden at the time, playing in his sandpit. Ronald had been summoned urgently from work. 'My boss is very good,' he told Celia. 'Very understanding. He's a family man himself.'

'Let me know if there's anything I can do,' Celia volunteered with quick sympathy. Beth immediately joined in to offer her own services. Ronald thanked them both but said he had no need to call on them, at least not for the present. 'Ben's over at his grandmother's,' he explained. 'She's looking after him for the present. He's very fond of her and he'll enjoy being in the country.' He had taken the child, at his wife's suggestion, over to her mother's yesterday afternoon. Her mother lived in a village fifteen miles away. She was in her sixties, healthy and active, well able to cope with a lively grandson. She would happily keep Ben for as long as was necessary.

'Please tell Phyllis we're thinking of her,' Celia said. 'Let us know how she goes on. If she would like a visit from either – or both – of us, do let us know.'

Ronald dropped Beth at the salon, then drove on to British Braids. As Celia got out of the car, he said: 'If you need a lift again tomorrow morning –' but she broke in: 'It's very good of you, but I don't think that will be necessary. I'm sure we'll have the car by then but if not I can fix up a lift with the chief accountant here. He goes past the end of the avenue on his way to work.'

She stooped by his window to thank him for his help, adding with her ready smile: 'Don't forget, if there's anything I can do, anything at all, don't be afraid to ask. I really do mean it. Just pop over to the house and let me know.'

In spite of the cloudy sky and cool breeze, Friday morning remained dry. Ivor Heyworth's funeral took place quietly at the Gosford church he had attended. He was laid to rest under the yew trees, beside his long-dead wife.

John Heyworth was able to have another chat with the solicitor afterwards and then returned to his uncle's house. He couldn't stay long; he had to get over to Cannonbridge and the traffic was sure to be heavy. He mustn't be late reaching Southview; he would have only a short time to say all that must be said to Celia.

He made a swift tour of the premises with the housekeeper, checking that all was in order. He had been delighted to find from his earlier detailed inspection that the property had been very well maintained. All in all, it was eminently saleable and should go quickly.

The housekeeper walked out with him to his car when he took his leave. She would be remaining in the house until it was sold. He thanked her again for all she had done and was continuing to do. He put an arm round her shoulders and kissed her lightly on the cheek. 'I'll be in touch again very soon,' he assured her. She smiled up at him, with tears in her eyes.

I've got to take my hat off to Uncle Ivor, he said to himself as he turned the car out through the gates. The old boy had left all his affairs in exemplary order, even taking out a large insurance policy to provide for inheritance tax, allowing the estate to be wound up with minimum delay.

Wilfrid Probyn always went home for lunch. He had formed the habit years ago, when his parents were old and ailing. Eva had never raised any objection; if she was out on one of her missions she would leave him something in the oven or fridge.

Today, as he crossed the car park on the dot of one o'clock, he saw that Celia Heyworth was already standing beside his car, glancing his way with an air of urgency. Her own car was still in dock, awaiting a spare part which wouldn't reach the garage this side of the bank holiday. As she caught sight of Wilfrid her features relaxed into a smile. What a lovely smile she has, he thought, by no means for the first time; it lights up her whole face.

Unlike Wilfrid, Celia didn't always go home for lunch. Sometimes she went shopping, picking up a hasty sandwich. Or she might meet a friend for a meal in a café. Once in a while she ate in the canteen. This morning, on the way to work, she had told Wilfrid she would be glad of a lift home and back again, at lunch-time, but she hadn't said why.

Now she jumped into the car the moment he opened the door. They were lucky with the traffic and it was only a few minutes later when he let her out at the top of Grasmere Avenue. She would wait for him at the same spot at ten minutes to two, for the return journey.

She hurried off to Southview and Wilfrid continued on to Sebastopol Gardens; he let himself into Nightingale Villa. Eva was in the kitchen and began dishing up the instant she heard his key in the lock. Over the meal she reminded him that she would be out when he got in from work in the evening. She had a meeting at four and was going on afterwards to the house of a woman she knew from the carers' support group. She had promised to sit with the woman's bedridden old mother, to allow the woman to attend the birthday party of a young granddaughter.

'I'm leaving a casserole in the oven for supper,' Eva added. 'Don't wait for me. I don't expect to be home before half past eight. Take what you want and then put the casserole back in the oven on a low heat. I expect I'll be glad of it when I get in.'

At a quarter to two, John Heyworth let himself out of Southview. He got into his car and drove out through the gates. Inside the house, Celia attended swiftly to her face and hair before leaving and then set off at a rush up the avenue. She drew a long breath to steady herself as she took up her stance to wait for Wilfrid. It had been a tiring forty minutes. She had found John's car drawn up by the front door when she reached home. John was inside the house, standing by the kitchen window, staring out. He had turned to face her as she entered the room, launching at once into his spiel, determined not to waste a moment.

Her train of thought broke off as Wilfrid's car came into view. He pulled up and she got in.

At the same moment her husband halted his car beside a phone box. He rang Sarah Brooke at her flat, by arrangement. A few minutes later he got back into his car. His first Melco appointment was in a town some miles from Cannonbridge and he mustn't be late. He'd just about have time now for a word with Beth Knight at the salon – if he could get to see her right away.

CHAPTER 7

Beth was about to go down to the basement storeroom to bring up more shampoo and conditioner when John Heyworth came into the salon, asking for her. He was able to have his word immediately, in a quiet corner. After he had gone she went off once again in the direction of the storeroom. But this time her mind was not on what she was doing; she was still thinking about what John had said to her. She opened the door leading down to the basement and descended the flight of steps without her usual care. She missed her footing and pitched forward, putting out a hand to save herself. She fell heavily and awkwardly, bruising her shins and spraining her right wrist.

She struggled to her feet and stumbled shakily back up the steps, tears in her eyes from the pain. One of the other girls sat her down and hurried off to speak to the proprietress. A few minutes later that lady's aunt, a brisk, grey-haired woman who acted as general factotum in the establishment, was driving Beth round to the doctor's surgery.

There was nothing broken, the doctor was happy to confirm. He strapped the wrist, wrote out a prescription for painkillers and told Beth to go home and rest. It would be some days before she could go back to work.

They stopped at a chemist's for the painkillers and then went on to Southview where Beth was very soon resting on her bed under the duvet, sipping hot milk, with the first dose of pain-killers inside her. She assured the aunt she would be quite all right on her own till Mrs Heyworth got in from work; the aunt could return to the salon.

The good lady took herself off and Beth drank her milk. She felt pleasantly sleepy; her thoughts began to drift. At home, her family would shortly be setting off for the seaside caravan; it would be nice if the sun shone for them. She wondered how Neil Leighton was enjoying his Spanish holiday. She hadn't yet had a postcard from him but maybe one would arrive tomorrow.

She finished her milk and set down the beaker. She snuggled back into her pillows and closed her eyes. She was soon fast asleep.

Shortly after three-fifteen, Ronald Marriott was standing outside the open door of his office, exchanging farewell civilities with a departing client, when his boss came along the corridor and hovered discreetly nearby until the client had gone. 'My next appointment has just been cancelled,' he told Ronald. 'I'm free now till we close. If you've nothing very special coming up, I can take over for you and you can get off to see your wife.' Phyllis hadn't lost her baby but was being kept in hospital for the present.

Ronald was delighted and thanked him warmly. They went into his office and he put his boss in the picture about his remaining appointments. 'Phyllis will be pleased,' he said as he turned to the door. 'She's not expecting me till this evening.' He had been popping into the hospital every day for a brief lunch-time call as well as for a longer evening visit of an hour or more.

He looked at his watch as he went out to his car. 3.35. Straight home first, to shave, wash and change, snatch a sandwich and a cup of tea. He could stop on the way to the hospital to pick up some little gift for Phyllis.

A quarter to five found him walking briskly in through the doors of the hospital, carrying a handsome basket of fruit, some glossy magazines and a gift-wrapped bottle of toilet water.

A relaxed holiday atmosphere prevailed at British Braids as the buildings emptied at five-thirty. Wilfrid Probyn was already sitting at the wheel of his car when Celia Heyworth came hurrying across the car park. A few yards away, Michael Anderson was walking towards his own car. He glanced over as Celia got in beside Probyn and closed the door.

The health-food shop where Teresa Anderson worked would be open on Saturday but Teresa had asked for and been given the Saturday off, in addition to the bank holiday Monday. She and her father were going to spend the weekend with her maternal grandparents in a Welsh market town. They intended setting off in the car after work on Friday evening, as soon as they'd had a bite to eat and attended to last-minute chores. Teresa was greatly looking forward to the trip. She was fond of her grandparents and hadn't seen them for some time.

She had hoped to get away from the shop sharp at six but had been delayed by a dilatory customer. She had missed her bus and had to walk.

As she let herself into the house, she could hear her father upstairs, in the bathroom. She went straight along to the kitchen and set about getting a quick meal on the table. In the utility room next to the kitchen the automatic washing-machine was in operation – her father was always punctilious about dealing with his work clothes at the end of the week. As she bustled about she glanced out of the window and saw Alec Morgan busy in the garden. He looked up and gave her a wave. He had promised to keep an eye on the place while they were away. Not only would he be sleeping in the house but he intended taking the opportunity to redecorate the bathroom. The colour scheme had been chosen and the materials bought.

Her father came downstairs in his bathrobe and transferred the load from the washing-machine to the tumble-dryer. He exchanged a few words with Teresa before going back upstairs to dress and throw a few last-minute items into his bag. Teresa checked the supper before hurrying off to wash and change, finish her packing.

Three-quarters of an hour later they were ready to leave. Alec would clear the table and tidy up. Michael had already taken his work clothes from the tumble-dryer and hung them on the line in the utility room, ready for use again on Tuesday morning.

In Joe Selwyn's view, the last call of the evening should always be made before six; that allowed time to catch a householder returning from work. Later than that, all you did was irritate folk by snatching them away from a meal or TV.

By 6.30 all the team had gathered, as they usually did around that time, at the spot where they had left the van. It was normally necessary to return to various dwellings to pick up the heavier pieces they had bought and for this purpose they went two or three at a time, according to the weight of the items involved. The greater part of what they bought was swiftly passed on to large-scale dealers and exporters.

As they loaded the van, the talk was of how the week had gone and their plans for the immediate future. There was a general air of satisfaction. Joe declared himself more than happy with the week. Two deals had given him particular pleasure, one a couple of days back and the other only this morning, both deals pulled off by Darrell Wilding. 'Keep it up, lad,' Joe exhorted him with an approving slap on the back. 'You're doing all right.'

But Darrell looked none too cheerful; he seemed tense and uneasy. When the talk turned to plans for next week he wasn't slow in speaking up. He'd had enough of Cannonbridge. He was all for moving on to fresh pastures, first thing tomorrow morning.

'You don't mean that,' Joe responded genially. 'You were all for staying on another two or three weeks, only this morning. It's Friday evening, you're tired and hungry, that's all it is. You'll think very differently tomorrow morning.' He gave a decisive jerk of his head. 'We'll definitely be staying here another two weeks, at least.'

The other three were in full agreement with Joe, and Darrell said no more on the way back to the digs. None of them thought of going home for the holiday weekend. Joe was a long-time widower, Darrell and the two brothers bachelors, the brother-in-law divorced and childless. They would take time off locally at a racecourse, a fair or a show.

Supper was almost over at Leacroft. The meal had been a good deal livelier than usual, Ellen Cormack had noted with pleasure. Instead of keeping his gaze lowered, speaking only in response to direct questions and then only in monosyllables, Simon had entered fully into the conversation, initiating topics of his own, engaging Thomas in an animated discussion about the family business, putting forward ideas that were certainly worth considering. He even went so far as to volunteer information about his own movements – something unheard of in recent times. He had, he said, spent the afternoon in the reference room of the public library, doing work for his course. Not only that but he also indicated how he proposed spending the evening.

'I'm going round to Lorraine's,' he said as he stood up from the table. 'We may go to a movie or we may take a run out into the country.' He had showered and changed before supper.

He offered to help clear the table before he left, but Ellen told him with a smile that she could manage, adding that he'd better get along to Lorraine's without delay or they'd be late for a movie.

Thomas and Ellen exchanged glances as the door closed behind Simon. The pleasure on Ellen's face was mixed with relief. If only things could be all right again between themselves and Simon, that was her dearest wish. She scarcely dared voice the hope that it was beginning to seem as if it might at long last be possible.

'Do you think there's anything in it with Lorraine Beattie?' she asked her husband.

'Simon's still very young,' Thomas said. 'But if there is anything in it, it might not be a bad idea. It might settle him down to have a steady girlfriend. And he could do a lot worse than Lorraine Beattie.'

Driving back to Lydhall on the motorway, with one-third of his journey still before him, John Heyworth was suddenly assailed by weariness. It occurred to him that he had eaten little all day. He pulled into the next service station.

His first action was to find a phone to ring Sarah Brooke at her flat. There was no reply. He went off to fill his petrol tank and have a wash, before ringing her number again. Still no reply. He went in search of food and strong black coffee, then he returned to the phone to tap out Sarah's number a third time. Again without result.

He abandoned the attempt and got back into his car for the last leg of his journey.

It was almost 8.30 when Eva Probyn got back to Nightingale Villa. As she garaged her car and approached the front door she could hear Wilfrid in the sitting-room, singing with loud exuberance one of the Gilbert and Sullivan songs, thumping out a spirited accompaniment on the piano.

He didn't hear her as she let herself into the house and opened the sitting-room door. When she spoke he gave a little startled jump and fell abruptly silent.

'You're in a good mood,' Eva observed on a quizzical note.

He flashed her a cheerful smile. 'I suppose I did get a bit carried away.' He sprang to his feet and darted across to give her a quick hug. He planted a forthright kiss on her cheek. He began to dance assiduous attention on her, pulling forward her chair and plumping up the cushions, inviting her to sit down while he went along to the kitchen to see to her supper.

She sat motionless after he had left the room. The expression on her face was one of not altogether pleased surprise.

The weather improved considerably over the holiday weekend. By noon on Sunday the sun was shining brilliantly; the skies were a cloudless blue. It was still fine and warm on Tuesday morning, for the general return to work. Wilfrid Probyn set off punctually for British Braids, halting at the end of Grasmere Avenue to pick up Celia and Beth. But this morning there was no sign of either of them. After a brief wait he started up the car again and turned into the avenue. As he pulled up outside Southview he gave a couple of toots on the horn. A minute or two later he tooted again. Another minute or two went by. He got out of his car and went up to the front door.

All was still and silent. He rang the bell. There was no response. He gave a brisk rat-tat on the knocker. Still no response. He went round to the side door, to the back door. At both he repeated his ringing and knocking, with no result. He wasted no more time but went back to the gate and along to the house next door; he had some acquaintance with the Marriotts.

He pressed the bell and Ronald Marriott answered it almost at once; he was dressed, ready for work. Wilfrid apologized for disturbing him and asked: 'I wondered if you happened to know if Mrs Heyworth decided to go away for the weekend after all. She told me on Friday she was staying at home but she may have changed her mind.'

Ronald shook his head. 'I'm afraid I've no idea. I haven't seen her for the best part of a week. Or Beth, either.'

Wilfrid frowned. 'I was supposed to be giving them a lift to work this morning but I can't get any reply next door. It's not like Mrs Heyworth. If she did decide to go away, I'd have expected her to give me a ring, to let me know she wouldn't be here this morning. She's never casual in that way.' He fell silent for a moment. 'I hope there's nothing wrong.'

'I think perhaps we should take a look,' Ronald said. They went rapidly over to Southview. Ronald rang and knocked, without result. Together they made a swift tour of the exterior.

No lights on anywhere. Doors locked, windows closed, curtains drawn back – except for an upstairs room at the back, where the curtains were three-quarters closed and the sash window open a few inches at the top. 'If they were going away,' Wilfrid said with conviction, 'they'd never leave a window open.'

'I can get in there,' Ronald said. 'If you'll give a hand bringing the ladder over.' They went hastily back to Rosemont and took the ladder from a shed. They carried it across to Southview and placed it against the rear wall. Wilfrid held the ladder steady as Ronald went up and let himself in.

The room was plainly Beth Knight's bedroom. It was orderly enough except for the bed. The duvet had been thrown back and the pillows showed the impress of a head. The bedroom door stood wide open. He went slowly out on to the landing, where he came to a full stop. He remained motionless, staring down.

Outside, Wilfrid still stood at the foot of the ladder, gazing up at the window, his brows drawn together in a frown. He heard the front door open and he went round there at once. Ronald was coming shakily down the steps, his face ashy pale. He looked dazed and nauseated.

'What is it?' Wilfrid demanded sharply.

Ronald gestured back into the house without speaking. He put his hands up to his face and staggered off into the shrubbery, where he was violently sick.

Wilfrid went up the steps and in through the front door. Flies buzzed. An unpleasant smell rose to his nostrils. He came to an abrupt halt.

Beth Knight was lying face down, sprawled across the lowest stairs, one arm outflung, the other bent under her body, her head turned to one side at an unnatural angle, her features contused and swollen.

He drew a ragged, gasping breath and stood leaning against the wall, his head lowered, his eyes closed. After some moments he opened his eyes. The kitchen door stood open. He made himself take a few halting steps towards it.

On the floor, just inside the door, he could see a pair of legs, female legs. He forced himself to stumble on, to look inside.

Celia Heyworth lay on her back among the buzzing flies, her arms flung out, her face and throat discoloured and swollen, her forehead smashed in.

Tears streamed down his face as he made his way back to the front door. On the mat inside the door lay a brightly coloured postcard. He went out, down the steps.

Ronald came lurching back from the shrubbery, wiping his face with a handkerchief.

'We must call the police,' Wilfrid managed to say.

'I'll go back over and ring from there,' Ronald said unsteadily. 'You'd better stay here.'

CHAPTER 8

Detective Chief Inspector Kelsey was a big, solidly built man with massive shoulders. His craggy features were dominated by a large, squashy nose. He had a fine head of thickly springing carroty hair, a freckled skin and shrewd green eyes.

In the early afternoon he made yet another tour of the Southview premises, inside and out. The forensic team was at work inside the house; every inch of the garden was being searched. The bodies had gone to the mortuary; the postmortem would take place at six o'clock.

There had been reports on local radio and a brief mention of the murders in a news bulletin on national radio. Local newspaper reporters were in evidence and one or two national dailies were showing interest. A sizeable crowd, including many children and teenagers at a loose end in the school holidays, had gathered in the vicinity.

House-to-house inquiries were in operation and several householders had spoken of the activities of the team of antique dealers in the neighbourhood. The dealers were still busy in Cannonbridge and had been promptly rounded up, to be interviewed by an officer who had known Joe Selwyn for years.

Joe had never been in trouble with the police, nor had any of his team. They freely acknowledged that they had been at work in the Grasmere Avenue area during the latter part of the previous week. It seemed they always tackled a district in the same fashion: three streets at a time. The brothers worked as a pair, dealing with the first street, up one side and down the other. Joe and the brother-in-law made a second pair, taking on the adjoining street. Darrell Wilding worked alone, in the third street.

The accounts they gave of their movements about the avenues tallied with what householders had told the police. Darrell Wilding had worked Grasmere Avenue on Thursday afternoon and Friday morning. He had called at Southview shortly before noon on Friday but had found no one at home. He had very definitely not made any second visit to the house.

After fingerprints of all five men were taken they were let go, on the strict understanding that no attempt would be made for the present to go elsewhere.

There was no sign of any break-in at Southview, no ransacking of any room. In the kitchen, behind Celia's body, a stool lay overturned. On the table in the centre of the room, tomatoes and runner beans were tumbled in a heap; a wilting lettuce lay on top. Beside the heap was a wooden rolling pin wrapped in a tea towel, the towel stained, with fragments of bone and tissue, strands of dark hair.

Celia Heyworth's body was fully clothed. According to Wilfrid Probyn, she was dressed in the clothes she had worn when she left work on Friday evening. Beth Knight wore a cotton wrapper over her underwear and nylon tights. Her shoes, placed neatly together, stood beside her bed. The dress she had worn to the salon on Friday was on a hanger hooked on the top of her wardrobe. The clothing of neither victim had been disturbed; there was no indication of any sexual interference. In both cases, rigor mortis had run its full course.

Beth's wristwatch lay on her bedside table, beside a bottle of painkillers and a beaker holding a little milky residue. There was no watch or jewellery of any kind on Celia's body, although Wilfrid Probyn stated with certainty that she always wore a watch and rings to work.

Wilfrid had also been able to enlighten them about the tumbled heap of vegetables on the kitchen table. It seemed they came from one of the clerks at British Braids, an enthusiastic gardener in the habit of distributing his surplus produce among the staff. It had been Celia's turn on Friday. She had commented on the vegetables to Wilfrid as he drove her home at the end of the day. He clearly recalled the carrier bag holding the vegetables; it was of white plastic, bearing the name of a local supermarket. Nowhere in the house, garden or dustbin was there any trace of the bag. Nor was there any trace of the shoulder bag, of dark brown leather, that Celia always wore to work. Wilfrid was positive she had been wearing it when he dropped her at the end of Grasmere Avenue at between 5.35 and 5.40 on Friday.

The electric wall-clock in the kitchen had stopped at four minutes to six. A radio stood on the worktop beneath the clock and both clock and radio were plugged into an adapter inserted into the socket in the skirting-board; the socket switch had been turned off. The Chief Inspector inclined to the belief that the clock might well show, near enough, the time the murders had taken place, almost immediately after Celia had entered the house, a view strongly reinforced in the Chief's mind by the fact that the vegetables had not been put away. The police doctor hadn't been able to narrow down the time as finely as that, but he had agreed such a time was well within the probable limits.

The salon proprietress had told them about the accident that had befallen Beth early on Friday afternoon. The aunt had described how she had driven Beth home to Southview after the visit to the doctor's surgery and the call at the chemist's. It was abundantly plain that but for her accident Beth would have remained working at the salon until 7.15 or 7.30 that evening – a particularly busy evening because of the approaching holiday.

The aunt had helped Beth remove her dress and shoes and put on her wrapper. She had removed Beth's watch and put it on the bedside table. She was sure Beth had worn no jewellery. She had settled Beth on the bed and then gone downstairs to make her some hot milk. She was positive the electric wall-clock was working when she was in the kitchen as she had checked the time by it; it had shown five minutes past three.

Beth had taken a painkiller with the milk. The aunt had opened the window and partly closed the curtains. Beth was quite happy to be left and had assured the aunt she would soon be asleep. The aunt had left the front door properly locked after her; she was always most careful in such matters.

One piece of information the salon proprietress supplied brought a sharp look to the Chief's eyes: a man had called at the salon shortly after two on Friday afternoon, asking to speak to Beth and promising not to keep her long. He had given his name as Heyworth. Beth had looked upset when he left and it was almost immediately afterwards that she had had her accident.

The news of the two deaths had been broken to John Heyworth by the Lydhall police and he was now on his way to Cannonbridge.

The news had also been broken to Beth Knight's parents by the local police. Her father had already been over to identify his daughter's body. He had been utterly devastated and had been able to throw no light on what had happened. Neither he nor his wife had ever set foot in Southview or had ever met Celia Heyworth or her husband.

But he could tell them who had sent Beth the holiday post-card, signed Neil, from Spain. That would be Neil Leighton, the son of a neighbour. He had recently been transferred to Cannonbridge and had got in touch with Beth. The only other friend he had heard Beth speak of was a girl called Teresa; he didn't know her surname. He understood she attended the same church as Beth and that she was still at school, but he knew nothing else about her.

The local police had contacted Neil Leighton's parents, who told them Neil had left for a touring holiday in Spain on Sunday, 22nd August and wouldn't be back until Sunday, 12th September.

The Chief came out of the front door of Southview and stood glancing about. There was no side or back gate to the garden. He crossed to the dividing fence to survey the empty property next door. According to the estate agents, there had been only three appointments to view the property since it had been put on the market: a retired couple, a middle-aged widow with a growing family and a businesswoman with elderly parents. The last of these, the retired couple, had viewed over a month ago. There had been no follow-up from any of them. All had come from well outside the Cannonbridge area.

As he turned from the fence he looked at his watch. Time he was on his way. John Heyworth would soon be arriving at the police station.

When Heyworth arrived he wore the set, grim look of a man nerving himself for a considerable ordeal. He was taken along to the mortuary to identify his wife's body and emerged in a distraught state. It was some time before he had recovered enough to be able to answer questions.

The first question was about Celia's relatives. Heyworth told them both her parents were dead. Her only close relative was an older sister, Abbie Yates, living in Wychford. Abbie and Celia had always got on well. The Chief had come across photographs of Abbie in an album in Celia's bureau. Every photograph had its neatly lettered caption, giving name, date and other details.

Heyworth told them he had last seen his wife at lunch-time on Friday, when he had called at Southview, by arrangement.

Could he recall if Celia had been wearing a watch or jewellery?

To the best of his recollection she had been wearing her gold wristwatch, given to her on her twenty-first birthday by her parents; it was engraved with the date and her maiden name: Celia Yates. He was pretty certain she had been wearing the three rings she usually wore: her platinum wedding ring, inscribed inside with the date of the marriage and the initials of bride and groom; her gold engagement ring – a solitaire diamond set in a plain, classic design – and a third ring she was fond of. This last ring, of gold, with a sapphire and diamonds in a highly decorative setting, had belonged to Celia's mother and grandmother; she usually wore it on her right hand.

Heyworth was driven over to Southview and asked to say if he thought anything was missing from the house. He was still in a shaky condition and found it difficult to focus his thoughts, but after a tour of the premises he told them that the only things that seemed to be missing were four small items from the sitting-room mantelpiece: a porcelain figure of a girl holding a basket of flowers, that he had given Celia on their first wedding anniversary; a Venetian bronze model of a tiger, that had belonged to his father; a Royal Worcester posy vase, painted with flowers, and a cameo glass scent bottle with a hinged silver top; the posy vase and scent bottle had both belonged to his mother. All four items, the Chief noted, were small enough to be thrust into pockets – or into the white carrier bag from which the vegetables had been tipped out on to the kitchen table. Other, larger, items of value in the sitting-room had been ignored.

Heyworth was sure all four items had been in place on the mantelpiece the last time he had stayed for the weekend; he would definitely have noticed if they had been missing. But he couldn't say if they had been there at lunch-time on Friday as he hadn't set foot in the sitting-room that day.

Had he noticed if the electric wall-clock in the kitchen was working that lunch-time?

Yes, he had glanced at the clock more than once and it had very definitely been working.

The Chief asked how long they had had the kitchen radio. Two or three years, Heyworth told him.

Was it always kept plugged into the adapter in the socket, along with the plug belonging to the wall-clock?

Yes, it was. The socket switch was always left on, the radio being turned on and off by means of its own control switch.

Night had fallen by the time the double postmortem was over. Chief Inspector Kelsey came out into the hospital corridor with the pathologist at the end of the long proceedings.

Celia Heyworth would seem to have suffered more than one assault, all from the front. At the time of the first attack she would have been standing, facing her assailant. A hand had been placed with great pressure over her nose and mouth, obstructing her breathing, while she was at the same time being gripped round the shoulders with the other hand. She would have become limp and lost consciousness almost at once. She had then been throttled – probably while lying down, having fallen or been lowered, insensible, to the floor.

She had survived – barely survived – both attacks. A matter of minutes later, she had been struck two savage blows to the front of the head, smashing in the skull. The first of these blows had killed her. The nature of the injuries was consistent with the blows having been delivered by the rolling pin, held in the cloth – presumably to avoid leaving prints.

Beth Knight had been attacked from behind, most probably as she turned to flee. Her neck had been seized in an armlock and her head forced back, breaking her neck and killing her instantly. Her attacker had then, for good measure, throttled her from behind, while at the same time bringing her head down with great force – most probably against the edge of a stair, fracturing her skull.

There was nothing to suggest that the attacks had been carried out by more than one person or that the attacker had been other than right-handed. No attempt at sexual interference had been made on either victim.

'Does all this suggest,' Kelsey asked, 'that the killer first attacked Celia, believed he had killed her by throttling, then dealt with Beth and did actually kill her? He then realized Celia wasn't dead. He went back and finished her off with the rolling pin.'

'Yes, that's what it does suggest,' the pathologist agreed.

One thing's for sure, Kelsey thought grimly: when we do catch up with the killer, he's not going to be able to plead manslaughter. He made very sure there was no spark of life left in either of his victims.

Celia had made an attempt to defend herself. She had well-manicured hands, the nails varnished a pearly rose-pink. Several nails had suffered damage as she had tried to fend off her attacker and had been left broken or bent. The end of one nail was missing. There was no human tissue under any of the nails but there were fragments of fibres, including one sizeable strand.

Beth would appear to have put up no struggle; hardly surprising in view of her injured wrist.

There had been no difficulty in discovering when and what each victim had last eaten and drunk. Celia had shared a snack lunch with her husband at Southview and had drunk a cup of tea and eaten a biscuit at her desk at British Braids, at four o'clock. It was the custom at the hairdressing salon to supply the staff with coffee and sandwiches at lunch-time on busy days. Beth had finished her brief lunch-break shortly before John Heyworth had called at the salon. She had also drunk a beaker of hot milk at Southview, at around ten minutes past three.

The pathologist's estimate of the time of death did nothing to shake the Chief's belief that the murders had taken place shortly before six.

One last question the Chief had for the pathologist: 'The strength required for these attacks – could a female have committed the murders?'

The pathologist gave a decisive nod. 'Yes, indeed.' Both attacks were within the powers of an ordinarily fit, strong and active female. 'Particularly,' the pathologist added, 'a female in a state of frenzy.'

Late as it was, John Heyworth must be questioned tonight. He had by now got a grip on himself and made no protest. An attempt had been made to contact Celia Heyworth's sister, Abbie Yates, but without success. It seemed Abbie was away on holiday, cruising the Norwegian fjords. She was expected back in Wychford on Thursday evening.

Kelsey began his questioning by asking Heyworth exactly when he had last had contact with his wife. Heyworth answered on a note of surprise: 'I've already told you: it was at lunch-time on Friday. I left Southview at a quarter to two.' He was able to be precise as Celia had made a point of the time, saying she must be in her place at the end of the avenue when Wilfrid Probyn stopped on his way back to British Braids. Heyworth was emphatic that he had had no further contact of any kind with Celia.

He supplied details of his two business appointments on Friday afternoon. He had left the office of the second customer, in a town ten miles from Cannonbridge, just before five and had immediately set off back to Lydhall.

Had his route taken him through Cannonbridge?

Yes, it had; that was the most direct route. No, he hadn't broken the return journey at Cannonbridge; he had driven through the town and headed for the motorway. He named the service station where he had halted for a meal. He had reached his flat in Lydhall a little after eight and had gone early to bed, tired after his long day.

Kelsey wanted to know if the two business appointments had arisen in the normal course and he had taken the opportunity to call in at Southview to see his wife.

No, he was told; that was not the way it had been. 'I had to attend the funeral of a relative, in Gosford, on the Friday morning,' Heyworth explained. 'I decided to fit in a couple of business calls in the afternoon, calls I'd have had to make before long, in any case. I thought I'd go on to Southview afterwards and stay there over the holiday weekend. I rang Celia but she told me she wouldn't be at home over the weekend. Beth had invited her to spend the holiday with her family and Celia had accepted. They intended setting off on Friday evening, as soon as Beth got in from work and had a bite to eat; they'd be leaving around eight. I was anxious to talk things over with Celia, get something settled about her move to Lydhall. I suggested calling in around six, after she'd got home from work but she said that would be no good, she'd be busy seeing to things before going off for the weekend. I insisted I must talk to her and would much prefer it to be face to face rather than over the phone. She said in that case it would have to be at lunch-time, so that was how we fixed it.'

Kelsey frowned. 'Your wife and Beth had no intention of visiting Beth's family.' Beth's father had told the Chief he had spent the weekend with his wife and children in a caravan at the seaside; they had returned home on Monday evening. Furthermore, but for her sprained wrist, Beth would have spent the whole of Saturday working at the salon.

'I knew nothing about that,' Heyworth countered. 'I only knew what Celia told me. Naturally, I believed her.'

Kelsey studied him. 'You called at the salon at around two o'clock and asked to speak to Beth. You must have gone there more or less straight from Southview. Why did you go there? What did you have to say to Beth?'

Heyworth came smartly back at him. 'There's no mystery about it. I wanted to be fair to the girl. I had to make sure she knew she'd have to leave Southview before long, the house was going to be put up for sale. I couldn't rely on Celia telling her that, fair and square. Celia was always soft-hearted. She'd let things drift on rather than come straight out with something she knew wouldn't be welcome, even though she was well aware it would have to be said sooner or later.' He jerked his head. 'And I'd guessed right. Beth was definitely under the impression she had no need to start looking for another place.' He drew a long breath. 'She was upset at the thought of leaving.'

'Did you discover from Beth that she wasn't taking Celia home for the weekend?'

He shook his head. 'The question never arose. I was in the salon only a few minutes.'

Again Kelsey studied him. 'Were you attracted to Beth?'

Heyworth looked levelly back at him. 'No, I was not. Not that I'd anything against the girl, she seemed pleasant enough. But I never wanted her living at Southview in the first place. I wouldn't have wanted any outsider living in the house. I knew nothing about it until Beth was already installed.'

'When you spoke to Beth at the salon, did she in fact dig in her heels? Did she tell you she had no intention of leaving Southview as long as Celia wanted her to stay?'

Heyworth shook his head. 'No, she said nothing of the sort. In fact, she was very cooperative. She said she'd start looking right away. If she didn't find something she really liked, she'd go into temporary digs and keep on looking.'

There was a brief pause and then Kelsey said, 'This talk you had with your wife at lunch-time, can you give me the gist of it?'

Heyworth launched at once into a rapid account. 'I put it to Celia that it was a full six months since I'd left Cannonbridge and she was still no nearer joining me in Lydhall. If it was the thought of leaving her job that was holding her back, there were plenty of good opportunities in Lydhall for someone like her, it wouldn't take her long to find something to suit her. She said she realized she hadn't been fair to me and she promised to think things over very seriously. She'd ring me on Wednesday evening to give me her decision. I pointed out that if she decided not to join me it would mean the end of the marriage. Things couldn't go on as they were and I had no intention of giving up my job in Lydhall to come back to Cannonbridge. She said she fully understood all that.'

'Was there a quarrel?'

He shook his head with vigour. 'There was no quarrel or anything remotely resembling a quarrel. She listened to every-thing I had to say. It was all very calm and rational. I said I'd be back next weekend to see estate agents; the house would be going on the market, whatever she decided. She made no objection to that. I said if she chose to stay in Cannonbridge she could look for a flat she liked and I would finance it. She thought that very fair.' He gestured sharply. 'So that was how we left it. We parted on friendly terms. We were always on friendly terms. We never quarrelled.'

Kelsey eyed him for some moments before asking: 'Do you have some other close relationship? With someone your wife didn't know about? Someone up in Lydhall, maybe?'

Again he shook his head with vigour. 'No, there's no one else. I loved my wife. I wanted her to join me. What I would really have liked would have been for her to give up working and start a family. That's what I've always wanted, a proper family life. I was sure that's what Celia would decide on, when she thought about it seriously; she couldn't just let the marriage go.' He suddenly put both hands up to his face and sat in silence with his head lowered.

'Do you carry life insurance on your wife?' Kelsey asked abruptly.

Heyworth's head shot up. 'Yes,' he replied, after a moment. 'We took out insurance on each other's lives when we were married.' He supplied details. The same figure for each of them, Kelsey noted; by no means excessive. He told Heyworth he would be checking the details of both insurance policies and Heyworth raised no objection.

Had Celia ever made a will?

Not to his knowledge, Heyworth answered. She hadn't had a great deal to leave. The house was in his name and she had never suggested it should be otherwise. As far as he knew, Celia had had no dealings with any solicitor.

'Was your wife a member of any staff pension scheme at British Braids?' Kelsey went on to ask.

Heyworth nodded. 'Yes, she was.'

'Will you receive any benefits under that scheme?'

Heyworth frowned. 'I've no idea. I never went into the ins and outs of it. I can't think I'd be entitled to very much, if anything at all. Celia was only there four years.' He made a dismissive gesture. 'They can tell you about all that at British Braids.'

At this point, Kelsey broke off to allow Heyworth a brief rest and some refreshment. When they resumed he began by asking: 'Do you know if your wife had any problems at British Braids? Any difficult relationships?'

Heyworth looked surprised. 'Far from it. She was very happy there. I'm sure that was at the root of why she was taking so long to make up her mind to leave Cannonbridge – she simply didn't want to give up her job.'

Kelsey sat regarding him before asking: 'Are you aware of any relationship your wife may have had with another man? At work or elsewhere?'

'I'm absolutely certain there was no one else,' Heyworth replied without hesitation. 'There was never the slightest suggestion of anything of the sort. Celia wasn't the type to play fast and loose.'

Kelsey switched tack abruptly. 'This relative of yours who died, whose funeral you went to – was it a close relative?'

'It was my uncle,' Heyworth told him. 'Ivor Heyworth, my father's older brother – the only near relative I had left. He was a good age, eighty-eight.'

'Did he have much to leave?'

'It seems he had,' Heyworth replied with energy. 'It turns

out he had substantial investments. I was astonished when the solicitor told me the size of the estate.'

'Do you come in for any of it?'

'It seems I do. I was even more astonished at that. I thought he might have left me some personal item or maybe a token legacy, but nothing more. I thought all he had was the house – that's no great size – and probably a few savings. He had his pension from the bank – he was a bank manager before he retired – but of course that died with him. He never had any children. He'd been a widower for a good many years. He was looked after by a housekeeper; she was with him more than thirty years. He made good provision for her. There are legacies to relatives on his wife's side and various bequests to charity.' He drew a long breath. 'I'm the residuary legatee.'

'When did you learn this?'

'The solicitor told me when I went to see him after my uncle died, five or six weeks ago.'

'Did you tell your wife about this inheritance?'

Heyworth looked him squarely in the eye. 'No, I did not. My first impulse was to tell her but then I changed my mind.'

'Why was that?'

'I didn't want her joining me just because of the money. I wanted her to do it because she loved me and wanted to be with me, not for any other reason. If she did decide to join me, then I'd tell her about the legacy when I came down, next weekend. If she decided not to join me I wouldn't tell her till it came to discussing financial arrangements for the divorce.'

'Did you tell her your uncle had died? That you were going to his funeral?'

'No, I did not. I just told her I would be down this way on business. She didn't know Uncle Ivor. She knew of his existence, of course, but she'd never met him. She knew I went to see him now and then but she never showed any interest in him.'

'You didn't keep his death a secret from her because you knew she'd be bound to ask if he'd left you anything?'

He shook his head with force. 'Absolutely not. It would never have occurred to her that he had anything much to leave. She'd have thought the same as I did, that most of what he did have would go to provide for the housekeeper.'

Kelsey asked if Celia had kept a diary and was told, to the best of Heyworth's knowledge, that she kept only a small pocket diary. There had been no sign of it at Southview and Heyworth thought it very likely it was in the missing shoulder bag.

Kelsey told Heyworth he would wish to scrutinize his bank account and that of his wife. Heyworth readily agreed.

When Kelsey let Heyworth go at last, he made it plain he expected him to remain in Cannonbridge for the time being. Heyworth told him he had had no other thought. He had friends and former colleagues in the area he could stay with, but he had booked into a quiet hotel he knew, a small, family-run concern. He preferred to try to come to terms with what had happened in comparative privacy.

CHAPTER 9

After a briefing on Wednesday morning, Chief Inspector Kelsey held a press conference, making a general appeal for information. Some of the national dailies carried a couple of paragraphs about the murders; one or two of the tabloids had provided greater coverage. Regional TV would be carrying an item in their early-evening news slot.

A tremendous air of shock hung over the town, allied to no small degree of fear, particularly among women in the better-class suburbs of detached houses – women living alone, or on their own during the day, with husbands out at work.

Shock was still evident at British Braids when the Chief and Detective Sergeant Lambert went along there after the press conference. Kelsey had no wish to disrupt production by making any attempt to address the entire workforce. He had George Drummond call in some of the supervisory staff, who promised to pass on the appeal for information. The Chief was especially anxious to hear from anyone who had had contact with Celia Heyworth during Friday afternoon.

The clerk who had given Celia the vegetables confirmed that he had brought them back with him after he went home for lunch and had handed them over immediately after returning to work.

The Chief asked Drummond and Wilfrid Probyn if Celia had made any comment to either of them about what had passed between her husband and herself over their snack meal at Southview. Had she said anything about the state of her marriage or her intention for the future?

Probyn told him Celia had seemed preoccupied during the drive back to British Braids. She had said nothing about her husband or her plans.

Nor, according to Drummond, had she said anything to him in the course of the afternoon that might suggest she was having second thoughts about staying on with the firm. Something had come up at one point where Drummond had referred to a project he hoped to get under way in the next year or two. Celia had discussed it with him with her customary enthusiasm, as if she fully intended to be part of all that was going forward. Drummond added that Celia had told him back in mid-July that she would not be joining her husband but would be remaining in Cannonbridge.

The Chief asked Probyn if Heyworth, as Celia's widower, would receive any benefits under the firm's pension scheme and was told he would receive a lump sum and a pension, neither of any great size.

The Chief went on to ask both men to account for their time from five-thirty on Friday. Drummond told them he had gone straight from work to call on an ex-employee, a valued worker who had taken early retirement twelve months ago after being diagnosed as suffering from Parkinson's disease. He was being devotedly cared for by his wife, who had also worked for the firm and had left at the same time, to look after her husband. Drummond was in the habit of calling in to see them every three or four weeks, after work, to ask how they were getting on; he normally made his call on a Friday. He had told his wife at breakfast last Friday that he would be calling in. He had stayed about half an hour, as he always did, chatting, drinking a cup of tea. He had got home around his usual time on these occasions, twenty past six or so. After supper he had spent the evening pottering in the garden.

The Chief asked if he had ever had acquaintance of any kind with Beth Knight, but Drummond told him he had never met the girl, never – so far as he knew – laid eyes on her. He did vaguely know that Celia had some young girl living with her; Celia must have had occasion at some time to mention the fact to him.

Probyn told the Chief that after dropping Celia at the end of Grasmere Avenue he had continued on home. His wife was out when he arrived. He had stayed in all evening, reading the paper, watching TV, running through his songs for the forthcoming theatrical production. His wife had come in at about eight-thirty.

The Chief asked if he had had any acquaintance with Beth Knight, apart from giving her a lift to work recently. Probyn replied that he had known Beth slightly from church, where he was a sidesman.

Did either man know of any significant difficulties Celia might have had at work?

No; they were both sure she had had none.

Did they know of any romantic attachment? Or of anyone with whom Celia had been on bad terms, inside the firm or perhaps in some way connected with it, as, say, a salesman or customer?

Again, both men shook their heads.

To the best of their knowledge, Celia had had no close female friend among the other employees, but Drummond sent for the woman who had been most closely associated with Celia in the course of her duties. She was a quiet, middle-aged woman, married, with a family. She told them she had seen nothing of Celia, away from work. She knew of no romance, no difficult relationships, nothing in any way amiss.

'Something I've just remembered,' Probyn said suddenly when the woman had gone. 'I don't know if it's of any use.' Celia had asked if he could drop her in town on his way home to lunch on Thursday; she was meeting a woman friend. He had gathered the woman was an old friend Celia now saw only once in a way; she had seemed pleased at the prospect of seeing her again. She had made no mention of the meeting afterwards. Nor had she at any point mentioned the woman's name or said where she lived or worked.

From British Braids, Sergeant Lambert drove the Chief to the hotel where John Heyworth was staying. He was busy making phone calls when they arrived but readily broke off. The Chief asked if he had any idea who the woman could have been who had arranged to meet Celia on Thursday, but Heyworth could make no guess.

They went next to the hairdressing salon. The salon was full but the atmosphere was hushed and sombre. The whereabouts of all the women working there on Friday evening – and the salon employed only females – were quickly established. They had all been busy at the salon, fully visible and accounted for. Apart from Beth Knight, the only employee not working there on Friday evening was one of the stylists, a married woman currently halfway through a fortnight's holiday in Italy, with her husband.

The proprietress spoke highly of Beth. She had shown natural flair for the work and had been well liked by both customers and staff. This good opinion was echoed by everyone else the Chief spoke to; he came across no suggestion of any trouble or clash of personalities.

Though friendly with all, Beth had not been on close terms with anyone at the salon. More than one employee recalled Beth sometimes mentioning a friend called Teresa, but no one could tell them any more about Teresa, nor did anyone know of any other close friend. It was the general view that Beth had had an open nature and had been in no way secretive.

But they were not left in the dark much longer about the identity of Teresa. A British Braids employee called into the police station during the lunch-hour, asking to speak to Chief Inspector Kelsey. He was a methods engineer by the name of Michael Anderson, who had been with the firm several years. He thought the Chief might be interested to know that his daughter Teresa, a schoolgirl of sixteen, had been a good friend of Beth Knight; he would go so far as to say her best friend. Beth had spent a couple of hours in their house on the Wednesday evening before the bank holiday.

It seemed that Anderson was a widower. He had spent the holiday weekend with Teresa, his only child, staying with relatives in Wales. They had got back to Cannonbridge late on Monday evening.

The Chief arranged to call at his house during the evening, to speak to Anderson and his daughter.

In the afternoon the Chief paid a visit to Celia Heyworth's bank. He was told there had been no movement in her account over the last few days and no unusual movement of any kind in recent times. She last drawn money – her usual amount – from the cash machine on the Saturday before her death.

No cheque book, no bank or credit card, no wallet, no driving licence or phone card had been found among Celia's things. It had been concluded that these items had very probably been inside the missing shoulder bag.

Later in the afternoon the Chief had both insurance policies checked; the details squared with what Heyworth had told them. There was no evidence from Heyworth's bank account of the existence of any additional – undisclosed – policy on Celia's life. Nor was there evidence of any irregularity or, indeed, of any significant fact.

*　　　*　　　*

A woman detective constable had called on Mrs Marriott in the Cannonbridge hospital during the morning, to check what her husband had told them about his visit on Friday afternoon. Mrs Marriott was still greatly distressed at the terrible happenings at Southview, but she was able to confirm that her husband had indeed visited her earlier than usual on Friday. He had arrived at the hospital at about a quarter to five and had stayed till just turned six – that was about the usual length of one of his evening visits.

She told the constable she and her husband had always been on pleasant, neighbourly terms with the Heyworths – and with Beth Knight, since she had been staying at Southview.

She could shed no light on what had happened.

Another officer had been busy checking various other statements. He had begun by checking the time Ronald Marriott had left work on Friday afternoon and had found that Marriott had indeed been given permission – as he had told them – to go off early and had left at about ten minutes to four.

The officer called next on the former employee of British Braids, disabled now by Parkinson's disease. He found him at home, with his wife; they were poring over the evening paper, which had devoted considerable space to the murders. They were both deeply upset by the horrific death of Celia Heyworth, whom they had known and liked. She had called to see them only a couple of weeks back.

They were both positive in their recollections of last Friday. George Drummond had looked in, straight after work, as was his habit. He had arrived at about twenty minutes to six and had stayed around half an hour, as he always did.

The officer went straight on to Drummond's house, to speak to his wife. She too had known Celia Heyworth and was appalled at the brutal manner of her death. She readily confirmed what her husband had told them about last Friday evening. He had mentioned at breakfast that he would be looking in on his ex-employees. He had got home at his usual time on such occasions: twenty past six. His manner and appearance had been entirely as usual.

Nightingale Villa was next on the officer's list. Mrs Probyn had driven in just ahead of him, returning from a stint at the Citizens' Advice Bureau. She took him along to the kitchen and made tea for them both.

She shared the general air of shock and distress at the murders. She had known both victims, from church, and had also known Beth Knight through being a client of the hairdressing salon. Yes, she fully understood the routine necessity to check movements.

'But I'm afraid I can't tell you what time Wilfrid got home on Friday evening,' she said with a regretful shake of her head. She had been out of the house from mid-afternoon, attending a meeting and then going on to sit with an old lady. 'All I can say is that Wilfrid was here when I got home at eight-thirty.' She thought back. 'I remember he was in good spirits when I got in.' She sipped her tea. 'He'd been going over his Gilbert and Sullivan songs.' She smiled. 'He was singing at the top of his voice, thumping away on the piano.'

The officer's last two calls were on the customers John Heyworth said he had visited on Friday afternoon. The two firms were in towns several miles apart, at some distance from Cannonbridge.

At each place the officer was assured that Heyworth had duly made his call, arriving and leaving at the times he had told the police.

Chief Inspector Kelsey gave the Andersons time to get home from work and have a bite to eat before he had Sergeant Lambert drive him round to the house.

The Andersons had just finished clearing up after their meal when Lambert set his finger on the doorbell. Kelsey ran a shrewd eye over father and daughter as he and Lambert were ushered into the sitting-room and offered refreshments, which Kelsey declined. Anderson seemed an intelligent, affable man, quiet and courteous. Teresa was still clearly upset but had herself well under control. She appeared sensible enough, anxious to be helpful.

Kelsey began by asking Anderson how well he had known either of the victims. Anderson replied that he had known Celia Heyworth slightly, from work; he had rarely had direct contact with her. Away from work, he had only once spoken to her at any length and that was some three weeks ago, when he had driven his daughter round to Southview to pick up Beth. The girls were going to a church social and in the ordinary way would have walked or gone by bus, but it was raining heavily and he had offered to run them there.

He had remained in the car while Teresa ran into the house

to fetch Beth. But Beth hadn't been quite ready and was still up in her room. Celia had come to the front door and called to him to come inside, as the girls would be some minutes. She gave him coffee and they sat chatting until the girls came down.

He had last seen Celia on Friday evening as she was leaving work; she was getting into Wilfrid Probyn's car in the British Braids car park.

Had he never encountered Celia at church?

Anderson shook his head. 'I'm not much of a churchgoer. My wife used to go regularly and so does Teresa, but weddings and funerals are about all I ever go to.'

Beth Knight he had known fairly well. She had spent many evenings with them and he had often chatted to her. He had greatly liked her. She was a sweet-natured girl, always amiable and helpful. He had last seen her on the Wednesday before the bank holiday, when she had spent the evening with them. She had been her usual cheerful self. He knew of no problems in her life.

Kelsey turned to Teresa, who had sat quietly by, dabbing unobtrusively at her eyes from time to time. She did her best to control any distress she felt at his questions, answering in a straightforward manner.

She had had no contact with Beth since last Wednesday evening. She had known Beth for about a year, since shortly after Beth had come to Cannonbridge. They had become very friendly and talked freely.

As far as she knew, Beth wasn't worrying about the question of accommodation. Celia had told Beth she didn't think she would be leaving Cannonbridge. She hadn't enlarged on the matter and Beth had been content to leave it at that.

The Chief asked if Teresa had met Neil Leighton; a second postcard from Neil, couched in loving terms, had now arrived at Southview.

No, Teresa hadn't met Neil, but Beth had talked about him and was clearly fond of him. To the best of her knowledge, Beth had never had a boyfriend before. She had been out a few times with someone else but it hadn't amounted to much. That boy's name was Simon Cormack. He was a couple of years older than Beth, a university student. He was the son of the Cormacks who owned the clothing business in the town. Teresa knew him slightly from church, which was where Beth had met him. They had gone out together during the Easter vacation.

No, Teresa didn't know why Simon and Beth had stopped seeing each other. Beth hadn't known the reason herself; there had been no quarrel. Beth certainly hadn't been upset over it, as her feelings had been in no way involved. Beth had found Simon interesting to talk to, quiet and invariably well mannered, but there had been nothing more to it than that. She had concluded that Simon had simply lost interest after going back to the university at the end of the Easter vacation.

Kelsey asked Teresa to cast her mind back to Friday evening. She told him she had got in from work at about six-thirty. That was a little later than usual as she had missed her bus and had had to walk. Her father was already home when she got in; he was upstairs in the bathroom.

Anderson confirmed that. He had left work promptly at five-thirty and had driven straight home. He had attended to a few matters he had to see to before going away for the weekend, then he went upstairs to shave and shower. Teresa was in the kitchen when he came down, a little later, to put his clothes in the tumble-dryer.

Kelsey broke in to ask what clothes they would be.

'My work clothes,' Anderson told him. 'The ones I'd taken off when I came home. I always put them in the washing-machine at the end of the week. I took them out of the tumble-dryer and hung them up to air in the utility room, before we went off, so they'd be ready to put on again for work on Tuesday morning.'

Kelsey asked what shoes he had been wearing when he came in from work on Friday.

'The same shoes I wore to work today,' Anderson replied.

'I'd like to see them,' Kelsey said, and Anderson went off to fetch them. Teresa sat in silence, looking pale and tired, until her father returned with the shoes.

'I'll take these with me,' Kelsey said, and Anderson made no objection. He resumed his account of Friday evening.

'I had a chat with Alec after I got in from work,' he recalled. 'That was before I went upstairs to shave.'

'Alec?' Kelsey queried. 'Was this a phone call you made?'

Anderson shook his head. 'No. I spoke to Alec here. He was out in the garden. Alec Morgan; I've known him all my life; we were at school together. He'd had a rough time this last year or two.' He sketched in a few details and went on to explain

Alec's current standing in the household and the arrangement whereby Alec had stayed in the house over the holiday weekend.

'Was Alec acquainted with Beth?' Kelsey wanted to know.

'Yes, of course,' Anderson said. 'He was often here when Beth came round. He used to walk her home – it didn't take him much out of his way and he'd have been leaving at about the same time, in any case.'

'What time did Alec get here last Friday evening?' Kelsey asked.

'I don't know when he arrived,' Anderson said. 'I happened to look out of the kitchen window and saw him working in the garden. I went out to have a word with him about one or two things I'd like him to keep an eye on while we were away.' He thought back. 'It would be somewhere about six-fifteen, at a rough guess, when I went out to speak to him, but I've no idea how long he'd been here before I got home.' They hadn't seen Alec since they'd got back from Wales, late on Monday evening. They'd found the house and garden in good order, the bathroom decorating finished. Alec had left the keys on the kitchen table, with a brief note.

They had expected him to call round as usual the following evening but by then the news of the murders had broken. When there was no sign of Alec, Anderson went round to his lodgings, but didn't manage to see him. The landlady told him Alec was out walking; she had no idea what time he would return. He had been devastated by the dreadful news. Anderson had left a message but Alec hadn't yet been in touch. 'I intended looking in again on my way home from work this evening,' Anderson added, 'but then I had to get straight back here, with you saying you'd be calling round.'

When they left the Andersons', Sergeant Lambert drove the Chief to the house where Alec Morgan was currently lodging. The landlady was a widow, a motherly, competent-looking woman in late middle age. The Chief asked if he might speak to Alec Morgan but was told he wasn't in. She didn't expect him back much before eleven, when she usually locked up for the night.

'He's been knocked sideways by these terrible murders,' she said with a melancholy shake of her head. 'I can't get him to talk about what's happened, he just wants to be left alone.' But she had at least managed to persuade him to eat a bit of bread and take a drop of soup this evening. He had taken nothing at all yesterday, after he heard the news.

'We'll be round again in the morning,' Kelsey told her. 'Ask him not to go out before we've had a word.'

They were back at nine-thirty next day. 'He seems quite a bit calmer this morning,' the landlady told them with manifest relief. 'He had tea and toast for breakfast.' He was in the sitting-room, waiting for them. She took them along and introduced them. Alec appeared steady enough, but worn-looking, with deep lines etched into his face. He may be the same age as Anderson, Sergeant Lambert reflected, but he could easily pass for ten years older.

The landlady left the room and Alec took his seat, facing the two policemen. Yes, he understood the routine necessity for this questioning. He was anxious to help in any way he could.

Kelsey began by asking if Alec had had any acquaintance with Celia Heyworth.

No, Alec told him; he had never so much as spoken to Celia. He had known her by sight, having occasionally seen Beth in the car with her and having sometimes seen her driving in or out of Southview as he went by.

Had he ever set foot in Southview?

No, never.

Did he think Celia an attractive woman?

'Yes, of course,' he replied without hesitation. 'Anyone would consider her attractive.'

Perhaps he had had some slight acquaintance with her through the church?

He shook his head. 'I'm not a churchgoer, I never have been.'

'What about Beth Knight?' Kelsey wanted to know. 'Did you consider her attractive?'

Again there was no hesitation. 'Yes, I did.'

'Are you divorced from your wife?'

Anguish showed in Alec's face. 'No, I'm not,' he returned brusquely. 'If my wife wants a divorce, she can have it. I won't stand in her way. I've never heard a word from her since she left. I've no idea where she is.'

Kelsey asked how he had spent last Friday afternoon.

He answered readily. He had gone out walking after lunch, at about two o'clock. It had been a long walk, such as he often took.

74

He hadn't gone back to his digs afterwards but had ended up at Anderson's place, as he frequently did. He had set about various jobs in the garden.

Had this long walk at any time taken him past Southview?

He couldn't say. He had been sunk in thought, as so often during his solitary rambles. He never much noticed or remembered where his feet took him. It would have been over one or other of his usual well-worn tracks, that was as much as he could offer.

Kelsey wouldn't let that go. Had he been in the vicinity of Southview at around two-thirty or three? Had he seen a car drive in, with Beth Knight in the passenger seat? Had he hung about, watching? Going a little way along the drive, maybe, keeping to one side, so as not to be spotted from the front door? Had he seen a woman helping Beth out of the car and into the house? Beth, with her right wrist done up in bandages? Had he seen the car drive out again, a little later, with Beth no longer inside it?

To each question Alec responded with a slow shake of his head. He hadn't laid eyes on Beth since Wednesday night. Tears rolled down his cheeks. He made no effort to dab them away but sat staring ahead with an air of fathomless grief. 'She was always so kind,' he said brokenly. 'So understanding.'

What time had he got to Anderson's house on Friday evening?

'I'm afraid I can't tell you that,' Alec responded. 'I didn't notice the time.'

'Can you say what time Anderson came in from work?'

He gave another slow headshake. 'I'm sorry, I don't know that, either. I would have heard him drive in but I wouldn't pay particular attention. He came out, later on, to talk to me about looking after the place over the weekend.'

'How did he seem? Did you notice anything about his manner or appearance?'

He thought back. 'I can't remember anything different about him. He seemed just as usual.'

No, he hadn't deliberately kept away from the Andersons since they got back from Wales. The last two days had passed in a terrible blur, since he had heard the appalling news from one of the other lodgers, on Tuesday morning.

CHAPTER 10

The Chief wished to speak to all three Cormacks together, so he called at Leacroft by appointment at seven o'clock. They had finished supper and were awaiting him in the sitting-room when he arrived. None of the three appeared at ease. They all confessed themselves still shocked and horrified at the two deaths; Simon, in particular, seemed distressed and tense. They all expressed themselves as ready to help in any way they could.

The Chief began by asking Thomas and Ellen for their recollection of the early part of Friday evening. Thomas told him he had got in from work as usual, at ten minutes to six. He had gone along to the kitchen and spent some time chatting to his wife about the business, as she busied herself with preparations for supper. He had then gone upstairs, his head still full of business, to take a bath and change. There were two bathrooms and a shower-room at Leacroft. He hadn't given a thought to Simon and had no idea if he was in the house or not.

At six-thirty he went downstairs for supper. Simon appeared punctually for the meal, freshly bathed and changed. Thomas particularly remembered the meal as being a good deal livelier and more cheerful than usual and for the sound ideas Simon had put forward for the future conduct of the business. At the end of the meal, Simon left Leacroft to go round to his girl-friend's house; he was taking her to a cinema.

The Chief asked Ellen to cast her mind back to the early part of Friday afternoon. She told him she had left the house shortly after lunch, to visit a friend. Simon had been upstairs in his room when she left. She had understood he intended spending the afternoon studying in the reference room of the local library, as he had often done of late.

She had got back home at around five-fifteen and had shortly afterwards set about preparing supper. While she was in the kitchen she heard Simon come in and go upstairs. That was what he usually did; he wouldn't normally call out a greeting or go along to the kitchen to speak to her. She hadn't looked at the clock when she heard him enter the house.

Could she say with certainty, the Chief interposed, if Simon had come in before or after her husband got home? Might it not have been while she and her husband were chatting in the kitchen that she heard Simon come in?

She frowned in thought but could give him no definite answer; she couldn't be certain. The Chief turned to Thomas and asked him to think back. Had he heard Simon come in while he was chatting to his wife in the kitchen? Thomas did his best to oblige but could make no more definite response; he simply couldn't recall.

Throughout these exchanges Simon had sat in silence, with his head lowered. Kelsey asked him now for an account of his movements on Friday, from, say, two o'clock onwards. Simon still didn't look up but gazed down at the carpet as he spoke.

He had left the house at about two-thirty to go to the public library, as he had been doing for the previous week or two; he had walked there, as he usually did. At about a quarter past three he had left the library, to take a short walk. He had called in, in passing, at the boutique where his girlfriend worked. He asked her if she'd like to go to the cinema with him that evening and she said she would.

He arranged to call for her at seven-fifteen and then returned to the library, where he remained until shortly before five-thirty. He walked back home, reaching Leacroft at about twenty minutes to six. He went straight upstairs to dump his books, shower and change. When he was ready, he found he had fifteen minutes in hand before supper, so he spent the time going through the notes he had made in the library, putting them in order.

'That was a very short time you stayed in the library after you first got there,' Kelsey observed. 'You were there barely half an hour before you were off out again, walking about.'

Simon moved his shoulders but made no reply.

'Did you speak to anyone at the library?' Kelsey asked.

Simon thought back. 'I spoke a few words to one of the assistants, that's all.'

Who was his current girlfriend?

Simon replied that her name was Lorraine Beattie. She lived

with her widowed mother in a cottage a few minutes' walk from Leacroft. He knew her from church; he had been going out with her since he came home at the end of the summer term.

'I believe you knew Beth Knight,' Kelsey said, and Simon gave a nod. How well had he known her?

Not very well, Simon answered. Again, he had come across her through the church. He had asked her out a few times during the Easter vacation but the relationship hadn't developed. There had been no disagreement, nothing like that. He had seen her about, on two or three occasions, since he got home. He hadn't stopped to talk and she had shown no wish for any conversation. They had merely smiled, exchanged a greeting and passed on. He was certain Beth had felt no more for him than he had for her.

How well had he known Celia Heyworth?

Scarcely at all, he answered. He had encountered her briefly, once or twice, when calling for Beth. Her manner towards him had always been pleasant.

Had he ever set foot inside Southview?

Yes, on two occasions. The first time had been for only a few minutes. He had called for Beth and she hadn't been quite ready. Celia had asked him in, to wait for her.

The second time had been when he brought Beth home at the end of the evening. They had been discussing proposals put forward by the local council for a pedestrian shopping precinct. They had differing views on the matter and Beth believed Simon had misunderstood some aspects of the proposals. She had asked him in while she looked out the local paper, to prove her point. He had stayed about half an hour. Beth had made coffee and Celia had joined them. She had taken part in the discussion which had been lively and good-natured on all sides.

'To go back to last Friday afternoon,' Kelsey said. 'Did you go past Southview after you left here for the library? Did you see Beth being driven in? Did you hang about and see her get out of the car? Did you see that she'd injured her right wrist?'

Throughout this fusillade of questions Simon kept shaking his head with vigour. 'No, I did not go anywhere near Southview,' he shot back as soon as the Chief came to a halt. 'I went straight to the library when I left here, I saw nothing of

78

Beth. I had no idea she'd had an accident and been driven home.'

The Chief regarded him for some moments. 'On your way home from the library at five-thirty, did you go by Southview then? Did you see anyone entering or leaving? Did you notice any vehicle in the driveway, or close by?'

Again, Simon shook his head. 'I didn't go past Southview on my way home. I have no idea if anyone entered or left around that time.'

Again, the Chief regarded him. 'You've given us your version of your movements that afternoon,' he said at last. 'I'm going to put to you now another version. When you left here you went by Southview. You saw Beth driven in, saw her get out of the car, saw her bandaged wrist. You saw the woman driving the car help her into the house. You hung about and saw the woman leave. You then went along to the boutique and spoke to your girlfriend. Then, and only then, you went to the library. You stayed there till almost five-thirty. But you didn't come straight home. You didn't get here at twenty minutes to six. I put it to you that it was turned six when you got here. And you didn't have fifteen minutes to spend on your notes after you'd showered and changed. It was time by then to go downstairs, for supper.'

Simon had started shaking his head again while the Chief was still in full flow. 'Not one word of that is true!' he burst out the instant the Chief finished speaking. 'I was never anywhere near Southview on Friday. I never laid eyes on Beth.'

'Did you know Beth had a new boyfriend?' Kelsey demanded.

Simon looked levelly back at him. 'No, I did not know. It would have meant nothing to me if I had known.'

And still the highly coloured postcards from Neil Leighton kept dropping through the letter box at Southview, cheerful and loving.

Shortly after a conference and news briefing on Friday morning, Celia Heyworth's sister, Abbie Yates, arrived at the Cannonbridge police station. She was still in a state of shock, her eyes swollen with weeping, far removed from the smiling woman Kelsey had come across in Celia's photograph album. She had got back from her Norwegian cruise last night, only to discover what had happened. She sat in the Chief Inspector's office, still scarcely able to believe it, trying her best to be of assistance.

She hadn't seen Celia for a few weeks but they had, as always, kept in regular touch by phone. They had always been on excellent terms and Celia had always talked freely to her. She had last heard from Celia on the Monday evening before she went off on her cruise. Celia had told her then that John would be calling in at Southview on Friday, to talk things over during the lunch-hour. Abbie believed John had had enough of Celia's stalling and would be demanding a definite decision. Abbie felt – and had said as much more than once to her sister – that Celia hadn't been altogether fair or straight with John over the whole business of the move to Lydhall. Abbie knew for a fact that Celia had encouraged John to go after the promotion, allowing him to believe she would without question follow him to Lydhall, a course of action Celia had never at any time had the slightest intention of pursuing.

Did Abbie know what Celia had intended with regard to the house? Had she intended staying on there for the foreseeable future? Would she have contested any attempt to get her to leave?

Abbie shook her head. 'No, I don't believe she would have dug her heels in over that. It was never exactly spelled out between us, but I'm pretty sure she took it for granted the house would be put up for sale once she told John she wouldn't be joining him.' Abbie was of the opinion that Celia would immediately have started looking for a flat for herself and that Beth Knight would have found other digs.

Did Abbie know if John had been aware of his wife's duplicity in the matter, and if so, had he resented it?

'I'm sure he was at least beginning to be aware of it,' Abbie replied. 'And he must have resented it. He's not a man to take very kindly to someone stringing him along, particularly his wife; he'd consider that a dirty trick – as, I must confess, I did myself.' Celia had told her a few weeks back that John had suggested she had only invited Beth to live in the house in order to complicate matters, provide herself with some sort of excuse for hanging fire over the move. 'But I'm positive that wasn't true.' Abbie gazed earnestly up at the Chief. 'I'm sure Celia genuinely took Beth in for company, and because she liked her; it suited both of them at that time for Beth to stay at Southview.'

Abbie had met Beth on a number of occasions when she had gone over to Southview. She had liked her and thought her very helpful to Celia in many ways.

The Chief recalled the photographs he had come across at Southview, in Celia's album. The most recent photographs in which Abbie figured had been taken in the spring, in the Southview garden; they showed Abbie alone, or with Beth or Celia. A folder containing prints of the same photographs had been found in a drawer in Beth Knight's bedroom. Kelsey mentioned the photographs now to Abbie. She told him she had a set of the photographs herself. They had been taken one fine Sunday afternoon towards the end of March, shortly after Beth had moved into Southview; that was the first time Abbie had met Beth. The garden had looked beautiful in the sunshine, bright with spring flowers and blossoming shrubs. Celia had produced her camera and they had taken photographs. Tears shone in Abbie's eyes as she looked back at that carefree afternoon.

Kelsey went on to ask: 'Do you know if Celia intended coming out into the open and telling John, when she saw him at lunchtime on Friday, that she definitely wouldn't be following him to Lydhall?'

'That's certainly what I advised her to do,' Abbie responded without hesitation. 'But she didn't say if she intended taking my advice. My impression – for what it's worth – would be that John wouldn't have been willing to put up with any more shillyshallying, he'd have insisted on a final decision there and then.'

The Chief was silent for some moments, then he asked: 'Would you ever have thought him capable of harming her?'

Tears shone again in Abbie's eyes. She appeared greatly distressed and it was some time before she answered. 'I don't know,' she replied at last. 'I just don't know. He was very much in love with Celia when he married her and I'm sure he was still very fond of her.' She clasped her hands tightly together. 'But who's to say what any man might be capable of if he was really angry? If he believed he'd been duped.'

She was sure Celia had had no difficulties at British Braids and equally positive Celia had never at any time had any extra-marital romance. 'I'd stake my life on that,' Abbie declared with total conviction. 'She simply wasn't that kind of person. And the last thing she would have wanted at this stage in her life would be to get tangled up with some other man; she could do without any more complications.' She gazed earnestly across at the Chief. 'She'd come to realize she wasn't cut out for domesticity and children. She regretted having ever married, she would have liked to be single, free to live her own life, do as she pleased. She wanted to make a good career for herself, that was the most important thing.' She leaned forward and spoke with great seriousness. 'It wasn't that she was trying to bamboozle John. She genuinely believed he'd be happier with some other woman, someone ready to make a real family life for him. Celia didn't want to be the one to say the marriage was over. She let things drift on, hoping he'd find someone else and the break would come from him.' She twisted her hands. 'It wasn't cowardice on her part, it was soft-heartedness. She would never want to hurt him.' She drew a long, sighing breath. 'I told her she was kidding herself, she couldn't break away without hurting him; it was doing no one any favour to keep putting off telling him.'

'This phone conversation you had with Celia on the Monday evening,' Kelsey said, 'did she say anything then about meeting a woman friend for lunch on the Thursday?'

Abbie thought back. No, she couldn't recall Celia making any such mention. Nor could she suggest who the woman friend might have been.

'Did she say anything that evening about the death of John's uncle, Ivor Heyworth?' Kelsey went on. 'Did she say anything about John going to his uncle's funeral on the Friday? Anything about John coming in for something under his uncle's will?'

This time Abbie didn't have to think back. She was positive Celia had said nothing about anything like that; she would very definitely have remembered. She only vaguely recollected that John had had an uncle. As far as she knew, Celia had never met him. She had certainly never heard Celia say that John had any expectations of inheriting anything from him.

Kelsey asked if there was anything else she could think of, however slight, that might in any way help to throw light on what had happened. Abbie sat in silence, her eyes closed, frowning, searching the recesses of her mind. 'There is something,' she said at last. 'I don't know if it amounts to very much.' Kelsey urged her to continue.

'It was just a silly lad,' Abbie said reluctantly. 'He had a bit of a crush on Celia. He got rather carried away and she sent him about his business.'

'Do you know who this boy was?' Kelsey wanted to know.

'Yes, I do,' she acknowledged. 'He's the son of the Cormack clothes people.'

'Simon Cormack?'

'That's right. He'd been going out with Beth Knight. He'd been round to Southview the odd time, picking Beth up or bringing her back. Beth sometimes had to work late and Simon started coming round to the house soon after Celia got in from work in the evening, when he knew full well Beth wouldn't be home for quite some time.'

'Did he make a nuisance of himself?'

'I gather he made some sort of approach to Celia. I don't know exactly what, she didn't go into details, but I don't think it can have been anything very much. Celia certainly wasn't at all nervous of him, from the way she spoke. I'm sure it was just some foolish infatuation, she was more irritated by it than anything. It looked to her as if he'd only been taking Beth out in order to get a foot inside the door of Southview – he'd known Beth, through the church, right from the time when she first came to Cannonbridge, but he only started dating her after she moved into Southview.'

'Did he know Celia before Beth moved in?'

'Yes, he did, but not to any great extent. He worked in the family store sometimes and Celia used to go in there. And, of course, the Cormacks live in the next avenue to Celia, so he'd see her about the neighbourhood. She wasn't a regular church-goer but she did go sometimes, so he could have come across her there, as well.'

'How did Simon take it when Celia gave him his marching orders?'

'Perfectly all right, as far as I know. Celia knew it wouldn't upset Beth if Simon stopped asking her out; she knew Beth hadn't lost her heart to him, or anything like that. She told Simon not to come near either of them again. He was going back to the university a day or two later, so that was the end of it, as far as I know. Celia certainly never mentioned him to me again, so I'm pretty sure she had no more trouble from him.'

'Did she tell Beth about all this?'

Abbie shook her head at once. 'No, she did not, she didn't see the need. She didn't want Beth to feel Simon had just been making use of her. She was pleased, later on, when Beth took up with this new boyfriend, someone she knew from back home. Celia liked him; she thought him a very steady young man, genuinely fond of Beth – and I gather Beth was really fond of him.'

'I take it Celia didn't say anything about this to Simon's parents?'

Abbie looked surprised. 'I'm sure she'd never have dreamed of doing that. She wouldn't think it at all necessary. She certainly never said anything to me about telling his parents.' She gave Kelsey a level look. 'Celia didn't make all that much of it herself. I wouldn't want to exaggerate it.'

'Do you know if Simon had any further contact with Beth?' Kelsey asked. 'Did he know she had a new boyfriend? Was he jealous of him?'

'I've no idea if he knew about the new boyfriend, or what his attitude might be, if he did know,' Abbie replied. 'I never heard of any further contact between Simon and Beth.'

An officer had meanwhile visited both the public library and the fashion boutique where Lorraine Beattie worked, in order to check what Simon Cormack had told them about his movements on Friday afternoon.

The assistants at the library knew Simon well; he had used the library for years. They all seemed to like him. They confirmed that he had been in a good deal lately and had been a familiar figure in the reference room, working at one of the tables. But as to whether he had been there on Friday afternoon, no one could state positively. Certainly no one could say he had been there at any particular time.

At the fashion boutique it was a different story. The manageress clearly remembered Simon calling in on Friday afternoon to speak to Lorraine. Not only that, she could also say at precisely what time he had called. She had been on her way through to her office to ring a valued customer about an urgent alteration; she had promised to phone at three-thirty. She had spent only a moment with Simon, anxious not to be late with her call. She told him he could speak to Lorraine but he mustn't keep her. He had called in on a similar errand once or twice before. He was always very courteous and never stayed more than a minute or two.

Kelsey had an appointment in the afternoon at the regional TV studios, to record an appeal for information. It would go out in the early-evening news slot and a clip from it would also appear on the main national news. John Heyworth had agreed to take part, as also had Abbie Yates and Beth Knight's parents.

On the way back to Cannonbridge from the studios, Kelsey called in at the forensic science laboratory, where he spent some time. When he got back in the car afterwards he sat sunk in thought as Sergeant Lambert negotiated the traffic. One of the laboratory findings, concerning the fibres caught up beneath Celia Heyworth's fingernails, seemed to offer a hope of leading somewhere. The fibres, in a subtle shade of light brown, included one sizeable strand. They had proved to be from a type of good-quality yarn, used mainly in hand-knitting and consisting chiefly of wool, with a small addition of various synthetic fibres.

As they approached Cannonbridge, Kelsey roused himself and glanced at his watch. He directed Lambert to drop him off at his flat and call for him again in three-quarters of an hour, to take him back to the station for a last stint before calling it a day.

He let himself into his flat, made himself a good strong pot of tea, far better than any canteen brew, and carried it along to the living-room. Two minutes to six. He switched on the TV and settled himself comfortably before it, to watch – hopefully without interruption – the interview he had recorded. It was not his own performance he wished to see; he had no vanity whatever in that regard. Nor was it the showing made by Abbie Yates or by Beth Knight's parents. His entire interest was in discovering how John Heyworth had come across. It was the movement of head and hands he wanted to catch, the tone of voice. But above all, the expression in the eyes.

The short clip was shown two-thirds of the way through the national bulletin; too short a clip for the Chief's purposes. The camera rested on Heyworth for no more than a few moments. The Chief drank his tea and waited with what patience he could muster for the regional news.

At last it came on; at last it reached the recorded interview.

He craned forward, fixing an intent gaze on Heyworth. When it was over he switched off the set, poured himself more tea and sat drinking it. Every moment, every gesture of Heyworth's had struck him as carefully controlled, in not the smallest degree spontaneous or instinctive.

As for the eyes, they had appeared guarded, devoid of expression. They had told him precisely nothing.

House-to-house inquiries went forward on Saturday morning, in an effort to discover if anyone had spotted John Heyworth's car – or Heyworth himself – in the vicinity of Grasmere Avenue, during the late afternoon or early evening of the fateful Friday.

The Chief Inspector had a number of calls of his own to make in the course of the morning, to ask questions about clothing, search through drawers and wardrobes, in an attempt to locate any item in light brown wool, possibly hand-knitted. His first call was at the hotel where Heyworth was staying. Heyworth was just finishing breakfast. He told them he had worn a grey suit that Friday – the darkest grey he possessed, because of the funeral – with a white shirt. He had worn no woollen waistcoat or pullover. An officer was dispatched to Gosford to speak to Ivor Heyworth's housekeeper; he returned to say she had confirmed Heyworth's account of what he had worn. And she had volunteered another piece of information: Celia Heyworth had never been to the house, had never visited the old man.

Sergeant Lambert drove the Chief next to Alec Morgan's digs, in the hope of catching him before he took it into his head to set off on one of his rambles. And they were lucky: they found Alec busy cleaning the downstairs windows for his landlady. He seemed a good deal steadier, answering questions without visible distress.

He couldn't particularly remember what he had worn that Friday afternoon but it would have been his usual gear these days: a T-shirt and jeans, a denim jacket. Whatever garments he wore would have been through the wash since then. No, he wouldn't have been wearing a woollen waistcoat or pullover, he was quite sure of that. He readily took them up to his room and stood calmly watching as they looked through his things. It didn't take long; he didn't have a great deal. The search threw up no garment of light brown wool, nor, when they went downstairs again, could his landlady recall his ever possessing such a garment.

Their next call was at Nightingale Villa, where they found Eva Probyn at home; her husband was out. She raised no objection when the Chief asked if they might cast an eye over Wilfrid's clothes. Their search proved fruitless. Eva, when questioned, could remember only one brown woollen garment of her husband's. He had owned an ancient cardigan, dark brown, when she married him. It had holes in both elbows and she had made him throw it out.

What had Wilfrid worn to work that Friday afternoon? It would have been one of his business suits and a white shirt, she replied at once. She couldn't say now which particular suit it might have been. They were all in various shades of navy blue or grey.

From Nightingale Villa they went to Rosemont, but the sergeant's ring at the doorbell went unanswered, as did his loud knock. They still had to call on the Andersons, but the Chief wanted to speak to father and daughter together and Teresa would be working at the health-food store until six. They could call round at about six-thirty and look in again at Rosemont afterwards.

At six-thirty they found both Andersons at home: Teresa in the kitchen, preparing supper, and her father at work outside, repointing the rear wall of the house. He abandoned his task without protest and came indoors. The Chief put his questions and Anderson showed them the work clothes he had worn that Friday. They had been through the washing-machine and tumble-dryer twice since then and were now airing over a line in the utility room, ready for work again on Monday morning.

'That Friday was on the cool side,' the Chief pointed out. Might not Anderson also have worn a pullover or woollen waistcoat? Anderson at once shook his head. He would have found such a garment much too warm for his work. A look through his clothes did produce a few pullovers, both long-sleeved and sleeveless, but nothing in any shade of brown, and nothing in the way of a woollen waistcoat. Nor could Teresa recall her father ever having owned any item corresponding with what they were looking for.

After leaving the Andersons' they tried again at Rosemont, with no better luck. But Lambert's ring at the bell on Sunday morning did bring Ronald Marriott to the door. It seemed his wife had been allowed to leave hospital, under strict instructions to take things very easily over the next month or two. Marriott had collected her from the hospital yesterday morning and had taken her over to stay with her mother, who had been most insistent that she could look after her daughter, in addition to Ben. She would make sure Phyllis had all the rest and care she needed. And Phyllis hadn't been too anxious to return to Grasmere Avenue in her present fragile state. She had been deeply distressed by the murders and preferred to be elsewhere for a while, where she wouldn't be continually reminded of the dreadful happenings.

'I'm going over there again this afternoon,' Marriott added. He showed them the casual jacket, the shirt and slacks he had changed into after leaving work that Friday evening, before his visit to the hospital. No, he had worn no woollen waistcoat or pullover. He made no objection to their going through his things, but they came across nothing corresponding to what they were looking for; the nearest was a machine-knit sleeveless pullover in a shade of dark fawn.

The Chief had one more question to ask before they left: had Marriott noticed Simon Cormack hanging round Southview at all, in recent weeks?

Marriott shook his head. No, he hadn't noticed him. Nor had Phyllis made any mention of seeing Simon hanging about. But Phyllis had sometimes had a neighbourly chat with Celia and it was possible Celia might have said something to her about it. Phyllis wouldn't necessarily have passed on any such remark to him; Phyllis was never one to relish repeating everything that came her way.

The Chief left his call at Leacroft till later in the morning, to give the Cormacks time to get back from the church service they always attended. They had barely reached home when Sergeant Lambert set his thumb on the bell.

Thomas Cormack admitted them, waving aside the Chief's apology for disturbing them on a Sunday; he asked how they might be of help. The Chief told him he had a number of questions to put to Simon, but he would first like to speak to all three of them together. Thomas at once summoned the other two and took them all along to the sitting-room.

Kelsey began by asking Ellen if she knew what clothes Simon

was wearing when he left the house that Friday afternoon. She replied immediately that she couldn't say. She had left the house before Simon, who had been upstairs in his room at the time. Nor had she seen him when he returned, as he had gone straight upstairs. By the time he came down for supper he had showered and changed.

The Chief then asked Simon what he had been wearing that Friday. Jeans, T-shirt and denim jacket, Simon answered. Any pullover or woollen waistcoat? Simon shook his head.

Kelsey spent the next few minutes looking through Simon's clothes, without result. He asked Ellen if she knew of any brown woollen garment Simon had owned in recent times, but she could recall none.

Back in the sitting-room again, Kelsey suggested that Simon might prefer the next part of the questioning to be conducted in private, but Simon responded at once that he saw no need for that. Kelsey then asked him exactly why he had stopped seeing Beth Knight.

Simon moved his shoulders. 'I just lost interest,' he replied. Beth frequently had to work late and she had a girlfriend she often went round to see. That didn't leave her much time for going out with him. 'There were no arguments or quarrels,' he declared. 'It simply petered out.'

'I put it to you,' Kelsey said, 'that you stopped seeing her for a very different reason. You called round to Southview more than once at a time when you knew Beth wouldn't be there, but there was every chance of finding Celia Heyworth in the house on her own. I put it to you that Celia considered you were making a nuisance of yourself. She believed you had never been genuinely interested in Beth but had only asked her out in order to gain access to the house. It was Celia you were really interested in. She gave you your marching orders and told you not to come near the place again, to leave Beth alone.'

Thomas Cormack frowned. He looked over at Simon with sharp inquiry. Distress showed plainly in Ellen's face and she, too, looked across at Simon. He didn't return their glances but gazed at the Chief with a faintly smiling air. 'I think you're rather exaggerating what happened,' he said easily. 'It's true I did call round a couple of times, expecting to find Beth, but she hadn't got in from work – I didn't know she'd be working late. Mrs Heyworth was nowhere near as upset as you seem to be making out. She was a bit short with me, I grant you. She had things to do and didn't want me underfoot, but that was all.'

The Chief gazed back at him. 'Did she or did she not tell you to clear off and not come back again? Did she or did she not tell you to leave Beth alone?'

Simon shook his head. He didn't appear in the least perturbed. 'No, she never spoke to me like that. She merely let me see I was in the way. I took the hint and left. That was all. I went back to university soon afterwards and the relationship with Beth – such as it was – came to a natural end.'

Ellen leaned forward, her bony face full of anxiety. 'I'm sure Simon would never have willingly done or said anything to upset Mrs Heyworth,' she said earnestly. Her husband flashed her a quelling glance and she subsided.

Kelsey regarded Simon. 'Could your conduct towards Celia Heyworth at any time be described as pestering?'

The slight smile returned. 'Most certainly not.'

'Were you jealous of Beth's new boyfriend? Did you feel she had no right to look elsewhere?'

Still the little smile. 'As I've told you before, I had no idea Beth had a new boyfriend and it would have been of no interest to me if I *had* known. I have another girlfriend myself.'

From the Cormacks', Sergeant Lambert drove the Chief to the Andersons'. Teresa had been to church and was now preparing lunch. Her father was again at work on his repointing. There was no sign of Alec Morgan.

Anderson told the Chief Alec hadn't been round since the tragedy. Anderson had called again at Alec's digs and finally got to see him. He thought Alec was beginning to come to terms with what had happened, though he still found it impossible to talk about. 'I think he finds it easier to keep away from us for the present,' Anderson said. 'I can understand that.'

Kelsey left him to get on with his repointing and went into the kitchen to speak to Teresa; she carried on with her lunch preparations as they talked. He asked if she had any reason to suppose Simon Cormack had been jealous of Beth's friendship with Neil Leighton. She told him no, she had no reason to suppose any such thing.

He asked her to try to recall everything Beth had told her

about the break-up with Simon, and any contact, however slight, Beth may have had with Simon afterwards.

Teresa did her best to oblige. Most of what she came up with revealed nothing new, but she did bring to light one little encounter between the pair that lit a gleam in Kelsey's eye.

It seemed Beth had come across Simon and Lorraine Beattie one evening on her way to the Andersons'. 'It was the evening she helped me make the curtains,' Teresa said, 'so that would make it about the third week in July.'

Simon and Lorraine had been going into the theatre. Simon had caught sight of Beth as she approached. Beth gave him a friendly smile but Simon merely looked back at her with stony indifference and turned away. An instant later Lorraine caught sight of Beth. 'It was the way Lorraine stared at her that really threw Beth,' Teresa recalled. 'It was so hostile and cold.' She looked up at Kelsey. 'She said she felt a shiver run down her spine.'

When they called at the Beatties' cottage a few minutes later, Lorraine answered the door to them. The Chief introduced himself and asked if he might have a word with her and her mother.

Yes, certainly, they could. Her manner was pleasant and helpful. She took them along to the kitchen, where she was helping her mother prepare lunch. Sergeant Lambert noticed a copy of a Sunday newspaper – a regional tabloid that had devoted considerable space to the murders – lying on the kitchen dresser, as if hastily thrust down.

Mrs Beattie asked if the Chief minded her going on with what she was doing; it needn't interfere with their talk. No, the Chief had no objection. Lorraine found them seats and then began stringing and slicing runner beans. Sergeant Lambert ran an appreciative eye over her as she worked: a good-looking girl, with a fine, athletic figure. She had an air of being very much on the ball.

Kelsey began by questioning Lorraine. Could she tell him what her movements had been that Friday evening? At exactly what time had she left the boutique?

She answered readily, in a cooperative manner. She had left the boutique at ten minutes to six and had gone straight to a nearby chemist's that stayed open till seven on a Friday. She had bought some perfume she had been saving up for. She had then walked home, as she usually did, arriving at about twenty-five past six. No, she hadn't kept the till slip from the chemist's but she could produce the perfume. She went up to her room and brought it down: a bottle of expensive French toilet water, very nearly full.

Mrs Beattie confirmed that Lorraine had arrived home at around twenty-five past six. She was able to remember because an in-law, the wife of a cousin of her late husband, had phoned a few minutes earlier, asking to speak to Lorraine. She needed an outfit for a special occasion and wanted to know if Lorraine could arrange a good discount if she went to the boutique for her outfit. Mrs Beattie told her Lorraine wasn't home yet but should be in shortly; she would get her to phone as soon as she came in. And this she duly did. Mrs Beattie gave the Chief the woman's name and address.

'I put it to you,' the Chief said to Lorraine, 'that your memory may be at fault here. You may have left the boutique earlier than ten to six. It may not have been on Friday evening that you called at the chemist's for your perfume. It may have been on some other day. You may have gone straight from the boutique to Southview.'

Lorraine gazed unwaveringly back at him. 'I most certainly did not. I would have had no reason to go to Southview.'

'Have you ever set foot in Southview?'

'No, never!' she declared. 'I've never even called at the door. I've never been inside the gate.'

'Did you know Beth Knight had been brought home from work on Friday afternoon, because of an injury to her wrist?'

She shook her head with vigour. 'No, I didn't know that. How could I possibly have known?'

'From Simon Cormack,' Kelsey returned at once. 'He could have been in the vicinity of Southview when Beth was driven in. He could have mentioned it to you when he called in at the boutique.'

Her tone was even more emphatic. 'He told me no such thing. He never mentioned Beth. He asked me if I'd like to go to the cinema. He said he'd been working at the library and was going back there. That's all.'

'Simon finished with Beth Knight months ago,' Mrs Beattie struck in. 'It's Lorraine he's interested in now. He's calling round this afternoon to take her out.'

92

'How well did you know Beth Knight?' Kelsey asked Lorraine.

She moved her shoulders. 'Hardly at all. I knew her a little from church and from going into the salon sometimes – nothing more than that.'

'Did you feel any hostility towards her?'

'No, of course not,' she responded sharply. 'I had no reason to. I had no feeling towards her, one way or the other.'

'Were you jealous of her?'

'Why on earth should I be jealous of her?'

'You may have thought Simon had a hang-up about her.'

'That's nonsense!' she declared brusquely. 'I don't believe he ever gave her a thought.'

'You may have felt she stood in your way.'

'That's a ridiculous suggestion.'

'How well did you know Celia Heyworth?'

'I knew her even less than I knew Beth Knight. She came into the boutique sometimes and I saw her at church once in a way; that's all.'

'Did you know Simon had made a nuisance of himself at Southview, hanging round Celia Heyworth?'

'I'm sure he did nothing of the sort,' she came back brusquely. 'She was years older than him.'

'How serious is it between you and Simon?' Kelsey wanted to know. Lorraine looked back at him without speaking. 'It's early days yet,' Mrs Beattie replied for her.

Kelsey went on to ask what Lorraine had worn to work that Friday. She thought back and then told him she had worn a tailored summer dress, stone colour.

Any cardigan or woollen jacket?

Yes, she had worn a lightweight woollen jacket. She showed him both garments. The jacket was machine knit; it had a stone-coloured background, discreetly patterned in shades of light and dark blue.

Did she own any knitted garment in brown? No, she didn't; brown wasn't a colour she wore. She made no objection when Kelsey asked if they might look through her things; the search yielded nothing.

Kelsey had one last point to raise: had Simon recently brought round any clothes for them to keep for him?

No, he had not.

Had Simon brought round anything at all for them to keep for him? A bag or suitcase, maybe? A parcel or bundle?

No, he had not. He had never given either of them anything of any kind to keep for him.

When they left the cottage they returned at once to Leacroft. The Cormacks looked surprised to see them back so soon but made no comment.

In the sitting-room, the Chief directed his attention at Simon. 'When you left here that Friday afternoon,' he began, 'I suggest you *did* go by Southview. You saw Beth Knight being driven in, being helped out of the car, saw she had an injured wrist. When you called in at the boutique, you passed that information on to Lorraine Beattie.'

Simon looked levelly back at him. 'None of that is true,' he replied calmly. 'I didn't go near Southview. I saw nothing of Beth that afternoon. I didn't know she'd injured her wrist and had been driven home. I was in the boutique only a minute or two. I never mentioned Beth; I had no reason to.'

As the Chief was about to put his next question, he noticed Sergeant Lambert eyeing with marked interest one of the family photographs ranged on a side table. The Chief followed his gaze and felt the hair prickle along his scalp. The photograph showed a smiling young woman, nineteen or twenty, perhaps, with a pretty face and dark hair. And more than a passing resemblance to Celia Heyworth.

'Who is that?' Kelsey asked, with a nod at the photograph.

There was a brief silence, then Ellen answered flatly: 'That's Faith. Our daughter.' Some quality in her tone, the way she had paused between the two utterances, hadn't looked at him as she answered, made the Chief say to Simon: 'Your sister?'

Simon made no reply but glanced across at Thomas and Ellen, his look edged with challenge.

There was another brief silence, then Thomas spoke up: 'Faith was Simon's mother. She died in a road accident in France, twelve years ago, when Simon was seven.' He drew a long breath. 'She was barely sixteen when Simon was born; she never married. It was agreed between us that Ellen and I would bring Simon up as our own child. We thought it best all round.'

'When did Simon learn the truth?' Kelsey asked.

Ellen clasped her hands tightly. 'He found out six years ago,' she said. She answered further questions without protest.

94

Simon said not a word throughout but sat motionless, with a face wiped clear of expression. When the two policemen left, a little later, Simon rose to his feet but didn't address another syllable to them, nor did he accompany them to the door.

As soon as they got back to the police station, Kelsey dispatched an officer to call on Mrs Beattie's in-law, the woman Mrs Beattie said had phoned her early that Friday evening.

The officer found her about to dish up lunch to her husband and schoolgirl daughter. She was a good deal surprised at his visit, but confirmed without hesitation that she had indeed phoned Mrs Beattie that Friday evening to ask about a discount at the boutique. And she was able to be fairly precise about the time. She had stood up towards the end of the early-evening news on TV to make her call; that would put it at about 6.25. Mrs Beattie had told her that Lorraine hadn't got in yet but would be in shortly. When Lorraine rang her a few minutes later, she came across as her usual friendly self, composed and helpful, in no way nervous or agitated.

The manageress of the fashion boutique occupied the flat above the business premises. The officer who had visited the boutique on Friday to ask about Simon Cormack's visit phoned the manageress at 8.15 on Monday morning to say he would like to question the staff about Lorraine Beattie's movements on the Friday before the bank holiday. While the questioning was going on it would be best if Lorraine could be occupied in some part of the premises where she would have no opportunity to speak to other members of staff before he had finished.

No problem, the manageress assured him. She would find Lorraine a job in the stockroom the moment she arrived. If the officer could come round right away he could start his questioning with herself. The staff would be arriving between 8.30 and 8.45; with luck he might be finished by nine, when the boutique was due to open.

The officer went round at once. He asked the manageress if she could recall the exact time Lorraine had left work that Friday. She did her best to recall, but it was ten days ago now. The boutique closed at six. It was rare for a customer to come in during the last half-hour, so, if there was nothing much doing around five-thirty, she usually let one or other of the staff get off, turn and turn about. She had very probably let one of them go that Friday but she couldn't now remember which one, or at precisely what time she had let her go.

As each member of staff arrived, the manageress had a word with her. Each was then in turn questioned privately by the officer, while Lorraine attended to the job in the stockroom, unaware that her name was being bandied about a few yards away.

As to who, if anyone, had left early that Friday, they were all in agreement: it was very definitely Lorraine. But the actual time she had left produced little agreement; their estimates varied between 5.20 and 5.45.

Other calls were also scheduled. A much-depleted house-to-house team was still making repeat visits to households where folk had not, for various reasons, been available on earlier calls.

Checks were made in the course of the morning at British Braids, to see if it was possible now to discover if either Wilfrid Probyn or Michael Anderson had worn a brown woollen pull-over or waistcoat to work that Friday. After the lapse of time no one could say anything very definite, but the impression left on the inquiring officer was that it was unlikely that Probyn would have worn such a garment and very unlikely indeed that Anderson would.

CHAPTER 11

The double inquest on the Southview victims was set down for three o'clock on Monday afternoon. Although the proceedings were expected to be brief and formal, the press, both national and local, was in attendance and a crowd of townsfolk gathered outside the courthouse.

The inquest was duly opened and adjourned; both bodies were released for burial. John Heyworth approached Chief Inspector Kelsey afterwards to ask if there was any objection to his returning to work. He could come back to Cannonbridge every weekend, in case he was needed, and he could return at any other time if the Chief deemed it necessary.

No, the Chief had no objection; it seemed a sensible arrangement.

On Tuesday, after yet another conference and press briefing, the Chief braced himself to tackle the paperwork, inexorably piling up. The case seemed to be getting bogged down in a mass of detail. What he yearned for was some positive breakthrough, some sudden burst of light to show him a single clear path out of the morass.

The search of the Southview garden and surrounding area had revealed nothing of consequence. Nowhere was there any sign of the missing ornaments, the wristwatch and rings, the shoulder bag. Nor had any use been made of the cheque book, the bank and credit cards that were thought to have been inside the bag.

They had discovered no sighting of John Heyworth, or his car, anywhere near Southview during the early evening of that Friday. Nor, in spite of various appeals, via radio, TV and newspapers, had they yet managed to run to earth the woman who had lunched with Celia the day before she died.

There was always the possibility in cases of this kind that the murders had been the work of some random psychopath or passing vagrant, but they had come upon nothing to suggest that this had been the case at Southview.

In the middle of the morning, the woman officer who had visited Phyllis Marriott in hospital went over to the village where Phyllis was staying with her son, in her mother's cottage. Her mother was out shopping and had taken Ben with her. Phyllis was sitting reading in a sheltered spot in the garden, in obedience to her instructions to rest.

The officer asked her to take her mind back to the weeks before the murders. Had she ever noticed Simon Cormack hanging round Southview during those weeks? Had Celia Heyworth said anything at that time about Simon making a nuisance of himself?

Phyllis wasn't surprised at the questions as her husband had told her the police had spoken to him on similar lines. No, Celia had said nothing of that sort to her. But there was something Phyllis had noticed herself, she added after some hesitation. It was nothing very much, barely worth mentioning. She didn't really know if she was doing right in mentioning it at all; it might give the wrong impression. She liked Simon; she had always found him quiet and well mannered. She had known the Cormacks for years, from church as well as from their store, where she had long been a customer. She would hate to say anything which might make undeserved trouble for the boy, might cast unjustified suspicion on him.

The officer pressed her to say what was on her mind, assuring her they wouldn't make more of it than it warranted.

Phyllis still looked far from happy. It was nothing much, she said again. It was just that she had caught sight of Simon slipping in through the side gate of the empty property next door to Southview, as she happened to be going by. It would be about a week before she went into hospital. She had wondered briefly what he could have been doing there, but had then forgotten it until Ronald mentioned the questions the police were now asking about Simon.

'Are you certain it was Simon you saw?' the officer asked. 'Could you have been mistaken?'

Her face relaxed. 'No, I'm not absolutely certain,' she

acknowledged with visible relief. 'I only caught sight of him for a moment. I could easily be mistaken.'

On Tuesday afternoon the Chief took a prowl through Southview, upstairs and down. He made a circuit of the garden, stared over at the empty property next door, at the tall horse chestnut tree. He crossed to the other side of the garden and cast an eye over at Rosemont, silent in the September sunshine.

Marriott, he thought suddenly. What do we really know of Ronald Marriott? He lived next door to the murder victims. It was Marriott, along with Wilfrid Probyn, who had discovered the bodies. He seemed a decent enough citizen, but the Chief had never found that much to go by in a murder case.

Marriott had lived at Rosemont no more than a couple of years. Where had he lived before that? What was his background?

I'll get DC Slade on to it, he decided. He can have a little ferret round, see what he can come up with. No one better than Slade at that kind of job. He could get going on it right away; he could make a start by having a word with Marriott's boss.

Slade's word with the boss, later in the afternoon, produced no dramatic revelations. It seemed Marriott had worked for the firm some five years, joining them on transfer from one of their branches, fifty miles to the north. His record was excellent. During his first three years in Cannonbridge, before his marriage, he had lived alone in a small flat. He was invariably quiet and well mannered, on good terms with his colleagues. He had never looked for a girlfriend among the staff; in fact, he had never seemed to have any girlfriend or to be interested in finding one. Work, work, and again work, had always appeared to be what concerned him. As far as anyone knew, he spent his evenings and weekends attending classes, or in solitary study. His marriage had taken them all totally by surprise.

At Slade's request, the boss supplied, via the computer, a record of Marriott's time with the branch of the firm where he had previously worked. His record there would seem to have been equally impeccable. He had worked there three years, having joined them from a firm of insurance brokers in a town forty miles to the north of the branch. At the time of joining, Marriott had given his home address as Willow Cottage,

Langmoor, Cumbria. During his time at the branch he had lived in digs in the town.

Early on Wednesday morning Slade set off to have a word with the firm of insurance brokers. They told him Marriott had spent two years with them, joining them at the age of nineteen from a small insurance company in a neighbouring town. He had given his home address on joining them as Melville House, Whitford, Cumbria. During his time with the brokers he had lived in a bedsit. Again, his record was impeccable. And again, as far as anyone could now recall, he had had no girlfriend while he was there, but had spent his leisure time studying.

Slade went next to the small insurance company in the neighbouring town. He was told there that Marriott had worked for them for three years, joining them straight from school as a junior clerk. He had given his home address as Melville House, Whitford – some twenty miles to the north. During his time with the firm he had lived in a bedsit. Again, he had been hard-working, conscientious and ambitious, his conduct irreproachable.

Slade set off without delay for Whitford. It proved to be a sizeable village, with evidence of a good deal of recent development. He went into a combined post office and general store in the centre of the village where he bought fruit, biscuits and chocolate for a snack lunch and then inquired for Melville House. The young woman serving didn't recognize the name. She explained that she and her husband hadn't lived very long in the village; they had taken over the business only a few months ago. But a middle-aged woman waiting to be served was able to help. 'There isn't any Melville House now,' she told Slade. 'It was pulled down some years back, not long after I came to live in the village. It looked to me as if it had been falling down for years before that. They put up starter homes on the land.'

Slade asked her if the name Marriott meant anything to her in connection with Melville House. She shook her head, but went on to say she knew someone who ought to be able to give him more information: a Miss Hogg, an elderly woman living in a cottage on the outskirts of the village. 'I believe she used to work at Melville House,' she explained. She walked with him to the door of the shop and gave him directions.

Slade looked at his watch as he returned to his car. It was

getting too close to lunch-time to call on Miss Hogg, if he wanted her to be in the right frame of mind to chat freely. He found a sunny spot by a patch of woodland to eat his lunch and then treated himself to a brief nap before seeking out Miss Hogg's cottage.

He found he had judged his timing just about right. Miss Hogg had washed up her lunch things and was out in the back garden, settling herself into a deck chair with a library book.

She came hurrying along to answer his ring at the doorbell. She was a cheerful, bright-eyed woman, happy to abandon her book for a chat about the old days, a pleasure that rarely came her way now. Slade told her who he was and explained that he was seeking information about a family called Marriott, who had lived at Melville House at one time. She assured him at once that she would be glad to help in any way she could. At her direction he brought out another deck chair from the garden shed and set it up near her own.

She declared herself well able to give him all the information he required; no one better than herself. She had gone to work at Melville House straight from school, just before the Second World War. There had been a married couple by the name of Marriott working at Melville House in her day. They had one child, a son named Ronald. 'Both the parents are dead now,' she told Slade. 'I haven't had any contact with Ronald for some time but I'm sure I can help you to get in touch with him.'

Ronald's mother, Olwen Marriott, had started out as a kitchenmaid at Melville House and had gone on in due course to become cook; she had been about the same age as Miss Hogg. She had married Clifford Marriott who was employed on general maintenance at Melville House; he was ten years older than Olwen. They had married during the war, when Clifford was called up. He had served in the army and had reached the rank of sergeant. He had been wounded in the closing stages of the war, suffering head injuries. He was believed to have made a good recovery but was ever afterwards subject to bouts of depression, troublesome but not incapacitating.

He had always been a serious, somewhat austere man and as the years went by he became something of a martinet, particularly with regard to the upbringing of his son, born when Olwen was over forty and had given up hope of ever having a child. She had been overjoyed at her son's birth and would

101

undoubtedly have gone on to spoil him, had Clifford not been determined to see that didn't happen.

'Ronald was always frightened of his father,' Miss Hogg said with a sigh, 'though he tried hard not to show it. He was a very well-behaved child, always careful never to step out of line.' There were no other youngsters at Melville House and Clifford Marriott wouldn't allow Ronald to mix with the village children. The Marriotts scrimped and saved to send him away to boarding school when he was eight; he went on later to a very minor public school. 'He wasn't at all happy at either of the schools,' Miss Hogg said with another sigh. 'He tried his very best, worked very hard, but you can imagine what it was like – going there from a good address and then the boys finding out his parents didn't own Melville House but were in service there. They made his life a misery. He never dared speak to his parents about it but he opened up sometimes with me. I offered more than once to have a word with his parents, see if they might let him leave and go to a local day school.' She shook her head. 'But Ronald wouldn't hear of it. He was determined to stick it out. He wouldn't let his father down.'

In the aftermath of the war, times grew progressively harder for the owners of Melville House, a childless couple getting on in years. One by one rooms were closed up, staff reduced. Marriott's bouts of depression grew more frequent. Shortly after Ronald turned sixteen his father disappeared. It was feared at first that some accident had befallen him and a thorough search was made of the grounds, without result.

For some time Olwen clung to the belief that he had gone off somewhere in one of his dark moods and would return none the worse when the mood lifted. But the days went by with no sign of him. She was forced at last to acknowledge that he wouldn't be coming back. Ronald left school and found himself a job as a junior clerk with an insurance company in a town twenty miles away. He lived in digs, coming back regularly to see his mother, who went on working at Melville House. 'Ronald was determined to get on,' Miss Hogg said. 'He wanted to make something of his life.' She had never heard of his having any girlfriend.

In the autumn, two years after Clifford Marriott's disappearance, a great storm blew up, causing widespread damage. Two of the tall chimneys of Melville House came crashing down through the roof. After the storm, when workmen were clearing the rubble from the attics – long crammed with a jumble of discarded items – they came upon an ancient rocking chair in a far corner, facing the wall. Seated in the chair, fully clothed in his working gear, was the skeleton of Clifford Marriott. Two letters were found in his pocket, one addressed to his wife and the other to the police. On the floor beside the chair was a tumbler holding a teaspoon; beside it, one quarter full, stood a container of cyanide, used in the past for destroying wasps' nests.

Miss Hogg shed a tear at the memory. She produced a box of newspaper cuttings and photographs, to show Slade. 'It made quite a stir locally,' she told him. Olwen had been heartbroken. She went on working at Melville House until the owner died – he was an old man by then. The owner's widow went into a nursing home where she died not long afterwards. Melville House passed to a distant cousin living in New Zealand. He never came near it but had it at once put on the market. But the fabric had been neglected and no one wanted the property; it would have cost too much to put right. It stood empty, going by degrees to rack and ruin. In the end a developer bought the land and the house was pulled down.

'Olwen and I had both left long before then, of course,' Miss Hogg added. 'We both left when the old lady went into the nursing home. I was lucky, I was able to rent this cottage. Olwen went to live with her niece, in a village ten miles from here. Ronald used to go to see her; he always helped her out financially, as much as he could. Olwen had a stroke after a year or two. She hung on for another couple of years. Ronald was very cut up when she died.' Miss Hogg hadn't been over to the niece's in recent years, nor had she seen or heard anything of Ronald since his mother's funeral. 'But the niece should be able to put you on to him,' she assured Slade. She gave him the niece's address: Willow Cottage, Langmoor.

Slade drove straight from Miss Hogg's cottage back to Cannonbridge. He made good time, arriving at the police station as the Chief was thinking of calling it a day.

Kelsey listened with close attention to what Slade had to say. He sat mulling it over after the door had closed behind the departing constable. Ronald Marriott would seem to have removed himself from Melville House by successive job moves of twenty, forty, fifty miles. He had stopped giving Melville House as his home address and begun giving Willow Cottage. Step by step, he would appear to have severed his links with the past.

Who can blame him? Kelsey thought. It was a past that seemed to have given him little joy.

I can't see that any of it gets us anywhere, Kelsey concluded as he rose to his feet. It doesn't throw up any lead we can usefully follow.

On Thursday morning the local weekly paper devoted considerable space to the murders. It repeated the general appeal for information and the particular appeal for the woman who had lunched with Celia Heyworth the day before she died, to come forward.

On Thursday evening Alec Morgan called into the police station in the course of a solitary ramble. He had been brooding over the fact that he hadn't been able to say exactly when he had arrived at the Andersons' house on the Friday of the murders. A recollection had risen up in his brain this evening as he walked about, a recollection he hoped might serve to prove how long he had been working in the Andersons' garden that Friday before Anderson got in from work.

It seemed the child of a neighbour of the Andersons, a little girl of five or six, had been playing with her ball in the garden next door and the ball had come soaring over the fence, a few minutes after Alec had started working. The child had come running round for the ball and had stayed chatting to Alec – she had sometimes talked to him before. After a few minutes she asked him the time. Her mother was going out for the evening and the baby-sitter would be along shortly, to give the child her supper and put her to bed. She was fond of the baby-sitter and wanted to be by the front gate, to greet her as she arrived. Alec now recalled telling the child the time: ten minutes past five. The child had thanked him and run off home.

The Chief at once dispatched a constable to check his story, but the child's mother was out when he called. She had gone to the cinema with a friend, according to her husband, but if the constable cared to return tomorrow morning, before nine-thirty, he would be sure to find her in; she never went to the shops before then.

And when the constable returned at nine next morning he found the woman expecting him. Yes, she had indeed gone out that Friday evening and she had employed her usual baby-sitter, as her husband would be working late that evening. She had asked the baby-sitter to be sure to arrive by five-fifteen as she had a bus to catch.

Yes, she did recall her daughter telling her she had run round next door after her ball and had been talking to the man working in the garden. The baby-sitter had arrived punctually and her daughter had, as always, posted herself by the front gate, ready to greet her.

But all that served to prove, the Chief reflected after he heard what the constable had to relate, was that Alec Morgan had been working in Anderson's garden at ten minutes past five that Friday. That left him with time enough to walk round to Grasmere Avenue after the little girl had run off home, get himself admitted to Southview and then return to his job in the garden, before Anderson went outside to have a word with him – that hadn't been till 6.15 or so. True, it wouldn't have given Alec a great deal of time inside Southview, but then the killer wouldn't seem to have taken long over his brutal work.

There was a change of tone in the postcard message from Neil Leighton that arrived at Southview on Saturday morning. He was still enjoying his holiday and the weather was still superb, but his thoughts were turning now towards home and seeing Beth again.

John Heyworth had driven back to Cannonbridge on Friday evening, booking in at the same hotel. Chief Inspector Kelsey had left a message for him there, asking him to come into the station first thing on Saturday morning. When Heyworth arrived the Chief put him through a long and thorough bout of questioning, going over everything Heyworth had told them, assailing his story from different angles, pouncing on point after point.

But Heyworth stood firm; he couldn't be budged in the slightest from what he had told them. He remained calm and courteous throughout, totally unshaken.

The Chief let him go at last, to keep his appointment with his uncle's solicitor in Gosford. Heyworth intimated that he would be going on afterwards to his uncle's house and would be given lunch by the housekeeper. He expected to be back in Cannonbridge around four, should the Chief wish to see him again.

When Neil Leighton got back from his holiday, reaching his lodgings late on Sunday evening, he found his father waiting for him, to break the terrible news.

After a night of little sleep, broken by horrifying dreams, Neil went along to the police station. There was little he could tell them. Beth had been very happy during the few weeks he had dated her; he was sure of that, sure she had no hidden anxieties. She hadn't appeared worried about her accommodation situation; she appeared to believe she would be staying on at Southview for the foreseeable future.

She had never said anything to suggest she was being in any way harassed by Simon Cormack – or by anyone else. Nor had she ever said anything about Simon pestering Celia Heyworth with unwanted attentions.

And then, on Monday evening, came the kind of break the Chief had been praying for. During the initial house-to-house inquiries, officers had called at a house on Grasmere Avenue, on the opposite side of the road from Southview and a little lower down. They had found no one at home and were told by a neighbour that the house was occupied by a married couple by the name of Kingwell, with a daughter, Judy, some nine years of age. The Kingwells had lived in the house for only six months or so, having moved from the other side of Cannonbridge. Both parents went out to work. They had gone away on holiday on the Friday evening before the bank holiday and wouldn't be back till the Sunday evening, nine days later.

An officer had accordingly returned on the Monday evening, after the Kingwells were expected back; he found both parents at home. They had spent the holiday with relatives in the next county and their daughter was staying on with the relatives; the private school she attended wouldn't start again for another week.

They could tell the officer very little. They had had only a nodding acquaintance with the Heyworths and Beth Knight. They had seen nothing, heard nothing, that Friday evening. Mrs Kingwell had got in from work as usual, soon after five. Judy had returned from her grandmother's just before 5.30, in time to watch a favourite TV programme. The grandmother lived close by and looked after Judy as occasion demanded. Kingwell had arrived home shortly before 6.30, somewhat later than usual, having been caught up in the holiday traffic. They had all three left the house an hour or so later, bound for the next county.

Many an officer would have left it at that, but this particular officer was an experienced man who took even the most routine of duties very seriously. He told the Kingwells he would be back in a week's time to speak to Judy. He would call around seven, to be able to talk to the girl in the presence of both parents. He would ask them to say nothing to Judy about his visit beforehand.

When he duly made his return call he found Judy a quiet, rather shy child, intelligent and sensible; certainly not one disposed to invent tales in order to attract attention. He had been speaking to her for a very few minutes when he realized she could be an important witness. He immediately broke off the interview to return to the station, telling the parents he – or some other officer – would be back shortly. In the meantime, he must ask them not to discuss anything relating to that Friday evening with their daughter, for fear of influencing her recollections. They readily gave their word.

The officer didn't return to the house. When the Kingwells' doorbell rang again soon afterwards it was Chief Inspector Kelsey and Sergeant Lambert who stood on the doorstep.

The Chief strove to put Judy at her ease. He allowed her to give an uninterrupted account of what she had seen before he began to question her.

She told him she hadn't noticed anyone in the vicinity of Southview as she returned home from her grandmother's that Friday evening. When her TV programme ended at six, her mother had come into the room to watch the news. Judy stayed watching with her for about five minutes and then went up to her room to check her holiday packing and make sure she was leaving her room tidy before going away, all the time keeping an ear open for her father's return. She was hoping he wouldn't be late, so they could get off in good time. After a few minutes she broke off what she was doing to go to the window, to watch out for him. There was no sign of her father, but she saw a young man come out very fast through the Southview gates and turn down the avenue. He wasn't exactly running, but going about as fast as he could walk without breaking into a run. That was what had attracted her attention: his pace, and the expression on his face. He had looked upset and frightened; she had seen his face clearly as he went by. She had returned to her tidying and five or ten minutes later, certainly no more than that, she had heard her father drive in. She had glanced at the clock when she heard him; it showed 6.25.

Yes, she knew who it was she had seen hurrying away from Southview. It was the young man who had called at her grandmother's house the previous day, asking if they had anything old to sell. Judy had opened the door to him herself. She had passed on his message to her grandmother who was busy in the kitchen and had returned to inform him they had nothing to sell. He had left at once; his manner throughout had been friendly and polite.

She was able to give an excellent description of the young man, a description the Chief had no difficulty in recognizing: it was that of the youngest member of Joe Selwyn's team: the newcomer, Darrell Wilding.

Had the young man been carrying anything as he left Southview?

Judy shook her head at once. No, she was sure he had not.

Could she say what he had been wearing?

She gave a decisive nod. She was sure he had been wearing the same, or very nearly the same, clothes both times: jeans and a denim jacket, a white T-shirt.

Any pullover, sweater or waistcoat? She shook her head.

Had his jacket been open or closed?

She was sure his jacket had been open as he stood on her grandmother's doorstep. She was equally positive it had been zipped up as he left Southview.

In that case, might he not have been wearing a pullover with a low V-neck, over the T-shirt? It wouldn't show with the jacket done up. The same might apply to a waistcoat.

She readily agreed that he could have been wearing some such garment.

Might he not also have been concealing something under the jacket? A lady's shoulder bag, perhaps, the strap slung round his neck, the bag lying close to his body.

108

Yes, that could have been the case.

Could he have been carrying small ornaments in inside or outside pockets of his jacket?

She screwed up her eyes in thought. His jacket did have large patch pockets on the outside; she remembered that from their doorstep encounter. But she couldn't say now if the pockets had appeared to bulge or sag that Friday evening.

No, she had said nothing to her parents at any time about seeing the young man. He had gone clean out of her head in the excitement of getting off on holiday. She had never given him another thought until the constable called to see her just now, to ask her about that evening.

They all went upstairs to Judy's bedroom and she showed the Chief where she had stood by the window. Yes, the Chief reflected, she would have had a good clear view of anyone leaving Southview and hurrying down the avenue. And her bedroom clock would seem to be a reliable timekeeper; it showed precisely the same time as the Chief's wristwatch.

It was turned 8.30 when the Chief got back to the station. Joe Selwyn's team was still operating in the area, still staying in the same digs in Cannonbridge. Joe had reported faithfully to the station twice a week, promising to inform the police if he thought of moving on, or if any of the team spoke of leaving. The Chief hadn't the slightest doubt where they would all be at this moment: in some pub. But which pub? It might be any pub in town, or some rural hostelry a few miles out.

Better leave things till tomorrow, he decided; get round to the digs first thing.

And first thing next morning he presented himself at the team's lodgings, accompanied by Sergeant Lambert and a handful of other officers. When the landlady answered their ring on the bell she stepped back in surprise at the sight of the group confronting her. But when the Chief introduced himself and explained the reason for their presence, her manner became markedly friendly and cooperative. She was, she informed the Chief with fond pride, the niece of a police officer who had served his whole career with the local force, retiring as a detective sergeant – it turned out – a couple of years after Kelsey had started out on his career. She was delighted to discover Kelsey had known her uncle.

He explained it would be necessary to search her own rooms

as well as those occupied by the team of dealers, but she took that in her stride; fortunately she had no other lodgers in the house at present. Any garden shed, garage, greenhouse or other outbuilding would also need to be included, Kelsey went on, but she merely nodded and waved her hand. 'Go right ahead,' she invited. 'Anywhere you like.' The Chief could take over the TV room as his base. If he needed to make any phone calls he was welcome to use the phone in her own sitting-room; it would be more private than the phone in the hall.

Joe and his team were in the dining-room, three-quarters of the way through their usual substantial breakfast. The Chief went in and informed Joe of the intended search, adding that none of the team could expect to go off to work that morning. The team left all response to Joe, who showed himself well disposed and helpful. The only one to display signs of unease was Darrell Wilding, who shifted about in his chair. He pulled out a pack of cigarettes and lit one, inhaling deeply, not looking at anyone.

The Chief left all but Darrell to finish their breakfast under the eye of a constable, while the search got under way. Darrell he took along to the TV room, where he asked for an account of his movements that Friday.

Still drawing deeply on his cigarette, Darrell repeated, almost word for word, what he had previously told them, stressing the fact that he had called at Southview once only, shortly before noon on Friday morning, had found no one at home and had very definitely made no return call.

'Why not?' the Chief demanded.

Darrell moved his shoulders. He replied that he only ever made a small percentage of return calls; it was all according to how things happened to work out on any particular day.

'We have a witness,' the Chief informed him, 'who saw you leave Southview not long after six that Friday evening.'

Darrell stubbed out his cigarette and at once lit another. 'That's not possible,' he maintained. 'Your witness couldn't have seen me, I was nowhere near Southview at that time. It was probably someone about my age and build, wearing the same sort of clothes.' He took a long drag on his cigarette. 'There are any number of guys about that look much the same as me.'

'But this witness had seen you face to face only the day before and is positive it was you leaving Southview that evening.' In reply Darrell merely shook his head and gave him a stubborn look.

What had he been wearing that evening?

'Much the same as I'm wearing now,' he replied at once. A denim jacket, white T-shirt and jeans. He couldn't say if it was these particular garments he had been wearing. Whatever he had worn would have been through the wash at least once since then. Clothes picked up any amount of dust and dirt in the course of a day's work. He took a bundle along to a launderette in town for a service wash two or three times a week; that was how they all dealt with their laundry.

No, he had very definitely not been wearing any woollen sweater or waistcoat that day.

The search of the team's personal belongings had revealed only one brown woollen garment: a long-sleeved, machine-knit cardigan, belonging to Joe Selwyn. Fairly new; a shade of brown a good deal darker than the fibres caught up in Celia Heyworth's fingernails; no sign of any rip or snag. But the cardigan would go off, all the same, without delay, to the forensic laboratory. None of the other members of the dealing team admitted to knowing of any other brown woollen garment owned by any one of them or recently got rid of.

The Chief spoke to Joe separately, asking him what he could recall of Darrell's behaviour that Friday evening. Joe thought back before answering with obvious reluctance that Darrell had suddenly changed his mind that evening about staying on in Cannonbridge. He had originally been very keen that they should work the town and had in fact wanted them to come this way some weeks earlier than they had done. Darrell had done well during their first week in Cannonbridge and had made some excellent buys. Then all at once, as they were load-ing the van that Friday evening, Darrell had declared himself in favour of moving on, giving no sound reason. No one had been disposed to listen to him and he had let the matter drop. 'I did notice,' Joe added, 'that he drank more than usual in the pub that evening.'

'And since that evening?' Kelsey queried. 'How's his drinking been since then?'

Joe drew a long breath. 'I've got to admit he's been knocking it back a bit.'

'Any other difference in his behaviour?'

'He's been pretty quiet.'

'I understand he started working for you in the spring,' Kelsey said. 'What do you know about him before that?'

'I knew his father well, years ago,' Joe told him. 'He's dead now. He was a good mate; he helped me out more than once. I came across Darrell now and then, after his father died. He seemed to be getting on all right. I bumped into him again back in the spring and he sounded me out about working for me. He'd been with a removal firm and they'd got a new foreman. Darrell had managed to fall foul of him in some way and it ended up with him being given all the worst jobs, always getting the blame when anything was broken or missing, so he gave in his notice. I agreed to take him on, give him a month's trial.' No, he hadn't asked for references, he hadn't seen the need; he was always content to use his own judgement. 'I've been more than satisfied with Darrell,' he declared with conviction. 'He's turned out to be a natural for the trade.'

The Chief had Darrell in again and asked him for the name of the removal firm he had worked for.

The fidgeting and cigarette-smoking started up again at once. Darrell gave the firm's name with marked reluctance.

Where was the firm's head office?

He named a nearby town.

Why had he left?

He hadn't got on with the new foreman. He'd been wanting a change anyway; the work was always heavy and often meant working late in the evening and over weekends.

Kelsey lost no time in dispatching a constable to the firm's head office and the constable returned before long with the results of his inquiries. It seemed Darrell had been with the firm some three years without trouble of any kind; he had always been an excellent worker. Then, last October, there had been a complaint from a female customer about Darrell's behaviour towards her in the course of her move. When Darrell was questioned he offered an account greatly at variance with what the woman had told them. The approaches had all been on her side; he had in no way responded. The complaint was purely the result of pique.

The incident, even by the woman's account, wouldn't appear to have been very serious, so Darrell was given the benefit of the doubt. He was also given a warning.

Three months later, in January, there had been an almost exact repetition of the incident. A second, far stronger, warning was administered.

When a third complaint along very similar lines was made in April, Darrell was instantly dismissed. He had made no attempt to fight his dismissal. There had been no approach since he left, from any prospective employer, asking for a reference. If there had been any such approach the firm would have felt, in the circumstances, unable to supply one.

The constable had gone on to ask if Darrell had been a member of any removal team engaged in recent times in moving any customer in or out of any property in Grasmere Avenue, or its immediate neighbourhood.

He was told yes; Darrell had been on a team who had moved a family into Grasmere Avenue from the other side of Cannonbridge, towards the end of March. The name of the family was Kingwell.

Kelsey at once tackled Darrell again. Darrell maintained, in between long draws on his cigarette, that he certainly had not been sacked by the removal firm but had left of his own accord. All three complaining customers had been frustrated spinsters. He had shown none of them more than ordinary politeness and helpfulness which had been totally misinterpreted by all three women and later grossly misrepresented to the firm, their accounts being spiced with a good deal of wishful thinking. They had singled him out because he had been the youngest of the removal team and, though he said it himself, easily the best-looking. The new foreman had never liked him and had been very happy to blow the matter up out of all proportion; it was Darrell's firm belief that the foreman had encouraged all three women to make their complaints official. In the end, Darrell had been forced to realize that the cards were stacked against him, under the new foreman. One or other of them would have to go and it clearly wasn't going to be the foreman. Darrell had no dependants, no mortgage to worry about, no reason to go on putting up with the kind of hassle he was getting, so he decided to jack it in. 'Best thing I ever did,' he declared as he stubbed out his cigarette and lit yet another. 'I have a better job now, better mates, no one on my back.'

'I understand you helped to move a family by the name of Kingwell, towards the end of March,' Kelsey said. 'They moved into Grasmere Avenue from the other side of Cannonbridge. The house is across the road from Southview, a little lower down.'

Darrell waved his cigarette. 'I may have moved them. I don't remember them. I can't remember every move.'

'Did you happen to come across Celia Heyworth or Beth Knight during the Kingwell move?' Kelsey asked. 'Did you have occasion to speak to either of them?'

'I've no idea,' Darrell came back at once, adding on a note of reasonable protest: 'I can't be expected to remember everyone I happened to see or talk to during every move.'

The search had now got as far as the team's vehicles, all three of them parked on the hard standing at the side of the premises. Joe Selwyn's car yielded nothing, as did the car shared by the two brothers. But with the van driven by the brother-in-law, the van in which Darrell Wilding always rode as a passenger, it was a different story.

On the underside of the dashboard shelf, in the farthest corner on the passenger side, a constable's probing fingers came upon a small, flat package, plastic-wrapped, held firmly in place by means of strong adhesive tape.

When the package was removed and opened out, it was found to consist of a plastic bag containing a man's handkerchief acting as a protective wrapper for a ring.

A lady's gold ring, probably an engagement ring, set with a fine solitaire diamond, in a plain, classic setting.

CHAPTER 12

Faced with this discovery, Darrell at first had nothing whatever to say, but sat with his head buried in his hands. When at last he brought himself to speak he raised his head and looked the Chief in the eye. 'All right,' he said heavily, with the air of a man who has come to the end of the road and is not in all respects sorry to have reached it, 'I'll tell you the truth.'

'And this time we'll have the whole truth,' the Chief responded briskly.

Darrell didn't reach for another cigarette but plunged straight into his tale. He had worked Coniston Avenue until a few minutes after six that Friday evening and had then decided to make a second call at Southview, as he would be going along Grasmere Avenue on his way to join the others at the van. It would be, say, eight or nine minutes after six when he rang the Southview door-bell. There was no response. Everything was quiet. He turned to leave and saw something sparkling on the gravel: the diamond ring. He picked it up and looked at it, he saw at once that it was valuable. He turned back to the house and tried the door; it yielded under his hands. He stepped quietly inside and at once stood riveted in horror, staring down at the body of a girl sprawled across the stairs, her head turned at an unnatural angle, her face battered and swollen. Beyond all question dead.

He remained transfixed for some moments, then he turned and left the house, releasing the catch on the lock, leaving the door securely closed.

He set off for the van with all speed short of running. He helped as usual with the loading, saying nothing to the others of what he had seen. His brain was at first paralysed with shock and it wasn't until it began to function again that he realized he still had the diamond ring; he found he had thrust it unawares into his pocket.

What to do with the ring? He saw with stark terror the danger he was in: he could easily stand accused of the girl's murder, for murder it very plainly was. He decided at last to do nothing, hang on to the ring for the time being, make up his mind what to do with it later.

He never had managed to make up his mind; he had just let the ring stay hidden in its corner, for lack of any better inspiration.

As soon as he came to a halt, Kelsey started in on him. Why had he gone into the house?

'I had a feeling something was wrong,' Darrell told him. 'A valuable ring lying on the ground. Everything so quiet. The door not locked. I thought someone might have done the place over.' He grimaced. 'I suppose I was just plain nosy. I wanted to see what was going on.'

Why hadn't he immediately raised the alarm? Run to a nearby house and phoned the police? Or at the very least told the rest of the team?

'I daren't let anyone know I'd been near the place,' Darrell retorted. The thought had instantly flashed through his mind that he would be the first suspect. The moment the police learned about the complaints against him at the removal firm he would be in deep trouble. He knew from that episode how difficult it was to prove you hadn't done something. His strong impulse was to flee the scene, keep his head down and his mouth shut, hope it would never be known he'd been anywhere near the house.

Why had he released the catch on the front door as he left?

Again, the reply came swiftly back: 'I didn't want anyone else walking in on it before I'd had time to get clear.'

What about the second body, the body of Celia Heyworth?

Darrell swore he had seen no second body; he had never glanced in the direction of the kitchen. He had never moved past the threshold. The first he knew of the existence of a second body was four days later, when the news broke.

Kelsey embarked on a series of rapid-fire questions. Had he snatched up the shoulder bag and hung it round his neck, concealing it under his jacket?

Darrell shook his head fiercely. He had seen no shoulder bag.

Did he remove jewellery and a watch from Celia Heyworth's body?

Darrell repeated that he hadn't seen Celia's body. The only

jewellery he had taken was the ring he'd picked up outside.

What had he done with the ornaments?

He knew nothing of any missing ornaments.

Why had he tipped the vegetables out of the carrier bag?

He knew nothing of any vegetables, any carrier bag.

Did he switch off the radio on the set or at the socket?

He had seen and heard no radio; the whole house had been silent. He had most certainly never touched any radio or any switch, anywhere in the house.

What time had the kitchen clock shown?

He had no idea. He hadn't set foot in the kitchen.

Still the Chief pressed on, back and forth, circling round, making sideways swoops, all without success. Darrell looked increasingly pale and nervous but never once contradicted himself, never once made any damning admission.

Kelsey then went off to speak to the rest of the dealing team. He asked Joe Selwyn if Darrell would have had any opportunity since that Friday evening to get rid of clothing or other items.

Joe acknowledged – again with manifest reluctance – that Darrell would have had ample opportunity in the course of various trips over the holiday weekend, as well as in their normal business forays since then.

All four were agreed that Darrell had at no time made any mention of finding any ring or of having come upon anything at Southview.

On one further point they were also fully agreed: Darrell had not been late in arriving at the van that Friday evening. He had indeed been the first to arrive. He could have had time then, Kelsey reflected, to secrete items temporarily in the van. But another question to the brother-in-law quickly put paid to that notion. The brother-in-law firmly maintained that Darrell had no keys to the van; he had never had any keys. The brother-in-law always kept them himself. Darrell had had to twiddle his thumbs until the brother-in-law arrived at the van, which, as near as he could now recall, would have been around 6.30.

Kelsey then returned to Darrell. He sat down opposite him and regarded him in silence. 'You've told me what you say happened,' he said after some moments. 'I'm going to tell you now what I think happened. At the time you moved the Kingwells into Grasmere Avenue Celia Heyworth chanced to take your eye. Maybe you spoke to her, maybe you just caught

117

sight of her. When you found yourself in the neighbourhood again, you remembered her. Maybe you deliberately fixed it so that it was you who worked Grasmere Avenue. You had this attractive female firmly located at Southview in your mind, but you had no idea there was a second female living there. You called at the house earlier in the week but got no reply. When you left Coniston Avenue that Friday evening you decided to try again at Southview, on your way back to the van. You didn't spot the diamond ring lying on the ground, because it wasn't there.

'You rang the doorbell. Celia had got in from work a matter of minutes earlier. She'd had time to switch on the radio, set down her shoulder bag and the carrier bag of vegetables on the kitchen table, but no more than that.

'She opened the door. You said something or made some move that alarmed her. She turned and ran back into the kitchen. You went after her. She screamed. You grabbed hold of her, clapped a hand over her mouth. She clawed at whatever woollen garment you were wearing. When she dropped to the floor you were sure she was dead. You'd no idea there was anyone else in the house. But Beth Knight was upstairs, lying on her bed. She was already starting to wake up when Celia came home. She heard the radio go on in the kitchen and thought she'd better go down and let Celia know she was in the house, tell her about her accident at the salon. She got off the bed and pulled on her robe.

'Then she heard Celia scream. She ran downstairs. She reached the kitchen doorway and saw you grappling with Celia, she saw Celia fall to the floor. She screamed in terror and turned to run back upstairs. You ran after her, grabbed her from behind, broke her neck, smashed her face against the stairs. You made very sure she was well and truly dead.

'Then you heard a moan from the kitchen. Celia was still alive. You ran back in and looked about for a weapon to finish her off. You snatched up a tea cloth and wrapped it round the rolling pin, to leave no prints, then you set about her again. This time you were very thorough; there would be no more moaning.

'You stripped Celia's jewellery – including the diamond ring – from her body; you took her wristwatch. You had to make the murders look like the work of thieves. You ran into the sitting-room and snatched up a few small items of value. You ran back into the kitchen, tipped the vegetables out of the carrier bag on to the table. You shoved the ornaments, the jewellery, the shoulder bag, into the carrier. You bundled it up and pushed it up under your sweater or waistcoat, zipped up your jacket over it.

'The radio was still on. You couldn't waste time looking for the right control, you turned it off the quickest way, at the socket. You left the house and went along to the van.

'At the first possible moment while the van was being loaded, with the others going back and forth, you hid the carrier bag somewhere well out of sight – under your seat, maybe, or inside one of the pieces being loaded, somewhere where you could get it out again later, to put it under your bed or in some other place where it could stay secure till you had a chance to get rid of it for good. You knew there'd be plenty of opportunity over the holiday weekend. Before you finally dumped the carrier bag you put in the sweater you'd been wearing, the sweater Celia Heyworth had clawed at.

'One item you'd taken from Southview you decided to keep: the diamond ring. You knew it was valuable and, unlike the ornaments and the other pieces of jewellery, it isn't readily identifiable. No engraved initials or dates, nothing distinctive about the setting, nothing to connect it directly with the murders. You saw no risk in hanging on to it for a while, then taking it to some pawnbroker in another part of the country. As good as money in the bank.'

He came finally to a halt. Throughout, Darrell had sat sweating and shaking, making no attempt to smoke. He looked very close to tears. 'This is why I never went near the police,' he said in trembling tones. 'I knew the moment I opened my mouth I'd find myself accused of murder.' He drew a long, shuddering breath. 'None of it's true. All you've just said, not one word of it's true. I've told you what happened. I swear to God every word of what I told you is the truth.' And he continued resolutely to maintain it during a fresh bout of questioning.

Later, at the police station, after the others had made statements and Darrell had been questioned yet again – still without in any way changing his story – Kelsey had another word with Joe Selwyn. He wanted to know what Joe's plans were for the immediate future.

It seemed Joe had intended moving on at the weekend but was now beginning to change his mind, thinking it might be best to leave earlier.

'I'd certainly advise you to move on right away,' Kelsey said, in a tone that brooked little argument. Word of the police visit to the team's lodgings had by now undoubtedly got about. All the initial rumours about the team's possible involvement in the murders would be surfacing again with renewed force. 'You won't be able to do any further business round here,' Kelsey added. 'And I don't imagine you'd find it very pleasant trying.'

Joe needed no further persuasion. 'What about Darrell?' he asked. 'What's going to happen to him?' He had already declared his intention of doing whatever he could to help Darrell. 'I owe it to his father,' he told the Chief. 'And I can't see Darrell as a killer.'

Kelsey chewed his lip. There was no evidence that Darrell had worn any kind of brown woollen garment that Friday, no evidence that he or any of the others had ever owned such a garment. The results of the tests on Joe's cardigan had now come through. They were totally negative, as Kelsey had expected.

Nor was there any evidence that Darrell had ever had in his possession the missing ornaments or any of Celia's jewellery – apart from the diamond ring, and his tale of how he had come by the ring might just be true. No evidence that he had ever had her shoulder bag or any of its probable contents in his possession.

None of Darrell's prints had been found at the murder scene. Checks had been made in Coniston Avenue and yes, Darrell would seem to have finished his last call there, as he had said, shortly after six. At the moment the kitchen clock was inadvertently switched off at Southview – four minutes to six – Darrell would appear to be very squarely placed in Coniston Avenue, talking to a householder who readily supported Darrell's timing. And Darrell's claim to have rung the Southview doorbell at eight or nine minutes past six certainly tied in with Judy Kingwell's recollection of seeing him leaving Southview at around six-ten, six-fifteen.

Judy's parents had been contacted and had come along to the police station. They both recognized Darrell as a member of the removal team when they had moved house, but neither of them could recall any untoward incident or behaviour on Darrell's part during the move. Judy hadn't been present while the move was going forward. She had stayed at her grandmother's until it was over.

All in all, Kelsey wasn't minded at this juncture to bring any specific charges against Darrell, but neither was he minded to let him walk out of the station, free to roam wherever fancy might dictate.

After some further talk with Joe he reached a compromise. Joe knew a reliable and upright citizen who ran a small family woodworking business in a town not far from Cannonbridge. Joe was sure he could arrange for Darrell to stay with the family for the present, occupying himself in the workshop, away from the public eye. He could report to the local police there as often as might be thought necessary.

Darrell made no protest when this arrangement was put to him. He appeared mightily relieved not to have been charged with any offence and agreed without a murmur to all conditions.

CHAPTER 13

The double funeral of the Southview victims was due to take place at eleven on Friday morning, at the church both had attended. Beth Knight's parents had never met Celia but they knew Beth had been fond of her; they knew also how kind Celia had been to their daughter. They felt it fitting now that she should lie beside Celia under the churchyard yews; they believed it was what Beth would have wished.

John Heyworth had let the Chief know he would be driving down from Lydhall after work on Thursday evening, in order to attend the funeral next morning. He would book in at the same hotel and would be staying there until Sunday evening.

The Chief woke early on Thursday morning with a single thought leaping in his brain: did Heyworth have some lady friend up in Lydhall? Had his wife's death smoothed the way for him into another relationship?

One more job for DC Slade, he decided as he got out of bed. He can nip up to Lydhall later today, have a little snoop round.

It was well into the afternoon by the time Slade left for Lydhall. When he had located Melco Polymers he didn't enter the car park but drove around the neighbourhood, keeping an eye out for pubs, cafés and snack bars. He spotted several likely-looking places which Melco workers, fancying a change from the canteen, might well patronize at lunch-time or in the evenings, for a drink after work.

He then drove to the furnished flat John Heyworth was renting in a converted turn-of-the-century dwelling in a pleasant residential suburb. He parked his car a little way along from the front gates and settled down to wait for Heyworth's return from work.

Ten minutes later Heyworth drove in. He didn't garage his car but left it standing by the front door. Slade got out of his vehicle and went up the path, intercepting Heyworth as he took out his doorkey. Slade made himself known and asked if he might step inside as he had one or two questions he'd like to ask. Heyworth's response was friendly and cooperative. He ushered the constable indoors and upstairs to the first floor. Inside the flat, Slade asked if he might look through Heyworth's clothes.

Heyworth looked surprised. 'That's already been done,' he pointed out. 'Two or three weeks back, at the hotel in Cannonbridge.' Quite so, Slade answered in his mind; now we'd like a look through your things here. Not that there was any realistic hope of finding anything after the lapse of time. But he didn't speak these thoughts aloud, nor did he inform Heyworth that the police had also gone through his belongings in Southview, in the same unavailing quest for a woollen garment in a subtle shade of light brown. All he said was: 'I won't be many minutes.' Heyworth made no further objection and led the way into the bedroom. He stood by as the constable made his search, which yielded nothing. He readily acquiesced when Slade told him he'd like to look through the other rooms. It didn't take long; there wasn't a great deal of storage space. Once again, the search yielded nothing.

When Slade had finished, Heyworth offered to make him tea or coffee, a sandwich, maybe. It would be no trouble, he was going to make himself something, in any case. He was driving down to Cannonbridge shortly, in readiness for the funeral tomorrow.

Slade accepted his offer and they sat chatting easily at the kitchen table. It was clear that Heyworth looked on the funeral as an inescapable ordeal, made worse by the presence of TV cameras, reporters, gawping crowds. He daren't leave setting off until tomorrow morning, in case of any delay on the motorway, which could mean arriving at the church at the last moment, harassed and agitated. He wanted to make sure of a good night's sleep after his journey, to be able to face the occasion with composure.

When Slade left, Heyworth walked down with him to the front door, plainly under the impression that the constable was about to leave immediately for Cannonbridge. His remarks implied that it seemed a long way to have come for so little result. Slade didn't enlighten him but went off at once to find himself a lodging for the night. That accomplished, he changed out of his dark suit and white shirt, into casual gear, and began a round of the pubs he had noted earlier.

He stuck to tomato juice and an occasional alcohol-free lager; he nibbled at bar snacks. He listened in to talk as unobtrusively as possible, he managed to infiltrate various good-natured groups, he struck up conversations, engaged in chit-chat of every description, and finally took himself off to his lodgings, no wiser than when he had left Cannonbridge. Before going to bed he took the precaution of telling his landlady he wasn't blessed with a big appetite, and a light breakfast would be ample. He knew he was in for a day of almost non-stop eating and drinking, however small he tried to keep his orders. The last thing he wanted was to handicap himself from the start with a typical landlady's offering of a vast plateful of assorted fried foods.

He was up in good time next morning, ready to make a start on the teashops and sandwich bars. He chatted where he could to waitresses and counter hands; he contrived occasional friendly exchanges with other customers. None of all this proved in the slightest degree productive, but he was by no means cast down. Things would surely look up during the lunch-hour.

A hundred miles to the south, the skies over Cannonbridge were blue and cloudless, with bright gold sunshine and a light breeze.

Even after all the attention the case had aroused, Chief Inspector Kelsey was surprised at the size of the crowds, the vast array of flowers.

Celia Heyworth's sister, Abbie Yates, was escorted to the funeral by John Heyworth. Beth Knight's family and relatives were there in force. Neil Leighton had joined them, together with a large contingent of friends and neighbours from the village, many of whom had known Beth from birth. George Drummond and his wife entered the church side by side with Wilfrid and Eva Probyn, followed by a representative group of workers from the various departments of British Braids. The proprietress of the hairdressing salon was accompanied by her aunt and her chief assistant. Many residents of Grasmere Avenue attended in a group, among them, Ronald Marriott, and Mr and Mrs Kingwell. Marriott's wife was still staying with her mother. She had suggested attending but had been greatly relieved when her mother and her husband had united in categorically forbidding it. They were all three aware that if she did attend she would spend most of the time in tears, doing no good to herself or the coming child.

Alec Morgan came with Teresa Anderson and her father. Kelsey managed a word privately with Anderson as the other two went into the church. He asked how Alec was behaving these days and was told he was now a good deal steadier and calmer. He had started coming round to the house again, doing odd jobs, working in the garden, much as before, but he never spoke of Beth or in any way referred to the murders. Nor did the Andersons ever raise these subjects with him, but let him go quietly along from day to day.

All three Cormacks were present. Simon looked pale and heavy-eyed. There was no sign of Lorraine Beattie or her mother. Simon was among those who stepped forward at the committal to cast flowers into the graves. Tears streamed down his face as he dropped a red rose on Celia's coffin. Beside him, Alec Morgan, his face drawn and grieving, let fall a white lily for Beth.

As the words of committal were spoken, a great sweep of swallows circled overhead and flew off through the high blue air to southern skies.

CHAPTER 14

Things did indeed show signs of looking up during the lunch-hour, DC Slade was pleased to find. In a bright, well-run cafeteria not far from the Melco gates, there was a sizeable influx of workers, all female, most of them chatting non-stop in voices far from hushed. By dint of joining the queue more than once and finding himself a place afterwards at tables in different parts of the room, Slade succeeded in overhearing a good deal of gossip. He stayed until the last bunch had gone back to work. But never once did he hear the name Heyworth spoken.

Nothing daunted, he continued his dogged tour of eating-places during the afternoon, with no better luck.

He wasn't beaten yet. In the early evening he provided himself with a newspaper and made for the pub nearest Melco. The television lounge was crowded but he managed to edge his way in and took up his stance against a wall. He found himself watching the national news. There was an air of hushed expectancy in the room, a lively stir of interest as the next item came on: the double funeral of the Southview victims. The audience craned forward to catch every word, peer at every face. Slade glimpsed Chief Inspector Kelsey and Sergeant Lambert on the screen. There was a sudden ripple of sound among the watchers as John Heyworth came into view.

Then it was over and the next item appeared. A surge of comment rose on all sides as most of those in the lounge got to their feet and headed for the public bar, talking as they went with animation. Slade moved with them.

He didn't have to bother sheltering behind his newspaper. He didn't even have to bother ordering a drink. For the next fifteen minutes he merely allowed himself to remain caught up in the crush before the bar, absorbing every scrap of opinion and observation as men and women struggled by him, clutching their drinks, exchanging loud greetings, calling out to each other. Ribald remarks, raunchy jokes, braying laughter.

He didn't have to wait in vain now for the name Heyworth to reach his ears. He heard it from all quarters.

And with it came another name, spoken with coarse humour and bawdy innuendo. The name of a woman, a colleague, it would seem. Judging by the freely flying comments, she was a good-looker, with an eye to the main chance, a hard nut to crack. As Slade left the pub he made a mental note of her name: Sarah Brooke.

It was late when he got back to Cannonbridge but he was at the police station early next morning, ready to make his report as soon as the Chief showed up.

Kelsey heard him out with sharp interest. As he sat at his desk a little later, mulling over what Slade had told him, he had a message from the desk sergeant: Mr and Mrs Kingwell had called in with their daughter, asking to speak to the Chief. Kelsey went along at once and took them to an interview room.

It seemed that when Mrs Kingwell had gone into her daughter's bedroom this morning, to wake her, she had drawn back the curtains and stood looking out. She had commented on the state of the garden belonging to the empty property across the road, complaining about weed seeds blowing over into their own beds and borders. Judy had got out of bed and joined her at the window. She had looked across and remarked casually: 'I haven't seen Simon Cormack up in the tree lately.'

Her mother at once questioned her. When she heard what Judy had to say she went downstairs and repeated it to her husband. They decided it warranted passing on without delay to the police.

Judy appeared self-possessed and at ease in the interview room. She told her tale in a straightforward manner. She was well able to recognize Simon Cormack; she had known him before they moved to Grasmere Avenue as she had often been into the store with her mother. Since the move she had seen Simon about the neighbourhood when he was home from university. She also knew him from church.

From her bedroom window she could see into the top branches of the horse chestnut in the garden opposite. When Simon was up in the tree he was well camouflaged. You had to look hard for quite a time to make him out, and then it was usually because he had moved or parted the leaves to look down. What had drawn her attention in the first place was that she had chanced to see him come down the footpath between the houses and let himself into the garden by the side gate. She knew the property was empty and she was curious to see what he was about. She had almost at once noticed movement among the branches of the horse chestnut and had spotted him settling himself into place. In all, she had seen him in the tree maybe half a dozen times, always in the late afternoon or early evening. If it crossed her mind when she was up in her room around that time of day, she would stand by the window to see if she could spot him; it had become a little game with her.

She had never said anything about it to anyone; she had never thought it worth mentioning. She liked climbing trees herself and she imagined it was a childhood habit Simon had never grown out of. She thought he had probably chosen the horse chestnut because it stood in the garden of an empty property. Maybe he liked to read up there. Or maybe he just wanted to get away to a little hiding place where no one could bother him. She didn't think that at all strange; she could well understand its attractions. She knew where Simon lived and knew there were no tall trees in the Cormacks' garden, so he couldn't have done any climbing there.

No, she had never said anything to Simon about seeing him in the tree. It would never cross her mind to do so. If a person had a secret hiding place, the last thing they would want would be for someone to let them know they knew about it.

When had she last seen him in the tree?

Not for some time, she replied at once. Pressed to try to recall more precisely, she told the Chief after some thought that it might have been six weeks or so.

What about the Friday before the bank holiday? Had she spotted Simon in the tree then? Kelsey asked her to think back very carefully before replying. She did as he instructed and then shook her head. She was certain she hadn't seen him in the tree that Friday.

When the Kingwells had left, the Chief dispatched an agile young constable to climb the horse chestnut, to discover what could be seen from that vantage point. The constable returned shortly to say he had had no difficulty in climbing the tree as there were ample footholds. He had come upon a secure niche high up where someone had clearly perched before. In suitable clothes he would be confident of not being easily spotted up there. By parting the leaves or branches here and there he was able to gain a good view of much of the front of Southview, the drive and front garden.

Kelsey lost no time in sending officers round to Grasmere Avenue to inquire from householders if there had been any sighting of Simon Cormack in the tree, close to the date of the murders. They could find no one who had ever seen him in the tree, but they did discover one old man who had been walking along Coniston Avenue a few weeks back and had seen Simon dart down the footpath. He had glanced down after him and had seen him slip in through the side gate of the empty property; he had wondered briefly what he could be up to. He couldn't recall the date more precisely; he often walked along Coniston Avenue.

The Chief had asked John Heyworth to call in at the station on Saturday morning and Heyworth duly presented himself. He told the Chief he had appointments in Gosford later in the morning, with his uncle's solicitor, the estate agent selling his uncle's house, and his uncle's housekeeper. Kelsey assured him he wouldn't detain him long. He produced the diamond ring found under the dashboard shelf in the antique dealers' van and Heyworth had no hesitation in identifying it as his wife's engagement ring.

He wanted to know where it had been found and displayed considerable agitation as Kelsey related the circumstances. Heyworth expressed astonishment and dismay that they had let Darrell Wilding go and took a good deal of persuading that there wasn't much of a case against him.

When Heyworth had finally calmed down, Kelsey suddenly fired a question at him: 'Have you a lady friend up in Lydhall?'

Heyworth looked taken aback. 'No, I have not,' he answered brusquely.

'What about Sarah Brooke?' Kelsey demanded.

Heyworth frowned. 'I've known Sarah a year or two. She's a colleague. I see quite a bit of her in the course of my work. But that's all there is to it.'

'Have you never taken her out?'

He moved his shoulders. 'We've had lunch together a few

times, to discuss work. I don't know if you'd call that taking her out. I certainly wouldn't.'

'Nothing more than that?'

He shook his head. 'Certainly not.'

Kelsey was silent for some moments, then he asked: 'Do you think the relationship is likely to develop now?'

Heyworth's eyes flashed. 'Good God, man!' he said with force. 'What do you take me for? I've only just buried my wife.'

CHAPTER 15

Once again, the Chief timed his call at Leacroft to arrive on the doorstep shortly after the Cormacks got back from church on Sunday morning. They didn't appear surprised to see him, merely resigned to the intrusion. Simon seemed in low spirits, his manner lethargic; he looked as if it was some time since he had enjoyed a good night's sleep. Kelsey explained that he had one or two questions to put to Simon. Thomas at once made it clear he would prefer any questioning to take place in the presence of himself and his wife. Neither Kelsey nor Simon raised any objection to that.

Kelsey jumped in without preamble. Was Simon in the habit of climbing the horse chestnut tree in the garden of the empty property next door to Southview, and remaining in the tree for some time?

Both Thomas and Ellen appeared startled at the question. They looked across at Simon, awaiting his reply with manifest anxiety.

Simon appeared in no way disconcerted. 'I've climbed the tree several times,' he acknowledged. 'Only since the property's been empty, of course, never before that.'

'Why did you climb the tree?' Kelsey wanted to know.

He shrugged. 'I've always liked climbing trees.'

'That's right,' Ellen struck in. 'He was always climbing trees as a child. We used to have a big elm in the garden, he made himself a den up there. The tree got the rot in it some years ago and it had to be cut down.'

'Why did you choose the horse chestnut?' Kelsey asked Simon. 'Why did you pick that particular garden? Was it because you could look down at Southview from the tree, you could watch the comings and goings there?'

Thomas and Ellen showed fresh anxiety at the question but Simon remained courteous and unflurried. 'Not at all,' he

131

replied. 'I chose it because the house was empty. And it's a good tall tree, with plenty of cover.' He smiled slightly. 'All I did up there was read, or think. I never stayed very long.'

'But I dare say when you were up there,' Kelsey suggested, 'you sometimes took a look down at the house or garden next door, when you heard someone drive into Southview, or ring the doorbell?'

'I may have done, once or twice,' Simon conceded. 'But when I'm reading I don't pay much attention to what's going on around me.'

'That's right,' Ellen interposed. 'You have to call his name two or three times before he even hears you, if he's got his head in a book.'

'When was the last time you climbed the tree?' Kelsey asked Simon.

He thought back. 'It would be some weeks ago now. I've been busy studying and going to the library.' He gave another slight smile. 'You can't really make notes up a tree.'

'Did you climb the tree on the Friday before the bank holiday?' Kelsey asked. Again, the question produced a display of anxiety on the part of Thomas and Ellen.

Simon shook his head. 'No, I did not climb the tree that Friday,' he replied evenly.

Kelsey didn't let it go. 'You could have been there in all innocence,' he pointed out. 'You may be afraid to say so now, in case you are unjustly suspected of some involvement in the murders. But if you were there in all innocence, you might be very helpful to us. You may have seen or heard something. You may have seen someone enter or leave Southview, or you may have noticed some other fact that could be useful.'

As Simon opened his mouth to reply, Thomas spoke up sharply. 'Are you trying to trap the boy?' he demanded.

Before Kelsey could respond, Simon said in a tone still equable, 'Whether it's a trap or not makes no difference. I didn't climb the tree that day. I never went near Southview that day. When I left the library at the end of the afternoon, I came straight home, I didn't go by Southview. I had no opportunity to see anyone entering or leaving.'

'If you did happen to be in the tree in the middle of the afternoon,' Kelsey persisted, 'you could have been aware that

Beth Knight had come home from the salon and was in the house alone.'

Thomas uttered a sound of protest, but Simon replied calmly: 'As I wasn't in the tree at any time that afternoon, I couldn't have known Beth was in the house on her own.'

'Maybe you were in the tree later that day,' Kelsey pressed on. 'Perhaps you were there when Celia Heyworth came home. Did you get down from the tree, not realizing Beth was in the house? Did you ring the bell, to bring Celia to the front door? Did you get yourself admitted to the house one way or another?'

Again Thomas uttered a sound of protest and again Simon replied, calm and unflustered: 'I wasn't in the tree at any time that Friday. I never went near Southview that day.'

Kelsey still wasn't to be put off. 'Did you in some way identify Celia with your own mother? Did you feel that both of them had treated you badly? Did you feel angry? Resentful?'

Simon gazed levelly back at him. 'I'm not a child, to confuse the identities of two women.'

'He was never interested in Mrs Heyworth,' Ellen put in, her face deeply creased in anxiety. 'He was never much interested in Beth Knight. Lorraine's the only one he's interested in.' She hesitated, then she drew a deep breath, clasped her hands tightly together and plunged on. 'They're getting married.'

Kelsey's head jerked round. 'Getting married?'

She pressed her hands even more tightly together. 'Yes. Next Saturday, at the church. They're getting married by licence.'

There was a moment's silence, then Kelsey said: 'Why all the rush?'

Another brief silence. 'Lorraine's pregnant,' Simon supplied in a voice devoid of expression. He looked far from joyful at the prospect of fatherhood.

Ellen found her tongue again. 'It's a pity it had to happen this way, but it's understandable when a young couple are very fond of each other. Lorraine's a dear girl. We know she'll make Simon a good wife.'

'There's never been any strong support for abortion in this house,' Simon said, adding in a tone of great bleakness: 'And the last thing anyone here would want would be for another child with Cormack blood to go through life as a bastard. One is enough by anyone's reckoning.'

A hush fell over the room.

Kelsey's next question was directed at Ellen: 'Do you propose telling the Beatties the truth about Simon's birth?'

But it was Thomas who answered: 'We've already told them, we thought it only right. They took it very well.'

'Very civilized of them, wouldn't you say?' Simon said to Kelsey. 'They might have been expected to run foaming mad at the revelation.'

'Are you going on with your studies?' Kelsey asked him. 'Are you going back to the university?'

Again it was Thomas who answered: 'That's been a matter of some discussion. We've all talked it over, Lorraine and her mother as well. We finally decided between us it's best if Simon leaves university and comes into the business right away.'

Simon gave the Chief a look edged with sardonic amusement. 'It's a great comfort,' he observed in a tone spiced with mockery, 'to have so many people so concerned with my welfare.'

'When exactly was all this decided?' Kelsey asked Thomas. 'When did you first learn Lorraine was pregnant?'

Thomas thought back. 'We were told about the pregnancy a couple of weeks back. Mrs Beattie rang me here just after I'd got in from work on the Monday evening – two weeks ago, tomorrow, that would be. She asked if we'd all be in if she called round about seven-thirty. She wanted to talk to us, she'd be bringing Lorraine with her. I told her I'd see we were all here when they came. I got it into my head she was going to ask if we could find an opening in the business for Lorraine. I was happy to go along with that. Lorraine's a bright girl, she has a good manner, she's in the trade already. I couldn't see any reason why she wouldn't do well with us.'

He moved his head. 'It was a bit of a bombshell when Mrs Beattie told us her reason for coming round. She came out with it right away, she didn't mince words.'

'Did you know about the pregnancy before the Beatties came round?' Kelsey asked Simon.

He shook his head. 'I hadn't the faintest idea. It was a bolt from the blue. Lorraine said she hadn't liked to tell me. It was her mother persuaded her to come round here and tell us all together.' He smiled slightly. 'It certainly made a dramatic moment.'

'There was never any question of anything other than marriage,' Ellen said with profound conviction. 'We could never agree to destroying life. We could never allow the child to be put up for adoption. And we couldn't have Lorraine being left to bring up the child as a single parent.'

Kelsey looked at Simon. 'Did you have any choice in the matter?' he asked.

Before Simon could reply, an answer was supplied by Thomas: 'What choice did he need? He has his Christian duty, his moral duty, his duty to the family, his duty as a citizen. Isn't that enough?'

CHAPTER 16

Strains of a Strauss waltz drifted out through the kitchen window of the Beatties' cottage as Sergeant Lambert halted the car. Once again they found Mrs Beattie preparing lunch, with her daughter's assistance. Neither appeared surprised or disconcerted to see the two policemen.

'I'm sure you won't mind if we carry on with what we're doing,' Mrs Beattie remarked pleasantly as she sat the two men down in the kitchen. She switched off the radio. 'Lorraine will make you tea or coffee, whichever you prefer.'

Kelsey thanked her but declined the offer. 'I understand you're getting married,' he said to Lorraine.

She gave him a serene smile. 'Eleven-thirty next Saturday morning, at the church,' she announced with pleasure. She began to busy herself again, preparing an assortment of vegetables.

'I expect you know the rest of it too,' Mrs Beattie observed to Kelsey. 'You'll have had it all from the Cormacks, I don't doubt.' She gave her attention again to her task. 'It'll be a very quiet affair, in the circumstances. There won't be a proper reception, just cake and champagne and a small buffet, at Leacroft, after the ceremony. The Cormacks offered to have it there, so that's what we settled on. We're all family now.' She glanced at her daughter with fond pride. 'Lorraine will be given away by a cousin of my late husband. His daughter's going to be bridesmaid. She's thirteen years old, a nice, sensible girl.'

She took down a bowl and began to assemble ingredients for a pudding. 'The manageress and the staff at the boutique are clubbing together to give Lorraine her outfit as a wedding present. She won't be wearing white, not in the circumstances.' Lorraine gave the Chief a demure little flick of her eyes. 'She's chosen a beautiful two-piece,' Mrs Beattie went on with relish. 'And Mrs Cormack took us both round the store the other evening, after it was closed. She let Lorraine pick out anything she wanted, anything at all. And she invited me to choose myself an outfit for Saturday – everything, hat, bag, gloves, as well. I got a very smart dress and jacket, with a lovely hat to match.'

She broke eggs into the bowl and began to whisk them. 'The honeymoon will be in Torquay. Lorraine didn't fancy going far afield, not in her condition. She didn't want to risk foreign travel, foreign food, she's got to take care. Torquay was my idea. It's very select and it won't be crowded this late in the season. You can usually rely on good weather down there, even at this time of year.'

Lorraine made no comment but worked steadily on, listening to her mother with an air of complacent approval. 'Mr Cormack's found them a furnished flat for when they get back from Torquay,' Mrs Beattie continued. 'Mrs Cormack and I are going to see it's all ready for them to walk into. It's only temporary, of course – the Cormacks are going to buy them a house. We'll see about choosing that after the honeymoon. Somewhere in this part of Cannonbridge, we thought, to be near both me and the Cormacks.'

She glanced across at the Chief. 'I know it's all going to work out very well. And Lorraine will be able to take an interest in the business. She'll enjoy that, she'll be very good at it. Mrs Cormack thinks so too. She's sure Simon will find Lorraine a great help. It can't be all that many years before Simon takes over the business.' She slanted Kelsey a significant look. 'I gather you know about Simon's birth. It came as a bit of a surprise to us, I must say, we neither of us had the slightest idea. Not that it makes any difference to anything, as far as I can see.' She fell silent for a moment, her hands idle. 'I remember Faith Cormack, Simon's mother. She was a pretty girl.' She resumed her task with fresh energy.

Kelsey turned to Lorraine. 'I understand you didn't tell Simon you were pregnant. The first he knew about it was when you turned up with your mother at Leacroft.'

'Naturally, Lorraine told me about it first,' Mrs Beattie interposed before her daughter could answer. 'Any girl would speak to her mother first. We talked it over and decided the best thing would be to be open and above board with Mr and Mrs Cormack, right from the start. We wanted any decisions to be made with their full consent.' She jerked her head. 'And we were quite right. They both appreciated the way we went about it. They both said so, more than once.'

'What would you have done if the Cormacks had decided there wouldn't be any wedding?' Kelsey wanted to know. 'Or if Simon had refused to marry Lorraine?'

There was a short silence, then Mrs Beattie said flatly: 'Lorraine would have had an abortion.' Lorraine gave no sign of dissent. 'But I was never in any doubt,' Mrs Beattie went on with conviction. 'I was certain Simon would marry her. The Cormacks are not the kind to go for abortion and I was positive Simon wouldn't be able to stand out against them.' She recollected herself suddenly. 'Of course he's very much in love with Lorraine. He'd never dream of letting her down.'

'Did you tell the Cormacks there'd be an abortion if there was no marriage?' Kelsey asked.

'Yes, I did mention that,' she acknowledged.

'How did they react?'

'They were horrified at the idea.'

'Why did you choose that particular day to go round to Leacroft to break the news?'

'Lorraine wanted to be certain there was no mistake, she really was pregnant, before anything was said. She had her pregnancy confirmed by the doctor on the Saturday morning. I talked things over with Lorraine on the Sunday and we decided to go round to Leacroft the following evening. There was no point in delaying any longer. The sooner a decision was made, the better.'

Kelsey regarded her for some moments, then he said: 'Let me put this to you. You were holding a very powerful card in Lorraine's pregnancy. You wanted to make sure you played it right, you had to choose your moment. That Monday was the day after we'd called at Leacroft to question Simon – we came on here afterwards, to talk to Lorraine and yourself. Was it that visit from us that decided you to make your move with the Cormacks? Did you believe things might be looking bad for Simon over the Southview murders, it might help to put him in a better light if he could show he wasn't at all interested in either Celia Heyworth or Beth Knight, it was Lorraine he wanted, Lorraine he was in love with.' He leaned forward. 'Did you decide it was by far your best moment to persuade the

Cormacks to agree to the marriage? You saw your chance and you grabbed it with both hands.'

Mrs Beattie regarded him coolly. 'You make me out to be a very scheming woman. All I am is an ordinary, hard-working mother, trying to do the best for her daughter in a difficult situation.'

'Maybe you had another card to play, as well as the pregnancy,' Kelsey hazarded. 'Maybe one or other of you knows something positive against Simon, in the Southview case, something he'd very much prefer the police not to know. Did you make it clear you wouldn't speak out, if Simon agreed to marry Lorraine?'

'Now you really are going over the top,' Mrs Beattie said with bland reproof. 'It's hard to know what you'll come out with next.'

She didn't have to wait long to find out. Kelsey turned to Lorraine. 'When you left work that Friday evening, I put it to you that you didn't call in at the chemist's, but you went straight round to Southview. You knew Beth was at home, you'd learned that from Simon. You believed Simon was still strongly drawn to Beth. You were determined to marry Simon, you saw Beth as the big obstacle in your way. Maybe all you intended was to tell Beth you were pregnant by Simon, appeal to her good nature, ask her to make it clear to Simon she would never look at him again.'

Lorraine gazed calmly back at the Chief. 'I never went round to Southview that evening, or at any other time. I've never had reason to. Simon was never strongly attracted to Beth, I'm certain of that. I'd no idea she was in the house that afternoon. Simon never mentioned her when he called at the boutique.'

Kelsey came swiftly back at her. 'Maybe it wasn't Beth you went round to Southview to see. Maybe you're right, and Simon no longer had his eye on Beth. Maybe you didn't know Beth was in the house. Maybe it was Celia Heyworth you went round to tackle. Celia came home at her usual time that day. Maybe you knew Simon was obsessed by her. He may not have told you in so many words but you're a bright girl, it wouldn't take you long to see how the land lay, especially when you saw how it might affect your own future. You thought it possible Celia could be amusing herself with Simon, leading him on. Maybe you went round to Southview to find out, tell her your situation, ask for her help, ask her to dismiss Simon once and for all. I put it to you Celia had just got in when you reached the house. Things got out of hand, you lost your temper. Beth heard the noise and came running down the stairs.'

Mrs Beattie could no longer keep silent. 'I've heard some tales in my time,' she declared, 'but this beats all. I know you've got your job to do and I dare say you'll try any idea that comes into your head, however daft it is.' She regarded him with maternal rebuke. 'You've got to remember Lorraine's condition. You mustn't go upsetting her.'

'It's all right,' Lorraine assured her mother. 'I'm not upset. The Chief Inspector knows there's not a word of truth in all that. He's just trying it on, seeing if he can get us both good and mad, get one or other of us to come out with something we're not saying, something he thinks we might know against Simon.' She gave the Chief a composed, half-smiling look. 'I'm afraid you're wasting your time, Chief Inspector. We neither of us know anything about what happened that day. And you can't try to make out you've found any of my fingerprints at Southview, because there couldn't possibly be any. I've never at any time been inside the gate, let alone inside the house.'

The weather grew brighter and warmer as the week advanced. Saturday brought blue skies and brilliant sunshine, a perfect day for the wedding of Simon Cormack and Lorraine Beattie. Eleven-thirty at the church, the Chief reminded himself over a hasty breakfast. He had a hundred and one matters to deal with, but he intended to go along to the church if at all possible.

Shortly before nine, John Heyworth called in at the station. He had to go over to Gosford again, to see the estate agent. He had found a message from the agent waiting for him when he arrived at his Cannonbridge hotel yesterday evening, to say there had now been a firm – and very reasonable – offer for his uncle's house. He must also see his uncle's solicitor again, and call on the housekeeper, to make sure she had reached a satisfactory decision about where she was going to live. And he must settle what must be done about his uncle's furniture and other items. 'I thought I'd better look in here first,' he told the Chief. 'To see if you wanted me.'

No, the Chief had no need to see him today.

'If anything does turn up and you do need to see me,' Heyworth went on, 'I'll be in the hotel all evening. It's very likely I'll have to go over to Gosford again tomorrow. There's a lot to see to at the house.'

Yes, the Chief would bear that in mind.

'I'd better also mention,' Heyworth continued, 'that I'll be away from Lydhall during the latter part of next week.' He would be setting off first thing on Wednesday morning, on one of his regular rounds of customers; he wouldn't be returning to Lydhall at the end of the week but would continue on to Cannonbridge on Friday evening, booking in again at the same hotel. And, once again, he would expect to have to go over to Gosford during that weekend. He supplied the Chief with the addresses and phone numbers of the hotels where he would be staying on Wednesday and Thursday nights, in case the Chief might need to get in touch with him.

Simon Cormack's wedding did indeed seem to be a very quiet affair. When the Chief arrived with Sergeant Lambert shortly before eleven-fifteen, they found a mere sprinkling of folk in the pews. Thomas and Ellen Cormack were both seated; they glanced swiftly round as the two policemen entered the church. Thomas said something to his wife and then rose and came down the aisle towards them. He expressed no surprise at their presence but indicated that he'd like a word with them outside. They followed him into the bright sunshine.

'Everything's going along without a hitch,' Thomas said. 'My wife's quite happy about it all, and Simon agrees it's for the best. He's properly settled in his mind about it now.' He considered his watch. 'He should be here any minute now. He's coming with his best man, David Reid; they were at school together.' He mentioned a village some miles away, where David lived with his parents. 'David fixed up a stag party for Simon, yesterday evening. Simon stayed the night with the Reids – he couldn't very well drive back home after the party.'

He looked at his watch again. 'I'll go down to the road, to see if there's any sign of them.' Kelsey followed as he set off down the path. They reached the road and Thomas stood glancing up and down. After a minute or two he began a slow pacing, back and forth, along the pavement.

The hands of the church clock moved inexorably on. The half-hour struck. Thomas halted in his pacing. 'They must be stuck in traffic somewhere,' he said. A car came into view and slowed to a halt. Mrs Beattie, resplendent in wedding finery, was ensconced in the passenger seat beside the cousin of her late husband; she wore an air of unassailable pride and satisfaction. Behind the pair sat Lorraine and her bridesmaid, Lorraine looking not in the least nervous, beautiful and elegant, in an ivory-coloured two-piece, her bridesmaid beguilingly pretty in palest primrose. None of the four showed surprise or displeasure at the sight of the two policemen flanking Thomas.

The moment the car came to a standstill, Thomas put his head in at the window and spoke to the cousin. Incipient frowns marred the expressions of mother and daughter as they heard

142

what he had to say. The cousin gave a brisk nod and the car moved off again, for a discreet drive round.

'I'm going to phone the Reids,' Thomas announced with sudden decision. He went rapidly back up the path and round to a side door leading into the vestry. Kelsey followed, stationing himself at Thomas's side as he made his call.

David Reid's father answered the phone. It became abundantly clear in a very short time that Simon and David were not on their way to the church. David Reid was not in the house, he was not even currently living at home. He was working in London and hadn't been home for several weeks. His parents knew nothing of Simon Cormack's wedding or of any stag party, nothing of any plan for David to act as best man; they had some difficulty in recalling exactly who Simon was. To the best of their knowledge, David hadn't kept up with Simon after their schooldays – not that the pair had ever been particularly friendly, even then. They knew of no communication of any sort from Simon in recent times; David hadn't mentioned his name to them.

Thomas looked dazed as he replaced the receiver. Now he had to face the distressing business of going back into the church, breaking the painful news to his wife and the others. Then he must return to the road, to await the reappearance of the bridal car.

When it came into view a second time the occupants were able to read the expression on Thomas's face as he stood on the pavement; it more than half prepared them for what they were about to hear. Neither Lorraine nor her mother displayed anger or agitation at the news; they made no response of any kind.

'You'd better come along to Leacroft,' Thomas told the four of them. The other guests, few in number, were already tactfully removing themselves entirely from the scene.

When the party reached Leacroft, Ellen insisted on some inroads being made into the buffet. Sergeant Lambert, himself never loath to oblige in such a respect, observed with interest that all four of the Beattie contingent addressed themselves to the refreshments with a good appetite; Lorraine, in particular, needed little urging.

The Chief busied himself asking questions. It seemed Lorraine and her mother had last seen Simon on Thursday evening, when he had been invited round to supper. His behaviour had been very much as usual. He had appeared in good spirits and talked of the wedding, the honeymoon, the future, as if he was looking forward to it all. He had certainly given no indication that he was having second thoughts about the marriage.

He had rung Lorraine yesterday evening, just before he drove away from Leacroft; Lorraine had got in from work only a few minutes earlier. He didn't stay long on the phone. He sounded loving and cheerful; he advised her to get to bed early, to make sure of a good night's sleep. He told her he would try not to stay up too late himself, at his stag party. Neither Lorraine nor her mother could throw any light on Simon's failure to show up at the church.

The Cormacks told the Chief they had noticed nothing out of the ordinary in Simon's manner or behaviour the previous day. He had chatted in seemingly good spirits during supper; he hadn't appeared at all uneasy or stressed. They had both been convinced he had fully accepted the path his feet were now set on. He had given no sign of anger or resentment; he had made no mention of the university course he had abandoned. Neither of them could offer any guess as to where he might now be, or why he had taken it into his head to vanish without a word.

He had left Leacroft shortly after supper, taking with him in his car a suitcase, containing, so they were given to understand, his things for the night and his clothes for the wedding. Ellen had walked out to the car with him when he left; she had stood watching as he stowed his case in the boot. He had opened the driver's door, to get in, and had then turned back towards her. He had put an arm round her shoulders, stooped and kissed her on the cheek – something he hadn't done for many a long day. Ellen put up a hand to her cheek now, recalling that moment with the glitter of tears in her eyes. She remembered, word for word, what he had said: 'You always did what you thought best.' It had seemed to her at the time a kind of absolution, as if, on the threshold of adult life, about to take on its responsibilities, he had looked back at the past with a more understanding eye.

A search of Simon's room, and of the two suitcases standing against the wall, packed ready for the honeymoon, revealed no letter, nothing to suggest what he might have been planning, where he might have gone, what his motives could have been. The rest of his clothing, his other personal belongings, his books

144

and notebooks, were all in his room, as usual. Something struck Sergeant Lambert: the total absence of any photographs in the room. No likeness of Thomas or Ellen. None of Faith. And none of Lorraine.

On Sunday afternoon, family parties took advantage of the continuing spell of warm, sunny weather to drive out from Cannonbridge to a beauty spot a few miles away.

A tract of woodland, bordered by grassy slopes, led down to a lake fed by streams. There was fishing; boating; a convenient car park. A number of picnic areas were set out with benches and tables.

At around half past three an elderly gentleman decided to walk up from the shores of the lake towards the trees. When he left the expanse of grass he strolled along a path taking him into the heart of the wood. Little sunlight filtered through the canopy of leaves and branches. Children's voices, calling to each other in play, from down by the lake, sounded distant and muted.

After some minutes he found himself approaching a more open stretch of woodland. Ahead of him a fine stand of towering beeches came into view. As he drew near he became aware of a raucous clamour overhead. He halted, tilting back his head to gaze up at the beeches.

Half a dozen jackdaws were darting about in agitated flight, swooping, dipping, circling. He strained his eyes to discover the cause of the commotion and drew a sudden gasping breath.

High above, he could just make out a slim figure, dangling from the topmost branches.

CHAPTER 18

By six o'clock the crowd of onlookers was dispersing, at the end of an afternoon that had turned out a good deal more exciting than they had envisaged when they had set out from home. The police doctor had left; the pathologist had also gone; the body had been taken to the mortuary.

Chief Inspector Kelsey left the scene with Sergeant Lambert and made his way to his car, bound for the Cannonbridge police station. No point now in rushing to break the news to the Cormacks or the Beatties; they must all four by now be only too well aware of what had happened. More than one video camera owner had been present in the crowd, snatching at the opportunity to record the unlooked-for drama, hopeful of selling his efforts to a regional TV station. And word had spread rapidly through the onlookers when the identity of the body became known, within a very short time of being brought down. A wallet discovered on the body held, among other papers, a driving licence, car insurance certificate and bank card; a gold watch on the wrist was engraved with name and date. The name – Cormack – was known to many in the crowd. It was common knowledge in Cannonbridge that detectives investigating the Southview murders had been asking questions about Simon Cormack's movements. And talk in the local pubs last night had been considerably enlivened by the news that Simon had failed to show up for his wedding and was nowhere to be found.

The Chief got into his car and leaned back against the upholstery. He closed his eyes as Lambert set the car in motion. The police doctor and the pathologist had been pretty well in agreement over the time of death, the doctor putting it between eight on Friday evening and two o'clock on Saturday morning, the pathologist between nine on Friday evening and four on Saturday morning.

The sash cord around Simon's neck was brand new. His car keys were in his pocket. His car was soon located, in a corner of the car park, near the lake. It had been left carefully locked. His suitcase in the boot had been neatly packed with his wedding clothes and his things for the make-believe overnight stay with the Reids. There were no letters, either in the case or on the body, but there were two photographs in Simon's wallet. A snapshot of Faith Cormack, aged about twenty, standing on the front steps at Leacroft, with Simon, as a four-year-old child, beside her. They were both smiling into the camera; they looked happy and carefree.

The second photograph was of Celia Heyworth. It was an excellent likeness and clearly showed a resemblance to Faith Cormack. The photograph had been cut in half vertically but the Chief knew what the missing half had shown. He recognized the photograph as one of those taken in the Southview garden when Celia's sister, Abbie Yates, had driven over one Sunday afternoon. He knew who it was that had stood beside Celia, in front of the superb show of yellow forsythia, that sunny afternoon in late March: it had been Beth Knight.

One of the amateur videos of the scene in the wood had indeed found a ready buyer, and clips from it duly appeared on regional TV in the early-evening slot. The Cannonbridge pubs were very soon buzzing afresh with speculation and gossip.

Shortly after seven, Sergeant Lambert drove the Chief over to Leacroft, where they found not only Thomas and Ellen Cormack, but also Mrs Beattie and Lorraine. The first wave of shock and grief had by now subsided. Ellen had managed to achieve a tenuous control over her emotions but the arrival of the two policemen plunged her back into a state of open distress; she strove valiantly to recover composure. Thomas was plainly devastated by the blow. He couldn't sit still but moved restlessly about the room, his face anguished.

The only perturbation Mrs Beattie displayed was in sliding repeated glances of anxious concern at her daughter, who showed no signs of agitation but sat upright and alert, saying nothing, watching and listening with unflagging attention to all that was going forward.

When Thomas left the house with the two policemen, to carry out the formal identification of the body, he said to the Chief in broken tones, 'Simon often used to cycle over to those woods when he was a boy. He always loved climbing trees.' He fell silent again, saying nothing more during the drive to the mortuary. When they arrived he sat motionless for several moments, then he nerved himself for the ordeal and got out of the car.

His agony as he identified his only grandchild was painful to witness. He stumbled as he turned away, and the Chief caught him by the arm. On the way out he said in a shaking voice: 'We gave him that watch on his eighteenth birthday.' On the way back to the house he wept in grief-stricken silence.

When the Chief left Leacroft for the second time, bound for the postmortem, he snatched a moment to call in at Southview, to glance through Celia Heyworth's photograph album again, as well as the folder of snapshots in Beth Knight's bedroom.

As he had remembered, the snapshot of Celia and Beth standing together in front of the forsythia was there in Celia's album but missing from Beth's folder. Beth could have shown Simon the photographs, he reflected, and Simon may have asked if he could have one. The obvious one for him to choose would have been the one of Beth standing alone by a damson tree in full snowy blossom. It was a good clear photograph, showing an excellent likeness of Beth, who looked happy and pretty. But his choice would appear to have fallen on the other photograph, less good of Beth but particularly good of Celia, relaxed and graceful, looking out at the camera with a lovely, warm smile.

And then, some time later, Simon would seem to have taken a pair of scissors and neatly excised Beth from the picture.

'Suicide, beyond any shadow of doubt,' the pathologist told Kelsey as they came out of the mortuary at the end of the postmortem on Simon Edward Cormack. Every death by hanging that the pathologist had ever encountered professionally had been either a manifest suicide or, very rarely, a case of misadventure – more often than not the result of some foolhardy schoolboy experiment that had gone wrong.

In theory it might be possible to commit a murder by forcible hanging, setting it up to look sufficiently like suicide to deceive the expert eye, but in practice it simply couldn't be done; there would always be telltale signs.

And very certainly it couldn't be done in the case of a fit young male victim, strong and athletic, where the hanging was scheduled to take place from the topmost branch of a towering beech.

On the way back to the police station the Chief sat mulling over the findings of the postmortem. The examination of the stomach contents had allowed the pathologist to be a little more precise in his estimate of the time of death; the nature of Simon's last meal and the time it took place had both been clearly established. The pathologist would now put the time of death at between eight on Friday evening and midnight.

They reached the station and Kelsey went wearily up the steps and in through the door. A number of messages awaited him. There had been several more phone calls from members of the public.

And a local shopkeeper, the owner of a DIY store, a man acquainted with the Cormack family, had called in to say that Simon Cormack had been into his store on Friday morning. He had seemed much as usual. They had chatted for a minute or two before Simon left with his purchase: a length of stout sash cord.

In Kelsey's mail on Monday morning was an envelope carrying a first-class stamp and a local postmark indicating that it had been picked up in the first collection on Saturday morning. The envelope bore a superscription in block capitals: ATTENTION DCI KELSEY ONLY. The address was written in a distinctive hand, small and cramped, a hand the Chief recognized at once as Simon Cormack's.

Inside the envelope was a single closely written sheet, formally set out: Simon's full Cannonbridge address at the head of the sheet, together with the date and time of writing – 4.15 p.m. on Friday; some two hours, the Chief noted, before Simon had phoned Lorraine to say he would shortly be off to his stag party and would see her at the church next morning. The handwriting showed no sign of unsteadiness.

Kelsey ran his eye rapidly over the sheet, then read it through again, slowly. Simon gave detailed directions for locating his body and his car, in case either had not yet been discovered. He had, he said, done his best to accept the future now mapped out for him, but without success. He felt only insurmountable depression at the prospect, a sense of being permanently trapped. He deeply regretted all the trouble his decision must cause, but could see no other way out.

He went on to state: 'I had no hand in the killing of either Celia Heyworth or Beth Knight. Nor have I any idea who might have killed them.'

The sheet was signed with his full name.

Kelsey had scarcely finished perusing it when he had a message from the desk to say that Mr and Mrs Cormack, together with Mrs Beattie and her daughter, had called in, asking to see him. He had them immediately brought along to his office.

All four appeared calm as they entered and took their seats, though Ellen looked as if she had only just dried her eyes. Two more letters from Simon had, it seemed, been delivered in the morning's post: one addressed to Thomas and Ellen, the other to Lorraine.

It didn't take Kelsey long to read them. Both were brief, formally set out, the handwriting steady. In both, Simon apologized for the trouble he was causing; in both, he declared himself innocent of any part in the Southview murders.

He made no protestation of love for Lorraine, but ended his letter to her by urging her to care for the baby and love it; he knew Thomas and Ellen would do all in their power to help.

He ended his letter to the Cormacks with the words: 'I realize that all along you both did what you thought was for the best. The truth is, I should never have been born.'

150

CHAPTER 19

The press were out again in force on Tuesday morning, for the opening of the inquest on Simon Edward Cormack. As was expected, the proceedings were brief and formal, the inquest being adjourned without any date being set for resumption; the body was released for burial.

Thomas and Ellen were both present. They had brought Lorraine and her mother with them and they all sat together. Afterwards, the Beatties left with the Cormacks, speaking a word to the Chief Inspector on their way out of the courthouse. They looked by this time a closely united foursome, Kelsey observed as he stood gazing after them. None of them made any response to the barrage of questions from the besieging reporters. They walked quickly past in a tight bunch, their eyes resolutely fixed on the ground, over to where the Cormacks had left their car.

At the press conference afterwards, one question kept obstinately popping up in various guises: would the police be continuing their hunt for the Southview killer or did they now consider there was no longer any need? To every manifestation of this query the Chief returned the same patient reply: the case was by no means over; the search for the murderer would continue with unabated vigour.

When the conference was over, Kelsey sat at his desk, reviewing the events of the past four weeks. He felt flat and dispirited. In spite of his positive statements to the press, he could see no clear path before him. The case seemed to have ground to a complete halt.

But very shortly after he reached this bleak conclusion there came another spin of the wheel and things were on the move again. A young woman, a Mrs Maureen Ryan, called in at the station, asking to speak to the Chief. He went along at once to see her. She was good-looking and smartly dressed but wore a stunned air, horrified and disbelieving.

151

'I understand you wish to talk to me,' she told the Chief. 'I had lunch with Celia Heyworth the day before she died.' She drew a long, shuddering breath. 'I simply can't take it in. I've only just heard what happened.' He took her along to an interview room, sat her down and plied her with tea. After a little while she declared herself ready to go on.

She told him she was Cannonbridge born and bred; she had known Celia since their schooldays. She worked for a bank and, on her marriage some years ago to a man who lived in Gosford, she had got herself transferred to the Gosford branch of the bank. She had always kept up with Celia to a certain extent after her move, but had seen little of her during the last year or two, largely because her own marriage had run into difficulties. After her divorce, a few months ago, she had decided to shake herself out of her despondency. She would take the best part of her annual leave in one go and treat herself to a holiday in Canada. Her older brother had settled there; he was married, with a family. Her widowed mother had gone out to join them a few years back.

Maureen had a great-aunt living in a village near Cannonbridge. Until recently the old lady had been reasonably fit and active, managing well enough on her own in her little cottage. When her health began to present problems she decided to sell her cottage and move into a residential home nearby. Maureen had arranged to drive over to the home to see her great-aunt, make sure she was happily settled, on the Thursday before she was due to leave for Canada. She rang Celia to see if they could lunch together on the same day. Celia had been delighted to hear from her and a time was fixed. They had duly met and lunched together.

After lunch, Maureen drove Celia back to British Braids; the next day she left for Canada. She had got back last night and was due back at work tomorrow. She had decided to drive over to visit her great-aunt today and had thought of meeting Celia again for lunch. She had rung British Braids this morning, asking to speak to Celia. She had at once been put through to George Drummond, to whom she repeated her request. Mr Drummond had then broken to her the grim news of Celia's death. He had asked if she was the friend who had lunched with Celia the day before she died. When she told him yes, he advised her to go at once to the police, who had been making strenuous efforts to find her.

At this point, Maureen dissolved into tears but soon recovered and held herself ready to answer questions. The Chief began by asking if Celia had made any mention to her of having been pestered by Simon Cormack − or any other man.

The answer to both parts of the question was no. Nor had Celia mentioned any trouble at work. She had told Maureen her marriage was definitely over, though she hadn't yet made that plain to her husband. 'I asked her, half joking,' Maureen added, 'if she had a boyfriend, and she came back at me, hot and strong. There wasn't any boyfriend and there never had been. And she had no intention of going looking for any other man − not for a long time, at least.' Celia had declared that she intended getting herself established on a sound, independent footing before she would even think of getting involved with anyone again. If she ever did get involved again she would make very sure it wouldn't be with some chancer trying to get his hands on whatever she'd secured by way of a divorce settlement.

That declaration had reminded Maureen of something she had meant to ask Celia. Maureen worked in the investment and securities department of the bank and had recently been engaged in listing stock certificates and valuing shareholdings for a Gosford solicitor who was administering the estate of a customer of the bank who had died in August. The customer's name was Ivor Heyworth; he had at one time been a manager of the Gosford branch of the bank. 'I asked Celia if Ivor Hey-worth was any relation of her husband's,' Maureen explained. 'His estate was worth quite a bit. I wondered if any of it might be coming her husband's way.'

Celia had told her John did have an Uncle Ivor who lived in Gosford and had been a bank manager; she had never met the uncle and knew nothing of his death. John hadn't said a word about it. 'She said,' Maureen went on, ' "I see what it is. John has been left some money in his uncle's will but he's going to keep quiet about it until he knows for sure what I intend doing about joining him in Lydhall." '

'Did she say if she intended asking John if he had been left any money?' Kelsey asked.

'At first she said she would ask him,' Maureen answered. 'She said John would be calling in at Southview at lunch-time next day, to talk things over, she'd ask him about it then. But then she had second thoughts. He could be going to tell her about it next day, so it might be better to wait and see if he did say anything before tackling him. If he didn't say anything, she still wouldn't need to ask him outright; she could get in touch with the uncle's solicitor and find out that way if there was any legacy. If there was, then she'd make certain it was brought into the divorce settlement.'

'Do you know if she definitely intended telling her husband next day that the marriage was finally over?' Kelsey wanted to know.

Maureen thought back. 'I remember her saying that the news about the uncle's death and the possibility of a legacy had put her situation in a new light. She'd have to think it over carefully before next day, decide how she was going to handle things.'

After Maureen had gone the Chief sat pondering. It came back to him that DC Slade had returned from Lydhall suggesting John Heyworth might, in spite of his denials, have a lady friend up there, a colleague of his at Melco. The Chief cast his mind back. Brooke, that was the name: Sarah Brooke.

It came back to him also that Heyworth would be setting off tomorrow morning on a round of business visits and wouldn't be back in Lydhall till Sunday evening.

CHAPTER 20

The fine spell showed no sign of ending. The sky was a cloudless blue as Kelsey set off for Lydhall on Wednesday morning. They encountered a good deal of traffic and it was ten minutes before midday when Sergeant Lambert pulled into the Melco car park.

They made their presence known to the management and Kelsey asked if he might speak to the chief personnel officer. Not that he entertained any great hopes of getting much past the lips of someone in that position – always one of the utmost confidentiality – but it was worth a try. They were taken along to Miss Forster's office, but the moment Kelsey laid eyes on her he knew he wasn't going to get very far. Nevertheless he went through the motions, with even less success than he had feared. There was no way the good lady could be persuaded that it was any part of her duty to answer questions of a personal nature about either Sarah Brooke or John Heyworth, and most certainly not about the possibility of some relationship – other than a purely business one – existing between the pair of them.

Never a man to waste further time on a cause so plainly lost, Kelsey took his leave of Miss Forster and sought out Sarah Brooke.

She made time to see him after the briefest of waits, displaying neither surprise nor unease at his unheralded arrival. A good-looking young woman, Kelsey observed; bright and intelligent. She seemed very sure of herself. He asked what time she would be going off to lunch. It might be convenient for them both if he saw her then, as he not only had some questions to ask her, but he would also like to take a look round her flat. Again, she showed neither surprise nor unease. Her manner was pleasant and cooperative as she told him she could get away almost at once, if he wouldn't mind waiting a few minutes while she handed over to someone else.

In a very short time the two policemen were back in their

car, following Sarah to her flat in a converted Edwardian dwelling. She left her car standing by the front door and took them up to the flat, the middle one of three. Very agreeably furnished, Kelsey noted; an atmosphere at once orderly and comfortable. Sarah offered them refreshments, which Kelsey declined.

He wasted no time on preamble, but began by asking what her relationship was with John Heyworth. A good, friendly, working relationship, she replied at once; nothing more.

Had she been seeing Heyworth, away from the work setting, before his wife's death?

Yes, occasionally, she told him without hesitation. They had sometimes gone out for a meal together in the evening. Once or twice they had gone to the theatre or cinema.

And since his wife's death?

She had continued to see him, she answered readily. More frequently than before, in fact. She felt he needed a friend now, more than ever. There was never any visit to a theatre or cinema now; they usually had a meal together at some quiet restaurant. Now and again she had cooked supper for him, either here or in his flat. He was clearly glad of her company; she felt it helped to prevent him brooding over what had happened.

Did she have any close relationship at present with any other man?

She shook her head. She had had one or two such relationships in the past, but nothing very serious. She wasn't looking for another at present, she was more concerned with making a satisfying career for herself. She added, with a direct look at the Chief, 'I don't consider my relationship with John Heyworth particularly close.'

Kelsey let that go. He asked if she would cast her mind back the best part of five weeks, to Friday, 27th August. Could she tell them what she recollected of her movements that day?

She had no difficulty in recalling the day, because of some trouble she had been having with a wisdom tooth at that time. She had left work earlier than usual that lunch-time, to keep a dental appointment at twelve-thirty. She had expected to go back to work in the afternoon but had felt unwell after leaving the dentist's and had rung Melco at about two-fifteen to say she would be taking the afternoon off. The dentist had given her some tablets. She took two and lay down on her bed to sleep. She had woken at around four-thirty, feeling a good deal better.

She had a cousin, a Mrs Gail Edney, younger than herself, divorced, living at the other side of Lydhall with her two small children. She went to see Gail fairly regularly and had promised to go round that evening, straight from work, in the usual way. She had thought, when she lay down on her bed, that she would have to ring Gail and cancel her visit, but in the event she had felt well enough when she woke up to go round, after all. She never liked to disappoint Gail if she could avoid it; Gail couldn't get out in the evenings because of the children and looked forward to her visits.

She had arrived at her cousin's around five-thirty and had stayed about four hours. She had then driven back to her flat and gone to bed. She supplied the Chief with the address of her cousin and her dentist.

Did she have any communication of any kind that day with John Heyworth?

No, she had no communication with him nor had she expected any.

Had she been aware of how he had intended to spend that Friday?

She knew he had some out-of-town business engagements but she hadn't known – nor would she have expected to know – the precise details of his schedule.

Had she known he was attending his uncle's funeral?

After a moment's thought she replied that she rather thought he had mentioned that.

Had she known John had been left the residue of his uncle's estate?

No, he had said nothing about that.

Had she known he had arranged to meet his wife at Southview that Friday lunch-time?

No, he had made no mention of that.

What had he said to her about his wife's death, during the last few weeks?

He had said very little about it and she would certainly never dream of broaching the subject herself. She felt he hadn't yet managed to come to terms with what had happened. He seemed to find plunging into work, keeping his mind occupied, offered the best remedy for grief and depression.

Did he have any views as to who might have committed the murders?

If he had, he hadn't expressed his views to her.

Had she never asked him his views on the matter?

She shook her head at once; she looked displeased at the suggestion. 'I would never think of asking him such a question,' she replied with distaste.

During John's time in Lydhall before the death of his wife, had she believed he genuinely wanted his wife to join him?

She gave a decisive nod. She was certain he had very definitely wanted Celia to join him. He had made no secret of it.

Did she believe at that time that his marriage was falling apart?

'I wasn't in any position to know,' she answered dispassionately. 'He never discussed his marriage with me and I wouldn't have thought it any of my business to ask.'

Had she ever had direct contact of any kind with Celia Heyworth?

She shook her head vigorously. No, she had never had any contact with her.

Had Celia ever attempted to make contact with her?

No, never.

Had she ever visited Southview?

Another vigorous headshake. Not only had she never visited Southview, she had never so much as set foot in Cannonbridge.

Kelsey sat regarding her in silence. 'As to the future,' he said after some moments, 'will you marry John Heyworth if he asks you?'

She looked steadily back at him. 'I have no gift for looking into the future,' she responded drily. 'I propose to do what I've always done: let the future take care of itself.'

Kelsey changed tack abruptly. Had she ever seen John wearing a brown woollen garment, such as a pullover, waistcoat, cardigan?

She pondered before shaking her head.

Had John ever given her any things of his to keep for him? A parcel or case, maybe?

She looked surprised but again shook her head.

Kelsey asked if he might look through her things and she told him at once to go ahead, look anywhere he wanted. If he had no objection, she would occupy herself while he was doing that

158

by making herself a snack – she would soon have to be thinking about getting back to work.

No, Kelsey had no objection. Again, she offered refreshment for himself and Lambert, and again Kelsey declined. While she busied herself in the kitchen, the two policemen made a swift, comprehensive search of the flat, entirely without result.

Before they left, Kelsey asked Sarah if they might take her fingerprints. She showed no surprise, made no objection, but agreed readily, assuring Kelsey that she fully understood the routine necessity.

Immediately on leaving, Lambert drove the Chief to Sarah's dentist. The receptionist told them the dentist was dealing with his final patient of the morning. He should be free in a few minutes if they cared to wait.

When he came along, he proved amiable and helpful. He consulted his records and confirmed that Sarah Brooke had indeed visited the surgery on Friday, 27th August. She had rung as soon as the surgery opened that morning, to ask for an emergency appointment, she was having trouble with a wisdom tooth. She had been found a slot at twelve-thirty and had duly arrived. He had dealt with the tooth; it had proved to be a very tricky job, which was why he particularly remembered it. He had given her some tablets to take over the next day or two, to ease any pain or discomfort.

Lambert drove the Chief next to the address Sarah had given them for her cousin, Mrs Gail Edney: a semi on a small council estate that appeared orderly and well run. Repeated rings on the doorbell produced no response. There was no sound from inside; all the windows were closed.

A curtain twitched in the adjoining semi and a woman came out to say she had seen Mrs Edney go out with the two children half an hour ago. She had no idea when they would be back; she hadn't spoken to Mrs Edney.

Their next call was at the house where John Heyworth rented his first-floor flat. Lambert rang the bell at each of the other three flats in turn, but only from the basement flat did he receive any response. An elderly lady, spry and sharp, came to her door and cast a circumspect eye over the two men. Her attitude didn't soften to any extent when Kelsey disclosed his identity.

To the best of her knowledge, the occupants of the ground-floor and second-floor flats were out at work; Mr Heyworth was away on business for a few days.

The Chief had the strong impression that he wasn't going to get very far with her in his inquiries about Mr Heyworth's lady friends, but he pressed on all the same.

His impression had been well founded. She declared herself as not having the slightest interest in such matters. She wouldn't thank anyone for prying into her own personal affairs and had never had any wish to pry into those of anyone else. She had always found Mr Heyworth courteous and friendly in such slight and infrequent contacts as she had had with him and, as far as she was concerned, that was the end of the matter.

The Chief consulted his watch as they returned to the car. Sarah Brooke would probably have left for work again by now. He told Lambert to drive back to her flat. When they reached the house he saw that her car had indeed gone.

They rang the bell at the other two flats in turn but received no response; they returned to the car. The Chief decided to have another stab at contacting Mrs Edney before leaving Lydhall and they set off again for the council estate.

But their second attempt was no more successful than their first; Gail Edney was still out.

Thursday was a busy mishmash of a day, with a press conference, a briefing, mounting paperwork to be dealt with, an interview to be recorded during the afternoon for regional TV, plus a steady trickle of personal calls from members of the public determined to speak to the Chief himself, each caller convinced he – or she – alone held the key to what had happened at Southview. Each one to be heard out, details recorded. Without, as far as today was concerned, discovering one iota of information offering even the most slender hope of shedding useful light on the events of that Friday.

Kelsey had made sure that regular checks were made of the current activities of various folk he had interviewed in connection with the case. Towards the end of Thursday morning, he cast an eye over the results of the latest checks.

Michael Anderson was continuing to work as usual at British Braids; his behaviour was in no way remarkable. Alec Morgan appeared to have pretty well recovered from his wretchedness and was now going round to the Andersons' much as he had done before the murders. He had begun looking in earnest for a regular job and had recently been called for one or two interviews.

Darrell Wilding continued to report faithfully to the police in the neighbouring town where he was billeted. Not only was he putting in a full day at the workshop, but he was occupying his leisure by making himself useful about the house and garden. He made no complaint about his enforced restriction. He got on well with the family and with his fellow workers. His boss had recently told a visiting constable that if things panned out all right for Darrell, he would have no hesitation in offering him a permanent job.

As Kelsey was digesting these facts he had a report from a fingerprint officer that made him sit up: a number of Sarah Brooke's prints had been found among those discovered at Southview. A thumbprint and three fingerprints on the lower end of the banister rail of the staircase; several fingerprints and the greater part of a palmprint on the polished arms of a chair in the sitting-room.

CHAPTER 21

Early next morning the Chief set off again for Lydhall. They called first at the council estate and this time found Gail Edney at home. She looked taken aback to find them on her doorstep. She was a harassed-looking young woman, no more than two or three years past twenty, thin and nervy, rapidly losing such looks as she had ever possessed. A brace of toddlers – a boy of eighteen months or so, and a girl of about three – wandered into the little hall and came to a halt at the sight of strangers. The boy clung to his sister's hand. Neither spoke. They pressed themselves back against the wall, subdued and timid in the presence of two large men. Their mother made no attempt to banish them, but picked up the boy and held him tight before her, like a kind of shield. The girl edged up to her and stood close to her side, sucking her thumb.

The Chief asked if they might come in, as he had one or two questions to put to her. Gail hesitated and then opened the door wide to admit them. She took them into a small, cheerless sitting-room and sat them down, but remained standing herself, facing them, with her back to the sideboard, still clutching the boy, the girl pressed close up beside her.

Kelsey began by asking if her cousin, Miss Sarah Brooke, had been in touch with her over the last day or two. She replied at once: no, Sarah hadn't been in touch with her at all this week.

Kelsey didn't let that go. Had Sarah not informed her of their own visit to Lydhall, their talk with Sarah, on Wednesday? Again she replied readily: no, she knew nothing of their previous visit.

Still he pressed her. Had she not received a phone call from Sarah at about twelve-thirty on Wednesday? To say police from Cannonbridge had called at Melco; Sarah was on her way to her flat with them; they might very well decide to look in on Gail shortly; Sarah would strongly advise her to take the two children and leave the house, make sure she didn't return for some considerable time?

Gail didn't waver in her response. No, Sarah had not phoned her at any time on Wednesday.

Kelsey then asked her to cast her mind back to Friday, 27th August, the Friday before the bank holiday. How had she spent that evening?

Her answer came back pat: Sarah had come round to spend the evening with her. It had been arranged a few days previously: Sarah was to come straight from work. But when Sarah turned up, at about five-thirty, she explained that she hadn't been at work that afternoon but had been in her flat, recovering from a session with her dentist. She was feeling a good deal better after a sleep but she wouldn't be staying late. She had behaved much as usual: helped with the supper and the washing-up afterwards, putting the children to bed. She had stayed chatting, watching TV, till about nine-thirty, when she went home.

Kelsey studied her for some moments. 'I imagine your cousin is good to you?' he hazarded. 'She helps you out sometimes?'

She stared defiantly back at him. 'What if she does? I make no secret of it. It's not against the law. She's been very good to me, she's helped me in lots of ways, and still does. And she's been very good to the children.' Her tone grew sharper and shriller. 'I don't know how I'd have managed without her, this last year or two. My husband vanished into thin air after the divorce. He went off abroad somewhere, I've no idea where. I've never had one penny of maintenance from him and it looks now as if I never will. Sarah's helped me out dozens of times. I'd have chucked myself and the children in the river before now if it hadn't been for her.' She suddenly burst into racking sobs. The boy stared anxiously up at her, his face puckered in distress; the girl began to whimper, pulling at her mother's clothes.

Kelsey said nothing until they had all quietened down, then he started off on a fresh tack, asking her what she could tell them about Sarah's relationship with John Heyworth.

Gail answered steadily enough. She had never heard the name. 'I can't tell you anything about her relationship with any man,' she added. 'Sarah never discusses that sort of thing with me.' Her tone sharpened again. 'But I'm positive she'd never make a fool of herself over any man. I'm sure she's well able to take care of herself in any relationship.'

Kelsey switched tack again. Had Sarah in fact never set foot in Gail's house that Friday evening? Had she asked Gail at some later date if she would be willing to confirm her statement that she had spent the evening here, with Gail and the children?

Gail answered at once, with a good deal of spirit. Sarah had very definitely spent that Friday evening here, exactly as Gail had just described to them. And Sarah would never ask her to tell lies for her.

Kelsey pressed her at some length but she could in no way be shaken in her account of that evening. When they left the house they called again at the dentist's surgery, with a fresh query. This time Kelsey was concerned with the way in which Sarah Brooke's dental appointment had been made. He was able to speak to the woman who had fixed the appointment and learned that Sarah had phoned at the beginning of that week in August, to say she was having trouble with a tooth, nothing very urgent. She made an appointment for the Saturday morning, 28th August. She usually came on a Saturday, to avoid having to take time off work. Then she had rung again, first thing on the Friday morning, to say the tooth was now giving her a good deal of pain and had kept her awake most of the night, she would be grateful for an emergency appointment. The woman had fitted her in at twelve-thirty that morning and cancelled the Saturday appointment.

On leaving the dentist's, Kelsey directed Lambert to stop by the next phone box. He rang Melco, asking to speak to Sarah Brooke and was put through at once. Sarah didn't sound surprised to hear from him again or to learn that he was back in Lydhall. He told her he had further questions to ask and it would be best if the interview could be conducted away from Melco. He suggested meeting at her flat, the sooner the better. She agreed at once, assuring him she would leave for the flat in ten minutes.

And she was as good as her word. She appeared unflurried and at ease as she stepped out of her car by the front door. The two policemen went across to greet her. She gave them a pleasant smile and hoped the interview wouldn't take too long. Kelsey made no response to that, but followed her indoors and up to the flat.

164

She offered them coffee which the Chief declined. She made some for herself and carried it into the living-room. She settled herself comfortably into an easy chair, facing them, and waited calmly for the Chief's questions. They weren't long in coming.

'I ask you again,' Kelsey began, 'if you have ever been inside Southview.'

She smiled slightly. 'I can see you know I have been inside the house. I did go there once, and once only.' She appeared in not the slightest degree disconcerted. 'I paid Celia Heyworth a visit on the Wednesday evening before the bank holiday.'

'You'd better tell us about it,' Kelsey said.

She gave a little nod. 'Celia was expecting me. I'd rung her the previous evening, to ask if she'd agree to see me. I wanted to know the truth about the state of the marriage – from Celia's angle.' She gave the Chief a forthright glance. 'I was getting fond of John but he was still very bound up with his wife. He'd been so sure at the start that she'd be joining him in Lydhall, but it was taking her so long to make a move that he was beginning to wonder just what she was playing at. He didn't want to believe she was stringing him along but it was getting to look very much like that.

'If she genuinely did intend joining him, then that would be that, as far as I was concerned. But if the marriage really was falling apart, then I could see no reason why I should hold back. I thought John and I were well suited, we could make a go of it. But I had no intention of going overboard without knowing exactly how things stood between them. I thought Celia might have reasons for hanging back that she was keeping to herself – maybe she had some boyfriend.'

She moved her shoulders. 'I can be patient if I have to be, but only up to a point; patience has never been my strong suit. I could see the situation between the two of them drifting along indefinitely, so I decided to take the plunge and ring Celia. I didn't go into any great detail over the phone, I just said I was a colleague of John's, we were on friendly terms. I had no wish to queer her pitch but I'd be grateful if she would allow me to come and talk to her, let me know how things stood between them, what her intentions were.'

She inclined her head briefly. 'She didn't seem surprised to be phoned out of the blue like that. She didn't sound at all angry or upset, more intrigued than anything. She was really very good about it, very pleasant and understanding. I got the impression she was pleased at the idea of meeting me and talking things over. That made me even more sure she did want out of the marriage.

'We fixed a time. I was to go straight from work the following evening. We'd be on our own; Beth Knight would be round at her girlfriend's. I asked Celia not to say anything about our meeting to John and she promised she wouldn't. She said she wouldn't even mention it to Beth, in case Beth let it slip sometime to John.

'I told John I wouldn't be able to see him on the Wednesday evening as I was going over to see my parents – they live about thirty miles from here. He still has no idea I went to Southview, not unless Celia told him, and I can't believe she did – she promised not to and he's never said anything about it to me.

'I stayed about an hour at Southview. Celia gave me coffee and biscuits; it was all very civilized. I told her frankly what my position was, that things hadn't gone very far between John and myself, we certainly weren't having an affair. I would be very happy to let it go further, but only if it was going to lead somewhere. I told her I was sure John would be delighted if she did decide to join him, but if she was heading for divorce, I believed I could make him happy, give him children, the kind of home life he wanted; I'd be ready to give up my job. I said it was possible I could be deceiving myself over the situation – John might not be interested in a future with me if the marriage *did* end; I could be sticking my neck out for nothing.'

'How did she take all this?' Kelsey asked. 'Did she open up?'

She gave a nod. 'Yes, she did. She seemed glad to. In fact, she seemed pleased that I'd come, that I'd spoken the way I had. She said as far as she was concerned the marriage was over, but she hadn't felt able to come out and say so openly to John. The marriage wasn't breaking up because of any failing on his part and she hadn't wanted to hurt him. She had been hoping all along that he would find someone else and things would resolve themselves that way, without ill feeling. She certainly wouldn't put any obstacles in my way. All she wanted was a fair divorce settlement.

'She told me John would be calling at Southview on the Friday. She said she would definitely tell him then she wouldn't be joining him, then she'd let things go on from there. I begged her again not to tell John I'd been to see her. I didn't want to risk frightening him off, making him think I was coming on too strong, before he'd even got round to thinking we might have a future together. She said I didn't need to worry. She gave me her word she would on no account tell him, or anyone else, about my visit.'

'Was that the end of it?' Kelsey asked.

She nodded. 'Yes, it was. I left and drove back here.'

He sat regarding her. 'I put it to you,' he said at last, 'that this meeting, if it ever did take place, was very far from being as friendly as you suggest. I put it to you that Celia was nowhere near as amenable or as frank as you say. I suggest she played her cards very close to her chest, that she heard you out and then told you, more or less: "I hear what you say. I dare say you'll learn in due course from John what has been decided between him and me."' He paused for a moment and then continued: 'Celia Heyworth was a businesswoman, and by all accounts a pretty smart one. If there was going to be a divorce, there was bound to be some hard bargaining. She was scarcely likely to show you – or John – all the cards in her hand. She'd want to think things over very carefully, in the light of what you had to say.'

Sarah opened her mouth to reply but Kelsey held up a silencing hand. 'Isn't the truth of the matter,' he went on, 'that you never phoned Celia to ask if she'd be willing to see you? And isn't it also true that things had gone a great deal further between you and Heyworth than you would have us believe? You were determined to marry him and you weren't too fussy how you set about it. If you could manage to hoodwink Celia between the pair of you, get her to agree tamely to what you wanted, well and good. If not, there were other means of getting her out of the way.'

CHAPTER 22

Again Sarah opened her mouth and again Kelsey raised a quelling hand. He went on: 'I put it to you that you brought forward your dental appointment from the Saturday to the Friday, not because your tooth had suddenly started playing up, but to fit in with a plan of action you had formed. My guess is that you said nothing to John about that plan, you were pretty sure he would never go along with it. You asked him to ring you after he left Southview at lunch-time that Friday, to let you know how things had gone between him and Celia. If they'd gone smoothly, then you could simply go back to work on Friday afternoon. If not, then you had the whole of Friday afternoon and evening before you, to put your plan into action.' He leaned forward. 'John did ring you that Friday lunch-time, after he left Southview, didn't he?'

She hesitated, then she said: 'He did ring me, but not to tell me how things had gone with Celia. There'd been a meeting at Melco that morning, at eleven. John couldn't be there because of going to his uncle's funeral, but he knew I'd be at the meeting. He was anxious to know how a particular point had been decided. He'd asked me to be sure his own point of view was put forward and I'd promised to do what I could. He said he'd ring me at lunch-time to find out the result of the meeting. I said OK. I'd come along here at lunch-time; he could ring me here, so we could speak about the meeting in private. He was on the phone only a couple of minutes. I told him things had gone very much as he had hoped. He was pleased to hear it and rang off.'

'Did he say nothing about his talk with Celia?'

She shook her head vigorously. 'No, not a word. He hadn't said anything to me about calling in at Southview. I'd only heard about that from Celia herself, so I couldn't very well ask him about it, much as I would have liked to know how things had gone. He'd have wanted to know how I knew he was meeting her.'

Kelsey regarded her again in silence, then he said: 'Why didn't you tell us earlier that John phoned you here that lunch-time?'

She moved her shoulders. 'I just forgot about it. It wasn't anything of any consequence. If I had remembered, I wouldn't have thought it anything that could interest you.'

He regarded her again. 'I put it to you that his phone call had nothing to do with any meeting at Melco. He rang you to let you know how things had gone with Celia. He told you she had found out about his uncle's legacy and she was holding out for a share of it; she intended digging her heels in over the divorce.' He stabbed a finger in the air. 'My guess is, you still said nothing to him about what you now intended to do, in the light of what he'd just told you.' He stabbed the air again. 'You made up your mind the moment you put the phone down. You intended to make sure John kept every penny of the legacy. And you'd also make sure there'd be no obstacle to your marriage, no long-drawn-out and expensive divorce wrangle, no division of property.' He stabbed again. 'And when you *did* marry John, there would be no first wife in the background, to spoil the pretty picture. So you put your plan into action. You rang Melco to say you weren't feeling too good after your visit to the dentist, you wouldn't be in again that day.

'You got into your car and drove down to Cannonbridge. You watched Celia go into the house. You went up to the front door and rang the bell. Celia answered it. You dealt with her the way you'd decided to deal with her, swiftly and permanently. You hadn't bargained for Beth being in the house, but no matter, you dealt with her as well.' He sat back. 'My guess is, John Heyworth still suspects nothing of all this.'

'That's hardly surprising,' Sarah retorted, 'since there isn't a grain of truth in the whole rigmarole. I never went near Cannonbridge that Friday. I spent the afternoon here, in this flat. I spent the evening with Gail. And I did drive down to Southview on the Wednesday, and only on the Wednesday. Every word I told you about that visit was the truth.'

'As to spending the Friday evening with your cousin,' Kelsey rejoined brusquely, 'Gail Edney is going to say precisely what you want her to say; she can't afford not to. She owes you a good many favours and she's undoubtedly counting on a good many more favours from you in the future. Her word wouldn't be worth tuppence in a court of law. You certainly did drive down to Southview at some time, you left your prints there. But I take leave to doubt it was on the Wednesday. Celia Heyworth had lunch with an old friend on the Thursday; they talked about her situation, the possibility of a divorce. If you'd been to Southview the previous evening, Celia would surely have mentioned your visit to her friend. To the best of my knowledge, Celia never uttered one solitary syllable to her about you.'

'I can't see any mystery in that,' Sarah responded calmly. 'Celia gave me her word she would say nothing about the visit to anyone. I believe she kept her word.'

Kelsey swept that aside with a wave of his hand. 'I believe it was only just now that you decided to admit to a visit to Southview, when you realized we knew you'd been there, you realized you must have left some trace. So you instantly invented the visit on Wednesday evening.' He fixed her with his eye. 'I believe you did go to Southview on only one occasion, but that occasion was on the Friday. I don't believe you ever phoned Celia, I don't believe she knew of your existence; I don't believe she had the remotest idea who you were when she opened the door to you that Friday evening.'

He did his utmost to shake her story, darting at it from every angle, attacking it this way and that, but without success. He couldn't shift her in the smallest particular.

When they left the flat, Kelsey had Lambert drive him round to Gail Edney's council semi. Gail had been out shopping, with the children; he caught her as she was returning. This time she was fully armoured against him. In the face of all his darts and swoops at her account of that Friday evening she remained positive and unshaken. Sarah had spent that evening with her and nothing would budge her from that.

They didn't drive straight back to Cannonbridge but broke their journey at Gosford, calling in at the bank where Maureen Ryan worked. The Chief was able to speak to her privately.

At his request, she cast her mind back with great care over her lunch-time conversation with Celia and was able to confirm very definitely that Celia had made no mention whatever of any visit from Sarah Brooke. But she went on to add in the next breath that in her opinion that didn't necessarily mean Celia hadn't received such a visit. Celia was well able to keep her own counsel when she chose. And if she had given her word on something, she could be relied on to keep it.

Furthermore, there hadn't been all that much time over lunch for Celia to say everything she might have wished to say. Maureen had had a lot to tell Celia about the break-up of her own marriage, her concern about her great-aunt, her trip to Canada. What with all that, on top of raising the matter of Ivor Heyworth and the possible legacy, ordering lunch and eating it, it was very soon time to be paying the bill and running Celia back to Melco.

Before they left the bank, Maureen had an idea of her own to put forward, with a certain amount of diffidence. 'It did just occur to me,' she told the Chief, 'that Celia might possibly have given some man the wrong impression – in all innocence. She had a very sweet smile and her manner was always friendly.' Some man she scarcely knew – or didn't know at all, a total stranger, maybe, might have got entirely the wrong idea from that smile, that manner; he might have fancied himself on the receiving end of a come-on.

As soon as they got back to the Cannonbridge police station, the Chief put men on to fresh inquiries in the neighbourhood of Grasmere Avenue, in an attempt to discover if there had been any sighting of Sarah Brooke's car, or of Sarah herself, in the vicinity of Southview, on either the Wednesday or the Friday before the bank holiday.

CHAPTER 23

John Heyworth was due back in Cannonbridge on Friday evening. First thing on Saturday morning, the Chief dispatched Sergeant Lambert round to his hotel, to ask Heyworth to call in at the station before going off to Gosford, or anywhere else. But before speaking to Heyworth, Lambert was to inquire from the hotel management if there had been any phone call for Heyworth yesterday evening, from a Miss Sarah Brooke.

Lambert duly inquired and was told yes, Miss Brooke had rung Mr Heyworth shortly after he arrived. The call had been a lengthy one.

Heyworth showed up, as requested, at the police station, anxious to be dealt with as quickly as possible, as he had a number of things to see to in the course of the morning. The Chief was equally anxious to lose no time and set about his questioning right away.

He began by asking Heyworth to go over once again what had taken place between himself and his wife during their lunch-time meeting that Friday. Heyworth swiftly recounted what he had told them previously.

When he had finished, the Chief said briskly: 'I will now put to you another version of what took place. I suggest it was very far from as amicable as you make out. I suggest that when Celia saw that you were going to make no mention of your uncle's death or the fact that you had just attended his funeral, you were going to say nothing about your inheritance under his will, she told you in no uncertain terms that the marriage was over. She had no intention of leaving Southview or of letting you sell the house. She pointed out that she could obstruct you legally if you tried to put the house on the market. She intended staying on at Southview and Beth would be staying on with her. She was going to make sure she got her fair share of what your uncle had left you. Furthermore, she now knew you had a lady friend in Lydhall; she had had a visit from Sarah Brooke two days earlier. You were scarcely in a position to accuse her of unfairness over the last seven months when you had plainly been guilty of double-dealing yourself, doing your best to manoeuvre her into a position where she would appear to be the one breaking up the marriage, so that you would have the advantage in any divorce settlement. But that wouldn't wash any longer, the cat was now out of the bag. She had no intention of handing you a divorce on a plate. If you wanted to marry your ladylove, you were going to have to bargain for a divorce, every inch of the way.'

Heyworth gave a vigorous shake of his head. 'There was nothing at all like that. Celia never once mentioned my uncle, or anything to do with his death. She said nothing about any lady friend. I don't have any lady friend, in Lydhall or anywhere else.'

'There's Sarah Brooke,' Kelsey rejoined.

Heyworth gestured impatiently. 'I've told you before and I tell you again: Sarah Brooke is a good friend and that is absolutely all. Celia said nothing about Sarah's visit to Southview.'

Kelsey jumped on that. 'So you *did* know Sarah had been to Southview.'

'I knew nothing about it at the time,' Heyworth snapped back. 'The first I heard of it was yesterday evening, when Sarah rang me at the hotel. She told me you'd been to see her and she'd had to admit she'd been to see Celia. She didn't want me to learn about the visit from you, she wanted to tell me herself, give me her reasons for going to Southview.' He gave the Chief a challenging glance. 'It wasn't an easy thing for her to do, explain to me why she went there that Wednesday evening; she has her pride. I could well understand why she hadn't said anything about it earlier, either to me or to you.'

Kelsey came smartly back at him. 'What makes you so sure she did call at Southview on the Wednesday? You say Celia made no mention of it to you.'

Heyworth frowned. 'Yes, of course she went there on the Wednesday, if she says she did. Why on earth would she lie about it?'

'She knows we found prints of hers at Southview, so she has to admit she went there at some time. She chooses to say it was on the Wednesday. But it could equally well have been on the Friday – though she could, of course, have paid visits on both days.'

Heyworth's tone showed anger. 'You're surely not trying to imply Sarah had some hand in the murders?'

Kelsey didn't answer that but asked: 'Doesn't it surprise you that Celia made no mention to you of Sarah's visit if it really did take place on the Wednesday?'

Another vigorous headshake. 'It doesn't surprise me in the least. Sarah told me Celia gave her word she'd say nothing about it, to me or anyone else. Celia always kept her word.'

'What exactly is your relationship with Sarah Brooke?' Kelsey wanted to know.

'You keep asking me that and I keep telling you,' Heyworth responded with exasperation. 'We're good friends and nothing more.'

'Are you telling me you've never been to bed with her?'

Heyworth gritted his teeth. 'That's precisely what I am telling you.'

'Do you intend to marry her?'

'I've never given the matter a thought. The last thing on my mind just now is any thought of marrying again.' He looked all at once worn and haggard. 'What kind of monster do you take me for? Celia's only been dead a matter of weeks.'

Kelsey changed tack. 'Did Sarah also inform you yesterday evening that she's admitted you phoned her at her flat that Friday lunch-time, immediately after you left Southview?'

Heyworth gazed levelly back at him. 'No, she said nothing about that.'

'But you did phone her at her flat that lunch-time?'

'Yes, I did.'

'You didn't mention that before.'

He frowned. 'It never occurred to me to mention it. I can't see what it could possibly have to do with the murders. It was purely a business call. I wanted to know what had happened at a Melco meeting. I'd fixed it with Sarah to ring her at her flat that lunch-time, to find out.'

'I put it to you that you arranged to ring her that lunch-time for a totally different reason: to let her know how matters had gone with Celia, if she was going to play ball, or to make a fight of it. I suggest that Sarah had particularly asked you to ring her, to let her know.'

'That is not so,' Heyworth broke in with sharp denial, but Kelsey ploughed on: 'Why did you immediately go on to the salon? Why did you need to speak to Beth Knight?'

'I explained that to you before,' Heyworth protested. 'I wanted to make sure Beth knew the house would be going up for sale in a week's time, and she'd have to start looking for somewhere else to live.'

'Wasn't it rather to check what Celia had told you about their plans for the holiday weekend? To discover if the two of them really were going away? And to find out what time Beth would get in from work that evening?'

Another forceful headshake by way of reply.

Kelsey leaned forward. 'You discovered from Beth that they were not going away for the weekend.'

'I never discussed the matter with her,' Heyworth retorted. 'I never mentioned the weekend.'

Kelsey pressed on, in a fruitless attempt to shake his account of that Friday. Heyworth didn't lose his temper but remained in command of himself. After some minutes he looked at his watch and asked civilly enough: 'Is this likely to take much longer? I'd appreciate it if I could get off; I have a lot to do.'

Kelsey looked back at him. Motive, method, opportunity: by any reckoning Heyworth's name must rank high on a list of suspects. But one tiny fact kept obstinately popping up in the Chief's brain, something he couldn't manage to square with the belief that Heyworth had been the killer. That fact was the little matter of the kitchen radio. If Heyworth's had been the hand that slew the two victims, why would he silence the radio by switching it off at the socket? Why didn't he switch it off on the set?

No answer occurred to him and he let Heyworth go off about his business.

A little later, Kelsey had the results of the inquiries in the area of Grasmere Avenue: the officers hadn't come up with any sighting of Sarah Brooke or her car, on either the Wednesday or the Friday before the bank holiday – any more than the initial inquiries had come up with any sighting of John Heyworth or his car in the neighbourhood of Southview, around the time of the murders.

175

Towards the end of the morning the Chief found himself back at his desk with a few minutes to spare. As so often at such moments these days, his brain began its untiring churning over of the events of the past five weeks, focusing now on this name, now on that. A face floated up before him, the face of someone he'd never really considered properly: Wilfrid Probyn.

He sat considering him now with sharp attention. It was Probyn who had been responsible for the discovery of the two bodies, Probyn who had gone next door and persuaded Ronald Marriott to help him effect an entry to Southview. Probyn had worked with Celia Heyworth for four years at British Braids. He had given Celia and Beth a lift in his car on the days immediately before the murders. He had no alibi for the time of the murders; he couldn't prove what time he had got home that evening.

Probyn's reputation at British Braids was that of a hard-working man, affable and obliging, quiet and unassertive. Someone on the staff had remarked of him that he wouldn't bat a fly. Kelsey drummed his fingers on the desk. The colleagues of half the killers in history had been ready to swear as much with total sincerity.

A picture rose suddenly to the forefront of his mind: Probyn as his wife had found him when she came home at eight-thirty that Friday evening. Probyn, that quiet, restrained man, had been sitting at the piano in great good spirits, exuberantly belting out his songs, thumping out an accompaniment.

Kelsey sat chewing his lips. It wouldn't hurt to have another word with Probyn. One-thirty or two o'clock might be a good time to call in at Nightingale Villa, catch Probyn and his wife at the end of lunch, before they had time to get off out somewhere for the afternoon.

And they did catch both the Probyns at home. Wilfrid was washing up the lunch things; Eva was upstairs, putting the finishing touches to her appearance, before driving over to her married sister's, to spend the afternoon.

Kelsey apologized for disturbing them but they waved his apologies aside. 'Did you want a word with me?' Eva asked. Kelsey told her no, it was her husband they wished to talk to. 'In that case,' Eva responded breezily, 'you won't mind if I get off.' She gave her husband a quick kiss on the cheek, assuring him she'd be back before supper, and took herself off.

'We'd like to take a look round,' Kelsey said in an easy tone as the door closed behind Eva. Wilfrid made no objection. He didn't return to his washing-up but followed them round. They volunteered no explanation as to what they were looking for and he didn't inquire; he stood watching in silence, his posture and facial expression far from relaxed.

When they arrived in due course at the door leading down to the basement, Wilfrid broke his silence. 'It's only my hobby rooms down there.' He attempted a carefree smile but his voice was taut. 'I've had the sole use of those rooms since I was a boy.'

'Do you still use the rooms?' Kelsey asked.

Wilfrid nodded. 'I set up a little gym down there some years back. I had my parents to look after and I couldn't get out much in the evenings and at weekends. I still use the equipment.' He attempted another jaunty smile. 'It helps to keep me fit.'

He turned as if to lead them off in another direction, but Kelsey laid an inexorable hand on the doorknob. Wilfrid said nothing more but followed them down the basement stairs.

There were three rooms, scrupulously clean and orderly, well supplied with storage space. One room housed gym apparatus, another a model railway layout; in the third, accurately accoutred troops refought the battle of Balaclava. 'I've always had a fondness for the Crimean War,' Wilfrid said with would-be cheeriness. 'Comes of being born and brought up in Sebastopol Gardens, I dare say.'

The contents of cupboards and drawers were laid bare, one after another; all beautifully neat. Wilfrid chatted compulsively the while, commenting with an effort at jocularity on all that came to light.

Kelsey drew back the door of a tall cupboard, revealing shelves stacked with magazines. 'Health and fitness,' Wilfrid said on a chirpy note, indicating the top shelves. 'Weight-lifting, body-building.' He pointed to the next shelves down. 'Model trains and train-spotting. Some of those go back more than thirty years.' He nodded at the shelves below. 'Model soldiers, war games.'

Kelsey took out a magazine here and there. The magazines concerned with bodily fitness were up to date but there were no recent issues, as far as he could see, in any of the other categories.

He selected a shelf at random and began to remove the stack of magazines. Probyn fell abruptly silent. In the space behind the stack more magazines were revealed – different-looking magazines, thick and glossy, each one tightly rolled, secured with a rubber band.

Kelsey picked up one of these magazines, slipped off its rubber band and unrolled it. He did the same to another. And another. Sergeant Lambert removed the front stack of magazines from a second shelf, and then from a third and fourth, disclosing each time a further cache of tightly rolled, glossy magazines. Every shelf told the same tale: all the hidden magazines were porno-graphic, the earliest dating back some ten or eleven years, the most recent being less than two weeks old. The earlier ones were soft porn, those bought during the last couple of years were undeniably hard-core.

Probyn's brow gleamed with perspiration. 'You won't say anything to Eva?' he suddenly burst out in tones of profound agitation.

Kelsey gave a single, silent shake of his head. Probyn appeared immensely relieved, but a moment later his look of relief van-ished and he burst out again: 'I had nothing to do with the murders, nothing at all. I dropped Celia off and came straight on here. I was here all evening.'

When the Chief made no response, Probyn's face creased in anxiety. 'You'll say you've only my word for that, I can't prove I came straight home.' Still Kelsey said nothing but continued · looking round the basement. Probyn fell silent, then he made a dart at the magazines and began to restore them swiftly to their original positions, rolled and secured as before.

When it was plain the basement held no further revelations, Kelsey crossed to the door leading into the garden and stood looking out. 'Do you do all the garden yourself?' he asked Probyn, still busy with his magazines.

Probyn gave him a fleeting nod. 'Yes, I do.'

'We'll take a look round outside,' Kelsey said.

Probyn nodded again. 'Go right ahead. I'll just finish these.'

The two policemen made a tour of the garden, keeping an eye out for signs of disturbance, but could discover none. They looked through outhouses, without result.

In the next-door garden a middle-aged man was at work among the borders. He glanced over at them from time to time with open curiosity but made no attempt to speak until Probyn came out to join the two men, when he could contain himself no longer and went up to the dividing fence. Probyn suddenly uttered an exclamation, jerking out a hand in the direction of his neighbour. 'He can prove what time I got home that Friday evening!' he said to Kelsey. He grinned with relief. 'He and his wife were going away for the weekend. He came over to give me his spare key.' He crossed swiftly to the fence, followed by the two policemen.

Probyn made no preamble but launched at once into his appeal: 'That bank holiday weekend — you remember, you were going away — ' but Kelsey raised a quelling hand and Probyn broke off. He apologized and effected introductions. The neighbour, whose name was Davis, looked even more consumed with curiosity. Kelsey asked him if he could indeed recall the Friday evening before the holiday. Davis replied without hesitation that he could recall it clearly. He had left work early that afternoon. He and his wife had been more or less ready to leave — they were driving to the airport, on their way to Amsterdam — and he was keeping an ear out for Probyn's return home, to ask him to keep an eye on the property and to hand over the spare doorkey, as he always did on such occasions. He heard Probyn drive in at his usual time: around twenty minutes to six. He had at once gone round and caught Probyn as he stepped from his car. Probyn had looked and behaved very much as usual; certainly in no way disordered or perturbed.

As Davis had handed over the key, he remembered something he wanted to tell Probyn. Davis's firm was putting out an advertising brochure and had accepted a highly competitive quote from a small, newly established printing concern, locally based, eager for business. The brochures had been delivered that morning, ahead of time; they were first class. Davis and his wife were ardent supporters of the local amateur operatic society, helping

179

in whatever way they could. Davis had told Probyn about the brochures, suggesting Probyn might get a quote for the society's next programme from the same concern; it was sure to be keenly priced. They had chatted about this for a minute or two and then Davis had gone back next door. That would have been at around ten minutes to six; he and his wife had left very soon afterwards.

Probyn had begun to look a good deal more relaxed as Davis talked. Kelsey thanked Davis for his cooperation and turned to go back into the house. On the way, Probyn had another recollection: he had phoned the operatic society's secretary that same Friday evening, as soon as he got indoors after talking to Davis. 'I wanted to catch her in case she was going away for the weekend,' he explained. 'I thought I'd better pass on right away what Davis had told me; I knew she'd have to see about the programmes pretty soon.' He gave the Chief the secretary's name and address. She was a single woman, living alone; she worked in a local office.

When they left Nightingale Villa, Kelsey told Lambert to drive him straight round to the secretary's flat. They got no reply to their rings on her doorbell, but as they turned to leave, the secretary walked in through the gate, carrying some shopping. It took her very few minutes to confirm what Probyn had told them. Yes, he had rung her about the society's programme that Friday evening. And yes, she could recall at what time he had phoned. She had just got in from work; that would put it at a few minutes before six. They had stayed talking on the phone for four or five minutes. Nothing in Probyn's manner had struck her as in any way unusual.

CHAPTER 25

The weather had grown markedly cooler over the weekend. The funeral of Simon Edward Cormack was fixed for Monday, two days before what would have been his twentieth birthday. The October day was crisp and cold, serenely golden. The funeral took place in the afternoon, at the local church, the church that had so recently seen the burial of Celia Heyworth and Beth Knight.

There had been no lessening of interest in Simon, on the part of either the townspeople or the media. A sizeable crowd gathered around the church; TV cameras were in evidence; there was no shortage of reporters.

The Cormack store was closed for the day. The entire staff assembled, on their own initiative, outside the store and walked together to the church, in an orderly group.

Thomas and Ellen brought Lorraine Beattie and her mother to the church. Chief Inspector Kelsey studied the foursome as they arrived. He had made it his business to keep abreast of developments in that quarter. The Cormacks were clearly going out of their way to treat Lorraine with every care and respect; they were also mindful of the need to show her mother attentive consideration.

Within a very short time of Simon's disappearance, even before his body had been found, Lorraine had begun to talk of abortion. The Cormacks had immediately responded with assurance of unstinting help of all kinds, if only Lorraine would renounce the idea. As soon as the Cormacks voiced their wishes, Mrs Beattie engaged a solicitor to represent the interests of her daughter and the unborn child. Some bargaining still remained to be done but it was certain now that agreement would shortly be reached. Lorraine and the child would be liberally provided for; there would also be provision for Mrs Beattie. Lorraine would in due course, if she wished it, be found a niche to suit her in the family business.

Today, in spite of her funeral attire and appropriately subdued mien, there was a noticeable air of calm satisfaction and well-being about Mrs Beattie, but it was impossible to read Lorraine's thoughts. She kept her gaze directed downward throughout; at particularly poignant moments she lowered her head still further and raised a screening hand to her face.

Eva Probyn was present. And Phyllis Marriott. Phyllis had returned to Rosemont with Ben a week earlier. Ben was now back at kindergarten and Phyllis, on doctor's orders, was still taking things easy. She had assured her husband and her mother that the funeral wouldn't be too much for her. She had been determined to attend; she had known the Cormacks for years; she had always liked Simon.

Many tears were shed at the committal. Thomas and Ellen could no longer restrain themselves and wept openly.

When it was all over and the crowds were leaving, Eva Probyn stood talking to the Chief. She turned her head and saw Phyllis Marriott making her way to where the cars were parked. 'Phyllis seems to be going along reasonably well now,' Eva observed. 'I do hope everything works out all right. I know her husband's very fond of Ben, but he'll be absolutely delighted to have a child of his own. He was desperately worried when Phyllis was taken to hospital. I caught him at the traffic lights, a day or two later, just after he'd been visiting her. He was so relieved she hadn't lost the child.'

Kelsey felt a ripple along his scalp. 'Exactly when would that be?' he asked on as casual a note as he could muster.

She thought back. 'I'd been to a meeting.' She mentioned the location, close to the hospital. 'I was on my way from the car park to sit with an old lady. She's bedridden; her daughter belongs to the carers' group; they live near the hospital. That would make it the Friday,' she concluded. She gave a decisive nod. 'Yes, it was definitely the Friday.'

'Which Friday would that be?' Kelsey kept his tone casual.

She was in no doubt. 'The Friday before the bank holiday.'

'Can you say exactly what time it was when you spoke to Ronald Marriott by the traffic lights?'

Again she thought back. 'I'd promised to be at the house for five-thirty, the daughter had a bus to catch. I looked at my watch when I left the car park. I remember it showed twenty past, so I knew I didn't need to rush, the house is only a few minutes away. That would make it five-twenty-five, near enough, when I got to the pedestrian crossing by the lights.' She had reached the crossing as the lights turned red and the oncoming traffic pulled up. As she stepped on to the crossing she saw that the first car in the stationary line was Ronald Marriott's. He spotted her and raised a hand in greeting. She stopped for a moment to ask after Phyllis. He smiled with relief and said: 'She's improving, coming along nicely now. I've just left her.' She told him how pleased she was, sent a message of goodwill to Phyllis and continued over the crossing. When she reached the old lady's house, the daughter said as she opened the door to her: 'On the dot, as usual.' And Eva had looked at her watch and jokingly corrected her. 'I'm actually one minute early,' she had said. 'It's only twenty-nine minutes past.'

Was she positive Marriott had said: 'I've just left her'?

Yes, she was.

Could she recall what Marriott had been wearing as he sat in the car?

No, she was sorry, she had no idea; she hadn't noticed his clothes.

CHAPTER 26

Phyllis Marriott was upstairs when Sergeant Lambert halted the car, a little way past the Rosemont gates. She had changed out of her funeral garb and was tidying her hair before the bedroom mirror. She glanced out at the sound of footsteps on the gravel and saw the two policemen approaching the front door. She didn't rush to admit them but went downstairs with care, keeping a steadying hand on the banister rail.

She greeted them with a pleasant smile and offered tea, which the Chief declined. 'We won't keep you long,' he promised. 'I know you must be wanting to rest. There are one or two points I'd like to raise, if you feel up to it.'

She declared herself ready to help in any way she could; she wasn't feeling particularly tired. She led the way into the sitting-room and took her seat opposite them. She didn't appear at all perturbed as she waited for the Chief to begin.

He asked her to cast her mind back to Friday, 27th August, to the visit her husband had paid her in the hospital, during the early part of the evening. Could she say at precisely what time he had left the hospital at the end of his visit?

'He got to the hospital earlier than usual that day,' she replied at once. 'He left just after six – about five past, I should think.'

'Do you clearly remember that he left at that time?' Kelsey pressed her.

She shook her head. 'No, I don't actually remember much about that visit at all. I usually tried to have a sleep before Ronald came, so I wouldn't be too tired. But with his being early that day, I'd only just gone off to sleep when he arrived, and I had to wake up again. I was very sleepy all the time he was there, I kept drifting in and out of a doze. Ronald was very good, he sat by me and held my hand.'

'Then how do you know what time he left?'

'I know because he mentioned it later, when there was all

the terrible business of the murders, when it first came out what had happened at Southview. I remember saying to him: "Do you realize that if you'd left work at your usual time that day, you might have seen the murderer going into Southview?" He said yes, he did realize that. And if he'd left the hospital earlier than he did, he might have seen the murderer leaving Southview. That was when he said he'd left the hospital a few minutes after six, he said it more than once. It made a big impression on him, that he could so easily have spotted the killer.'

'Can you say what your husband was wearing that Friday evening when he came to the hospital?'

She looked momentarily puzzled at the question but thought back and then shook her head. 'It's five or six weeks ago now. I wouldn't expect to remember after all this time, even if I hadn't been half asleep that evening. Ronald always wore a business suit and a white shirt when he came into the hospital at lunch-time, but he used to change into casual clothes before he came along in the evening. Not always the same ones, of course – he has a lot of casual clothes.'

Could he have been wearing a pullover or woollen waistcoat that evening?

Not a woollen waistcoat, she replied at once; he didn't own any. 'But I suppose he might have been wearing a pullover,' she added, 'if it was chilly. I can't remember now if it was.' She glanced at the clock on the mantelpiece. 'Ben will be home any minute now. One of the other mothers is bringing him back from kindergarten for me, for the present. Then Miss Vernall comes to take him off to her flat for tea, and to feed the ducks in the park afterwards. She lives quite near here. She used to work for my first husband; we've been friends a good many years. She's retired now. She's being very helpful with Ben. He's so full of energy, he can be rather tiring. She keeps him out till six-thirty; that gives Ronald time to change and have a cup of tea before he takes over in the evening. He's very good with Ben, they think the world of each other. They play games in the garden, then Ronald puts him to bed. He does even more to help at weekends, he more or less takes over completely.' She smiled. 'You must think I'm being very lazy, but it's doctor's orders – I have to take care.'

There was the sound of a car driving in and her face lit up. 'That will be Ben now.' She left the room and went to the front door. There was a murmur of voices, then the car drove off again. Phyllis put her head round the sitting-room door to say she wouldn't be long, she was taking Ben upstairs to change out of his school things, have a little wash and tidy, ready for Miss Vernall. They heard Ben chattering in a lively fashion as the pair went upstairs.

Kelsey glanced about the room in silence. Sergeant Lambert knew better than to interrupt his thoughts.

There were a good many photographs in evidence. Kelsey stood up and walked about, examining them. Wedding photographs of Phyllis and Ronald. Phyllis with her first husband. Ben's christening. Phyllis as a girl, with her parents. Snapshots of Ronald and Ben, playing together in the garden. Nowhere any photograph of Ronald at any earlier stage of his life.

He crossed to a side window overlooking a stretch of garden where a grey-haired man in overalls was sweeping up fallen leaves.

Phyllis came back with Ben, who was now dressed in colourful play clothes. He chatted animatedly to the Chief about his day at kindergarten while his mother went to the kitchen to find scraps of bread for the ducks. She had barely returned when Miss Vernall walked past the window. Ben ran out to the front door to greet her and pull her by the hand into the sitting-room. She was a capable-looking woman, a few years past sixty, with an amiable manner. When Phyllis effected introductions she didn't appear surprised to discover the two visitors were policemen.

'I want to wear my new stripy gloves,' Ben proclaimed suddenly, as he was about to leave with Miss Vernall. He looked up at his mother. 'I know where they are. Can I go up and get them?'

'Yes, all right, then,' she smiled. 'I suppose it is quite chilly today. My mother knitted them for him while we were staying with her,' she said to Kelsey as Ben darted off. 'He thinks they're very smart, he chose the colours himself.'

Ben was back down again a couple of minutes later, proudly waving aloft the new gloves. He held them out for the Chief to admire. The gloves were striped in blue and brown, trimly cuffed in brown. 'Granny had some wool left over,' Ben explained. 'She made them out of that.' He jabbed a finger at a cuff. 'The brown wool is from the pullover she made for Daddy.' The wool was a subtle shade of light brown. Kelsey's heart thumped against his ribs.

'Mind you don't lose your gloves,' Phyllis warned as Ben

186

tugged them on. She gave him the paper bag of bread, escorted the pair out into the hall and waved them off.

'Your mother knitted a brown pullover for your husband?' Kelsey asked as she came back into the room.

She nodded. 'Yes, she made it for his last birthday. It's a lightweight, sleeveless pullover.'

'May I see it?' he asked.

She looked surprised but answered readily: 'Yes, if you wish.' She went off upstairs. It was some little time before she returned, frowning, to say: 'I'm afraid I can't put my hand on it. I've looked through his things, but it doesn't seem to be there.'

'Perhaps he's wearing it to the office?' Kelsey suggested.

She shook her head at once. 'He'd never wear anything casual to the office. He's very particular like that.'

'Have you seen him wearing it lately?'

She thought before answering: 'No, I don't think I have.'

'Do you happen to remember if he was wearing it that Friday, when he visited you in the hospital?'

Her frown came back. She shook her head slowly. 'I'm sorry. I can't remember.'

'I'm afraid we're going to have to search,' Kelsey said.

'Search?' she repeated on a baffled note, staring up at him. 'What for? For the pullover? Why should you want to do that?'

He didn't answer her query but went on to say: 'I'm talking about a full search, you understand, inside and out. We'll need to get some men in. If you give your permission we can go straight ahead and arrange it. If you refuse permission it means getting a search warrant. We'll get it all right. It will involve some delay but we'll still carry out the search.'

'There's no need for any warrant. You can carry out your search.' She clasped her hands tightly together. 'We've nothing to hide. What is it you're looking for?' He still made no answer to that and she didn't press him. She glanced at the clock. 'Ronald will be here soon. Can't you wait till he gets here?'

'Who is the owner of this house?' Kelsey asked.

'I am,' she replied. Again she asked: 'Can't you wait till Ronald gets here?'

Kelsey gave a decisive shake of his head. 'I'm afraid not. Do I take it we have your permission, as owner, for the search?'

She nodded slowly. 'Very well, then. Search if you must.'

By the time Ronald Marriott turned his car in through the Rosemont gates the search was well advanced. So far it had yielded
nothing. The garden and outhouses had been dealt with; they
hadn't taken long. The gardener had worked at Rosemont for
many years, having been originally taken on by the father of
Phyllis's first husband. He assured the Chief that neither of the
Marriotts ever did any gardening; he looked after everything
entirely on his own. He would unquestionably have known if
there had been any disturbance of the ground, anything secreted
in an outbuilding. He was positive there had been nothing of
the kind.

The men had been through the cellars, the ground floor and
first floor and were busy in the attics when Ronald garaged his
car and came looking for his wife, demanding to know what
was going on.

Phyllis was in the sitting-room, lying back on the sofa, trying
to relax. A woman officer from the team, the officer who had
interviewed Phyllis on two previous occasions, made a point of
looking in on her from time to time, to be sure she was all right.

Phyllis sat up at once at the sight of her husband. 'Thank God
you're here!' she exclaimed with fervour. Tears glittered in her
eyes.

Ronald dropped to his knees beside her and put an arm round
her shoulders. 'You mustn't fret,' he urged. 'It's bad for the
baby.' He glanced up as Kelsey appeared in the doorway. 'Can't
you see you're upsetting my wife?' he said with heat. 'She's
supposed to have rest and quiet.'

'Your brown pullover,' Phyllis said in a rush. 'The one Mother
made for your birthday. Where is it? I can't find it.'

He stared at her. 'My brown pullover?' he echoed on a baffled
note. 'What do you want that for?' He glanced up again at
Kelsey. 'Have you a search warrant for all this?'

'We didn't require a warrant,' Kelsey replied calmly. 'Your wife, as owner of this property, gave permission for the search.'

'Your pullover,' Phyllis said with renewed urgency. 'Where is it? I looked in your things but it isn't there.'

'It must be there,' Ronald returned. 'What on earth do you want it for?'

An officer came into the room and spoke to Kelsey in low tones.

'You'd better come up to the attic,' Kelsey told Ronald, who got to his feet, frowning. Phyllis began to rise from the sofa but Kelsey raised a hand. 'No need for you to come, Mrs Marriott. You'd do better to stay where you are and try to rest.'

'I'm coming with you,' she declared with finality. Ronald made to give her an arm but she shook her head. 'I'm perfectly all right,' she assured them both with a touch of impatience. 'There's no need to fuss.'

They left the room and ascended the stairs in silence to the first floor, then up the narrower flight leading to the attics: three rooms containing an assortment of objects accumulated over the last hundred years.

As they entered the first room, the female officer left what she was doing and picked up a chair from the jumble of furniture. She tested its strength before setting it down beside Phyllis, who waved it away without a word.

In a corner of the attic, under a pile of rugs, the team had come upon an old wooden trunk. Inside was a pair of velvet curtains, neatly folded. Under the curtains were two bulging bin bags of black plastic, their necks tightly secured with twine. It was when they undid the twine and looked inside the bags that they had at once ceased operations and alerted the Chief.

Kelsey nodded to them now to proceed. The bags were carried across and set down in a space cleared in the middle of the floor. The contents were removed, one by one, to be logged, bagged, tagged. Phyllis stared down in stunned silence as the articles were lifted out. Ronald stood rigid, gazing straight ahead.

The first item to emerge was a white plastic carrier bag bearing the name of a local supermarket. Out of the bag came a Royal Worcester posy vase, painted with flowers; a Venetian bronze model of a tiger; a cameo glass scent bottle with a hinged silver top; and a porcelain figure of a girl holding a basket of flowers. These were followed by a gold wristwatch engraved with a date and a name: Celia Yates; a platinum wedding ring, inscribed with the date of Celia's wedding, the initials of bride and groom; a sapphire and diamond ring with a highly decorative setting. And a shoulder bag of dark brown leather, its contents seemingly undisturbed.

Inside the second bin bag was a bundle of men's casual clothing: slacks, shoes, jacket and shirt.

And a hand-knitted, sleeveless pullover, in a subtle shade of light brown.

The upper part of the front of the pullover showed a number of snagged threads. Caught up in one of these was the curving tip of a fingernail, varnished a pearly rose-pink.

'It isn't true!' Phyllis said in an anguished half-whisper. She twisted her hands tightly together. 'It can't be true!' She looked up at her husband. 'Tell them you didn't do it!'

Ronald remained rigid and silent, staring straight ahead.

'You didn't do it!' Her voice rose. 'You couldn't have! Tell them!'

He didn't look at her. 'It's no use,' he mumbled. 'I'm sorry.' Tears ran down his face.

She uttered a terrible cry. 'You mean you did it? You killed them both? *Why*? Why did you do it?'

Ronald looked across at Kelsey with pleading. The tears ran unchecked down his face. 'Can we get this over with?' he implored.

Kelsey spoke the formal words of arrest, of caution. Phyllis scarcely waited till he had finished.

'Why?' she burst out again. 'What made you do it? I have to know!' The woman officer laid a quietening hand on her arm but she shook it off.

Ronald stared down at the floor. 'I never meant to kill them,' he said in a rush. 'Either of them.'

Kelsey halted him with a raised hand and repeated the formal caution. The instant he ceased speaking, Ronald plunged on again, still staring down at the floor.

'I'd just got back from the hospital, I was upstairs in the bedroom. I looked out of the window and saw Celia go by. She'd asked me to let her know how Phyllis was. I went over to tell her.'

He closed his eyes and drew a long, shuddering breath. 'She looked pleased to see me, she gave me a lovely smile. She asked

190

me in, asked me how Phyllis was.' He drew a gasping breath. There was silence in the room, except for his voice running on, pouring it out.

'I thought she liked me, she was always so nice, so kind and friendly. I thought about her a lot, I was sure her marriage was breaking up, she must often be lonely. She'd said for me to come over if I wanted anything, if there was anything she could do, I could come over any time. I could hardly believe it, hardly credit my luck, but I began to think she might care for me. I couldn't stop thinking about her. She was so lovely. I'd never known anyone like her before. I'd never had much to do with women, I'd always been shy of them. No one like her had ever smiled at me the way she did.'

His voice grew ragged. 'I never meant to harm her. It was the last thing in the world I intended. She got it all wrong, she didn't understand, she was frightened, petrified. I never meant to kill her, to kill either of them, it all went wrong. She started screaming. I was terrified. I couldn't think, I had to stop her. I couldn't let her go on screaming. It would be the end of everything for me, I could lose it all. I had to quieten her but she wouldn't stop.'

He drew a long, sobbing breath. 'Beth came running down the stairs. I was in a blind panic, I'd no idea she was in the house. She looked in at the kitchen door. She screamed and started back up the stairs, still screaming.' He made a helpless gesture. 'I had to go after her. I had to stop her.'

He fell briefly silent. 'I heard a sound from the kitchen: Celia moaning. I had to go back.' His voice broke, he shuddered convulsively. 'I went back in and picked up the rolling pin.'

Later, as they were about to leave the attic, Ronald nerved himself to risk a direct glance at Phyllis. He opened his mouth to speak to her but she shrank back in horror, throwing him a look of such appalled repugnance that the words died on his lips.

A few moments later they came out of the attic. An unshaded light bulb cast a cold white glare over the stairs. Ronald walked slowly down the narrow flight with lowered head and bowed shoulders, the Chief ahead of him, Sergeant Lambert behind, a constable bringing up the rear. Phyllis followed at a little distance, with the woman officer close behind. No one uttered a word. Down in the avenue the homegoing cars went by.

The leading group rounded a bend in the stairs and disappeared from view. Phyllis held tight to the rail, her face ashypale in the harsh light. Her steps began to falter. The woman officer craned forward with a look of concern.

Phyllis halted suddenly and bent double, clutching at herself. The woman officer sprang to her side and laid hold of her arm. 'What is it?' she demanded urgently.

In the same moment the constable came back up the stairs, inquiring as he approached: 'Are you coming down? Is anything wrong?' He broke off at the sight of the two women and uttered an exclamation.

Phyllis doubled up again with a groan. She sank down on to the stairs, her face twisted in anguish. 'You'd better get me to the hospital,' she managed to jerk out, in a voice riven with pain. 'It's all over. I'm losing the baby.' Her shoulders shook, she dropped her head on to her arms. She began to weep, with great racking sobs, as if she would never stop.